Left to Chance

ALSO BY AMY SUE NATHAN

The Good Neighbor

The Glass Wives

Left to Chance

— A NOVEL —

Amy Sue Nathan

St. Martin's Griffin

www.stmartins.com

Library of Congress Cataloging-in-Publication Data

Names: Nathan, Amy Sue, author.
Title: Left to chance / Amy Sue Nathan.
Description: First edition. | New York : St. Martin's Griffin, 2017.
Identifiers: LCCN 2017026876| ISBN 9781250091116 (softcover) |
ISBN 9781250091123 (ebook)
Subjects: LCSH: Self-actualization (Psychology) in women—Fiction. |
Self-realization in women—Fiction. | City and town life—Fiction. |
Homecoming—Fiction. | Domestic fiction. | GSAFD: Love stories.
Classification: LCC PS3614.A85 L44 2017 | DDC 813/.6—dc23
LC record available at https://lccn.loc.gov/2017026876

Our books may be purchased in bulk for promotional, educational, or business use. Please contact your local bookseller or the Macmillan Corporate and Premium Sales Department at 1-800-221-7945, extension 5442, or by email at MacmillanSpecialMarkets@macmillan.com.

First Edition: November 2017

10 9 8 7 6 5 4 3 2 1

For Judith
Look what I have to show you!

Acknowledgments

It all started with tacos.

The first time I met my literary agent and friend, Danielle Egan-Miller, I offhandedly shared the seed of this story while we were eating lunch. Everyone at the table shared best friend stories, and we all cried. Then Danielle called me three times the following week to convince me that this was the novel I should write next. She was right! Danielle, here's to many more years of tacos and stories.

Brenda Copeland and St. Martin's Press took a chance on me six years ago. Brenda, we'd have made a great team even if we didn't look like sisters. I know you helped me become a better writer. Huge thanks to Holly Ingraham for eagerly adopting me and *Left to Chance,* and to Jennie Conway, Nancy Sheppard, and Jessica Preeg of St. Martin's Press, and Clancey D'Isa of Browne and Miller Literary Associates, for your diligence and enthusiasm.

A big hug to my daughter, Chloe, who is responsible for Shay's handwritten note, and for patiently helping me restructure this book using stacks of brightly colored index cards during one very long afternoon (okay, and night). My only regret is Chloe's permanent index card phobia. My son, Zachary, always responded quickly to my "What's a good word for . . ." texts. Who needs a thesaurus? It is very cool to have grown-up kids. I am extraordinarily proud of them. I'm also fortunate to have my parents, brother, aunts, uncles, and cousins giving me their unbridled support. Now, from not-so-far away.

Renee San Giacomo, Fern Katz, Alice Davis, Ilene Banach, Deborah Okleshan, Carole Farley, Larry Blumenthal, Elaine Bookbinder, Pamela Toler, Joanna MacKenzie, Abby Saul, Janie Chang, Holly Robinson, Barbara Claypole White, Sharon Snider, Orly Konig, Cathy Lamb, Robert K. Lewis, Renee Rosen, Lydia Netzer, and Katie Moretti contributed time, insights, answers, or friendship (or a hearty combination thereof)—all equally important when writing a novel. Manny Katz, please note that sisters Violet, Lily, and Heather were named intentionally. Professional Women's Network (PWN), an impressive group of women in Chicago's South Suburbs, embraced me and my books, which they continue to do from a distance. Book Pregnant and WFWA provided much-needed camaraderie, and Tall Poppy Writers, individually and as a group, have added value to my life and my career in immeasurable ways.

Readers, librarians, booksellers, and bloggers were all so hospitable and warm, online and in real life. Bloom, a special Facebook group where readers gather, has been a source of fun and support. A special shout-out to the Manhattan-Elwood Public Library District in Illinois, for always welcoming me with a full house *and* a specially painted door. A hug to Lynn Rosen, my new neighbor at Open Book Bookstore in Elkins Park, Pennsylvania, along with author and friend Nomi Eve, for their warm welcome when I moved "back home."

Last but not least, this book would not exist without my sister-

Acknowledgments

friend since tenth grade, Judith Soslowsky. She experienced a health scare a few years back, and when I received the call that she was okay, Teddi's story came to me fully formed. I never could have written a book about the impact of losing a lifelong best friend without having a lifelong best friend. She champions and challenges me and cracks me up and can make me cry. And this can happen in one phone call. Sometimes I think it's a shame everyone can't have her for a best friend. But you can't. She's mine.

And, yes, Jude, I'm making this about you.

Come to think of it, Danielle and Judith are two smart, trustworthy, strong women who have my back in different ways. Both are tall and have black hair. Neither has been seen in the same room as Wonder Woman.

Just sayin'.

A man travels the world over in search of what he needs and returns home to find it.

—GEORGE A. MOORE

Left to Chance

Chapter 1

GETTING PICKED UP ONCE meant flirting and free drinks. Today it meant hurrying through the airport in comfortable shoes.

I wove in and out of the slow-walkers and rushed past restaurant outposts selling breakfast, lunch, and dinner. The sweet, buttery aroma wafting over from the gourmet popcorn shop didn't slow me down, but when I reached a flower stand called Eliza's, I paused. I could resist the bongo-like buckets overflowing with roses, carnations, sunflowers, and the assorted I-missed-you bouquets. What caught my eye was the faux-vintage signage and the way the flowers were shielded from the imaginary sun by an awning, all meant to mimic Victorian London. It didn't hurt that the stand also sold energy drinks and earbuds. Nostalgia and irony. I resisted pulling out my camera.

My phone dinged as the carousel spit out my suitcase. I wouldn't make Shay wait more than a few moments for my reply. I'd known Shay—Shayna—since the day she was born. I remembered when she'd babbled and burped, when she'd first walked and talked. Now she was a thumb-typing, artistic tween who held a piece of my heart tighter than ever before, mostly from afar.

But today, and for the next week, Shay and I would be face-to-face. First, we'd reminisce about meeting in Chicago last summer—tea at The Drake, climbing the wall at Maggie Daley Park, the miniatures at The Art Institute, and finding our way to the bottom of a tin of Garrett popcorn. We'd replay every detail but save the best fun for last, recalling how the hotel's pastry chef let Shay decorate her own cake, which we later ate for dinner. Then we'd tick off the rest of the list: school, Shay's art, friends, reality TV, and maybe, could it be possible—boys?

I couldn't wait to see her, hug her, spend time with her.

I also couldn't wait to leave.

Shay: Dad will be a few minutes late.
Me: Aren't you with him?
Shay: In art class sorry. ☹ ☹
Me: Ok.

Not okay. I didn't want to spend an hour and a half alone in the car with Miles. Shay was the bridge, the bond, the buffer. And Shay wasn't coming.

I paced between the signs for taxis and shuttle buses. Car after car slowed as it passed, then kept moving, or stopped for someone else. I watched bear-hug reunions and aloof hellos. I smiled at every woman driver who passed. I even stifled a few waves. My insides rolled. This had to stop.

Celia would not be picking me up.

A horn beep-beeped and a white sedan pulled alongside the curb. I slung my camera bag over my shoulder and tipped my suitcase toward the trunk, my eyes on my old friend as he stepped out of the car. Miles's hair was gray and a little thin, more than it had been when I'd seen him a year before—or since, in the pictures he'd posted on Facebook. He'd lost weight.

I met Miles at the trunk. We reached our arms around each other and hugged hard, but quick. Miles wasn't just thinner, he felt more fit than I remembered. What had been soft was now solid. But his newfound physique couldn't hide the lines around his eyes. He looked tired.

"Thanks for coming all the way out here," I said.

"Not a problem. I hope Shay texted you. She had a project to finish for art class." Miles shooed my hand from my suitcase and lifted it into the trunk. "What've you got in here, Ted? Bricks?"

No one in my life now called me Ted. It sounded unfinished, yet smooth and familiar.

"Nope, just rocks."

Miles smiled and just like that, memories broke through. Was he remembering, as I was, our long-ago friendly teasing during Scrabble matches and Pictionary marathons with Celia? We'd always joked that with Celia as his wife, and my best friend, we were practically related.

I touched his arm before I could stop myself. "Good to see you, Mi. This is weird for us, isn't it? To be here, I mean?"

"A little bit, yes."

"We okay?"

"As okay as we're going to be, Ted."

"I would have come back sooner if you'd asked me." I wasn't sure that was true. "Let's not do this now. You being here is important to Shay, so it's important to me."

"I hope that's true."

"If it wasn't true, I wouldn't be here," I said.

"I guess not." Miles's tone was soft, his words slow, leaving space for his thoughts. And mine. "You look good."

"Oh, God, Mi—I'm a mess. But thanks." I knew how my hair smashed to my head after a long airplane sleep. I had a natural tan that sometimes hid the fact that I was thirty-nine, but not after two flights. My skin tone was the reason most people thought I was Italian or even Greek, not descended from the Russian Jews who had journeyed west—which meant past Cleveland—from New York's Lower East Side in the 1890s.

"I have to admit, once we got used to the idea, it was exciting to think you'd be our wedding photographer. I just want you to know that, under the circumstances, we really appreciate everything you're doing for us."

Our. We. Us.

Miles and . . .

My breath caught.

Not Celia.

Violet Frank.

His fiancée.

And *I* was going to photograph the wedding. That's what Shay had wanted. That's why I was here.

"Ready?" Miles asked.

No, I wasn't ready at all, but within moments I was headed toward the place that had haunted me for the past six years, the town I grew up in, and ran from, on the day of Celia's funeral.

Chance, Ohio, was no place for wimps.

I was on my way, regardless.

A straight stretch of rural highway connected the Robertson Regional Airport to the road leading to my hometown, tucked in the northeast corner of Union County. Or it *had* been a rural highway. The last time I was here the "highway" had been two lanes flanked by cornfields. Now the road was the blackest black with bright yellow lines. Newly paved and painted, it was four lanes wide. Two lanes out of town I understood, but two lanes in? I stared out the window at the cornfields. I loved the way the light played off the stalks at different heights, how the clouds cast a shadow that seemed to go on for miles. But I knew that as soon as I saw the fields, the exit would be near. Hey! Where were my cornfields?

"There's an outlet mall?" I hadn't meant to say it aloud.

"I'm sure Shay will talk you into going. It's her favorite place. She says it has everything."

"There's enough space in the parking lot for—"

"For a hotel. And a water park. I know. It's exciting, isn't it?"

"Someone is building a hotel and a water park?"

"Not yet."

"Who would go there?"

"Everyone," Miles said. "There's a new road off Route 33 now, so it's easy access. Small-town feel, big-town amenities. The mall has done a lot of good things for the area, Ted. And it's only the beginning."

"What are you doing? Running for mayor?" I was kidding.

Miles was not.

"No," he said with a smile. "The county board of commissioners. Just decided yesterday!"

I could have sworn a light sparked off his front tooth.

I tried to imagine Celia as a politician's wife, all buttoned-up business suit, pearls, and coiffed hairdo. Nope, couldn't picture it. Celia was an artist, a teacher, an expert tailor. Politics, even small-town politics, would have eaten her up and spit her out.

The expectations, the gossip, the mandatory mingling. Or maybe Celia would have changed its landscape with her caring conversations and handmade clothes. I shivered. It didn't matter what kind of political wife Celia would have been or what she could have done. Violet would be the one on the campaign trail.

"So, how's *your* life?"

"It's good. Lots of traveling, lots of interesting people."

Miles drummed the steering wheel.

"What's it really like working for Simon Hester?"

People always wanted to know about Simon "The Hotel Man" Hester. He had landed on at least one big most-eligible-bachelor or best-dressed list per year since he was twenty-five, almost twenty-five years ago. That kept some women interested in him. At first, that had kept me *from* being interested.

"I like working for Simon."

"I saw that write-up in *San Francisco Magazine.*"

"You get *San Francisco Magazine?*"

"There's this thing called the Internet now. And yes, we have a real copy too. You're a celebrity."

"Hardly. I take pictures of some celebrities and some fancy places. The Hester hotels have an A-list clientele. That's thanks to Simon, not me."

"That article had more than a few paragraphs about you."

It was all part of Simon's branding. He bragged about—promoted, he had said—all the weddings and corporate events we handled, and how I shot the most important ones. Since A-listers always want to be considered *most important,* they started requesting me as their photographer.

"The article was about modern hoteliers." I shouldn't have used that word—it made me sound like an industry insider. Which I was. I just didn't want to sound like one around Miles.

Not yet, anyway. "I wasn't the only one mentioned in the article. Or in the photo. You remember me because you *know* me. Just like the other people in the photo. Everyone who knows them thinks they're famous too. Believe me, none of us are."

"Well, you were the only one from 'a small town in Ohio.' It would have helped our image if they had mentioned Chance by name."

Chance had an image?

"So, no problem getting away, with your schedule and all? That article made Hester sound like kind of a hard-ass. But I guess you'd have to be . . ."

"Simon's a very nice man. I've told you that before." There was a time I'd have talked to Miles about Simon for real, but that time had passed. "No, it wasn't a problem at all. Nothing for Shay would ever be a problem."

It hadn't been a problem. It had been a nightmare.

I'd never taken off so much time before, and now I was handing over supervision of two weekends of weddings in New York and San Francisco, weddings that had been booked more than a year in advance. I'd rescheduled outdoor photo shoots at our new resort in Scottsdale and had canceled models, wardrobe, and makeup in Denver. I'd sweet-talked my assistant, Annie, into making the calls for me and for helping me find the perfect apology gifts, likely gourmet meals or spa services, for the wedding couples. Luckily, the corporate attorneys were loophole experts.

Back in San Francisco, I'd color-coded and organized everything, then e-mailed with cc and bcc, finally backing up to an external drive and the cloud. I was ready to leave for eight days. Then, this morning over coffee, Simon had thrown a curveball into my game plan. But I wasn't going to think about that now.

What mattered was that I'd promised Shay I'd come home, and I had.

"Where's your favorite hotel?" Miles asked.

"I don't have a favorite."

Miles wanted an answer. They always did. "I always like Aspen in the summer. Palm Springs is always nice in the winter."

"Too bad we only have Nettie's on Lark."

"I'll love staying at Nettie's. It's full of memories."

"I don't know about that. It's been renovated, but it's not a hotel at all, you know. You're in for a DIY vacation."

As long as DIY included decent cell reception, I'd be fine. I pulled out my phone. I'd just hold it. In case an urgent message came through. I needed to check in with Annie, but really, after the two flights all I wanted was a bath, a drink, and a nap before seeing Shay.

"If you need to check in with work, I don't mind," Miles said. "You can tell your boss about the land if you want."

I didn't know if Miles was kidding and didn't ask. "No, it's fine. Tell me what's new with Shay."

"You text her all the time, I'm sure you know all about her art class. She's really enjoying it."

"She's a natural."

Miles glanced at me. "I know."

A lump grew in my throat. "How are your parents?" I asked.

"Excited about the wedding. Yours?"

"They're in Portland now."

"Celia always admired their adventurous spirit. Sometimes I think she envied it."

I shrugged. "I guess."

We'd pass one more cornfield and then exit the highway, while most cars would keep going and going toward bigger towns or parts unknown. But again, not a stalk in sight. Out of the rich soil grew a Cineplex. My stomach lurched. I pressed my lips together as we rounded the exit, drove past the gas stations and string of fast-food drive-thrus that our exit was previously known for. *Last Exit for 50 Miles*. Then just over four miles down the road, we turned left onto Main Street. The stoplight was red.

There was a stoplight in Chance? Until I was twelve, there wasn't even a stop *sign*.

"I can't believe this."

"Not the Chance you remember, huh, Ted?"

"No. It's—"

"Progress."

I should have agreed. I should have been happy. But this seemed *wrong*. Main Street looked posh. Preppy, even. The Chance I knew was gritty on the outside, pretty on the inside. The place I knew didn't have filigreed street signs so glossy they looked freshly painted—or lampposts to match. And what was with the overflowing baskets of fuchsia impatiens dangling from them? And the awnings. Forest-green awnings decorated every window and doorway from the computer doctor on one corner to the eye doctor on the other. Where were the mismatched signs that had been there my whole life? Those had made sense, announcing goods and services, not flaunting a designer color scheme.

It was as if Chance had turned its back on itself.

I stared at the storefronts. I had never noticed the marble arches between the businesses, or how the ivy trailed across the bricks and along the bottom of the windows. I snapped a few pictures with my phone so I could study them later, before coming back with my camera.

"I'd love to see Shay tonight. Just a quick visit? I want to go to sleep early, but . . ."

"It's Gallery Night for her summer art class. That's why she had to stay back, to set up her sculpture. She wants you to come, of course. I'll pick you up."

"Tonight? Really?"

"You can't say no, Ted. She's over the moon that you'll be there."

"Right. Of course. Of course I'll go."

Crap.

That didn't give me much time to check in with Annie, unpack, shower, change clothes, apply a little makeup. It gave me no time to just be in Chance *without* seeing people I knew. People I'd left behind. Exhaustion swept through me. Was that what accounted for my hallucination? As Miles cruised past the alley where Celia and I had hidden to smoke cigarettes the summer before we'd started high school, I could swear I saw her standing with her back against the brick wall, a grown-out perm (an ill-fated attempt to have hair like mine) pulled up in a ragged ponytail. And there I was, sitting cross-legged on the ground with pack of Parliaments in my lap. We'd thought no one knew what we were doing, but we were grounded. Twice.

My arms and legs tingled, almost itched. Curls crept across my forehead like spiders. The air from the A/C burned my eyes, and the vibrations from Miles tapping the steering wheel pricked my nerves. I felt the ripples and stitching in the leather seatback through my no-wrinkle dress.

Since when was I the goddamn Princess and the Pea?

Chapter 2

NETTIE'S ON LARK, ITS official name, had been a boarding house until the 1950s, at which point it shifted into a trendier-sounding bed-and-breakfast. After that it was an *inn,* which meant: no breakfast. Now, rooms were listed on vacation rental sites and described as vintage, charming, and cozy. Painted in whimsical pale blue and yellow, the house mimicked the sky and the sun in a child's drawing. The turret had made Nettie's on Lark the castle of my childhood daydreams. In college, I had cleaned the room at the top of the spiral staircase and found there was nothing royal about it, except that it was a royal pain in the ass. Celia and I had dubbed it the "Rapunzel room" and each week we'd flip a coin. The loser was the one to clean it.

"Thanks again for the ride. I know it was a hassle."

"You took two flights to get here. It was the least I could do."

"What time tonight?"

"Seven-fifteen. I promised Shay we'd be early."

"I'll be ready."

The trunk popped. "You sure you'll be okay here alone? There's no room service, you know."

"No one waits on me at the hotels," I said. "That's not who

I am." That wasn't completely true. The staff did wait on me when I was with Simon, and they would have when I was alone, if I'd let them.

"You don't even have a car to get around."

"I don't have a car anywhere. I walk." Or drive golf carts, or take cabs, Uber, or limos.

Miles fiddled with his keys. His voice softened. "I still miss her, Ted. Every day. Every single day. I still can't believe she's really gone." Then he looked at me. "But you should also know, Violet's an angel. I love her very much."

After high school Violet went off to Kent State or Kenyon or maybe Kentucky and stayed or moved somewhere else. I had no idea. She hadn't even been a peripheral person in my life until she and Miles had connected a few years ago after she'd returned for a reason I'd never asked about. At first, Shay had mentioned that she'd gone somewhere with her dad and Violet. A picnic, I think. Or maybe it was a ball game. Then it had been that her dad and Violet were dating. Shay's texts were full of "we," and "they," and "all of us." Then it had been the bombshell that they'd gotten engaged. It didn't matter. Not really. I wasn't here to disrupt anything, change anything, or offer my opinion. I was here to take pictures and spend time with Shay, catch up with old friends, and then go back to my real life. "I'm happy for you. And for Shay. I'm sure Violet is lovely."

"I know you're thinking about Cee. It's harder to forget about her when you're not on the other side of the country."

"You think I've forgotten her?"

"Not completely, no."

Miles had no idea when or how or what I thought about Celia. He never asked; I never told. I didn't infringe on his grief or his time or his privacy and I didn't invite him into mine. I tempered my breathing, moved my hair off my neck so the sweat would evaporate.

"Do you really want to talk about this now?"

"Not really, but Shay's asking a lot of questions lately, more than ever before. I want you to be honest with her, tell her whatever she wants to know. Within reason. She's twelve. And whatever you do or don't do while you're here, do not leave without saying good-bye to Shay."

"I would never—"

"You mean *never again*."

I wished my phone would buzz or my hair would catch fire.

"So, seven-fifteen?"

"Promise me you won't do anything to upset her."

"Of course I won't. What aren't you telling me? I know I only see her once a year, but she asked me to come back, and I'm here." I thought that would count for something.

"A fancy weekend once a year doesn't take the place of being there day after day for a kid. No matter how much she likes your shopping sprees on Michigan Avenue."

"I know that."

Miles's tone was so calm that he sounded rehearsed. "Shay's not a baby anymore, but she's still dazzled by you. You're the fancy one, the one who got away, the one who spoils her and lets her leave her life behind for a weekend. And I'm glad. But now you're here, and this is our world. Shay's world. Everything here is very real. Including her mother."

"What do you think I'm going to do to her? I'm here because of Shay, Miles. Believe me, I wouldn't be here taking pictures at your wedding unless she'd asked me. She made an excellent case for me coming back and doing this; she only used about a third of the guilt she could have. That kid should be a lawyer."

"She wants to be an artist."

"Of course she does." I looked down. "It's not easy for me to be here."

Miles stared out the windshield again. "I realize that."

"So let's agree I'm here because Shay asked me to be here. Whatever else I've done or haven't done, can we just table it for now? Please?"

Miles nodded and I opened the car door before I inhaled all the oxygen.

"Hey Ted," Miles said as I stepped out. "Don't you wonder what Celia would have thought of your leaving? I mean, I think she'd be very proud of your success, but—"

"No, I don't wonder." I shut the door, careful not to slam it.

I didn't have to wonder.

I knew.

The door was unlocked, but there was no one to greet me: no registration desk, no sleek computerized check-in, no key card or concierge. This was Nettie's on Lark, which meant that I was met by an envelope propped up on the walnut mantel in what had once been the parlor. It was still a parlor of sorts, with a mauve velvet settee and chair that looked decidedly uncomfortable. A key tied to a grosgrain ribbon dangled from a coat tree on hiatus for summer.

Welcome, Teddi Lerner.
The wireless code is Nettie6.
You have the house e-mail and phone number.
Texting or e-mail is the best way to reach me.
Welcome back to Chance,
Nettie

Anyone who owned Nettie's was called Nettie. According to the booking site, the current owner lived in Columbus, but wanted a reminder of an uncomplicated, small-town childhood. Chance was definitely small town. "Uncomplicated" was subjective. The new owner would have learned before his (her?) purchase that Chance residents, committed to maintaining town history, had the inn proclaimed a historic landmark in 1952. The name couldn't be changed.

It was just a town tradition to call the owner Nettie.

The Garden Suite was at the end of the hall. It was as if I'd entered a champagne cave—the color, not the bubbly wine. The tacky brass bed I remembered had been replaced by a four-poster draped with an ivory lace canopy. The fringed pillows and bedspread shimmered with shades of iridescent pink. A small oval table flanked by two wing chairs had been positioned between the floor-to-ceiling windows. One dresser had drawers, but its mate had been repurposed to hold a marble sink. Underneath the sink, on a shelf, sat a small black refrigerator, as if this were a dorm room in a time-travel novel. A bookcase held well-read versions of classics, as it had when I'd borrowed them in college, reading the books I'd pretended to read in high school. I skimmed the spines for my favorites: Austen, Hemingway, Bronte, Orwell. I didn't look in the bathroom but imagined no new owner would have removed a claw-foot tub. I held on to hope that something here had remained the same.

My visit felt like a layover in an alternate universe. Perhaps unpacking would ground me. One by one I removed my dresses from my suitcase, smoothed the skirts, adjusted the shoulders and necklines, and slipped each one onto a wooden hanger in the small, not-renovated closet. I stored my almost-empty suitcase under the bed, and placed my camera bag on top. I plopped next to it and fell back.

I pulled out my phone and Bluetooth headset.

"Hey," Annie said. "How were your flights?"

"Fine. They're always fine. Tell me what's going on there."

"Nothing. How's your homecoming so far?"

"Come on, tell me. What have I missed?"

"You've been gone less than twenty-four hours. We are still standing tall without you."

"What about the Thomas retreat? Do they want full coverage and social media shots?"

"Two days."

"Two days? That's not enough. Who talked to them?"

"Devereaux."

"Are you kidding me? He couldn't upsell his own grandmother."

"Calm down. I'm kidding. I told them you were out of town and that I'd get the info together and call them tomorrow."

"Don't do that to me! E-mail me all the information. I can put together a proposal tonight—oh, no I can't. I have plans."

"That sounds promising."

"It's a local, um, art show."

"Oh, now they produce art in Mayberry!"

"It did produce me, you know."

"Touché!"

"Someone very important to me is one of the artists, so I have to go. I mean, I want to go. I'm excited to go."

Annie and I were coworkers, and buddies based on work. I didn't lie to her. I never lied. I just left things out—like my entire personal life before I'd arrived in San Francisco. All she knew—all anyone knew—was that I grew up in a tiny Ohio town and that my parents traveled around the country in a Winnebago, the latter being a distracting bit of family trivia that had nothing to do with me. As far as I could tell, no one who met me in Chicago (my first stop after leaving Chance) or San Francisco or any city I'd worked in was interested in my past. They were only interested in my present. And in my pictures. Simon *had* met my parents during their swing through Petaluma, but that was the only time.

"When you get back we need to talk. I have a proposition for you that will change your life," he'd said, as he handed me a bowl of steel-cut oats with organic dried cherries and maple syrup he'd brought back from Vermont and now had on a regular monthly shipment. "Just don't get too distracted while you're gone. Keep your eye on the prize."

"More weddings."

"You never know where you'll meet our next happy couple."

When I'd opened my mouth to reply he just kissed me, essence of oatmeal and all.

Annie's voice faded as I noticed a basket in the corner of the room by the door, looking as if Little Red Riding Hood had skipped through.

"Did you send me something?"

"No, I don't even know where you're staying, remember? You wouldn't tell me."

"Right." I knelt by the basket and opened the lid to find a bottle wrapped in a blue cotton kitchen towel. Pinot Noir from a local winery.

"I've got to go. I'll call you tomorrow. I mean, I'll call Mr. Thomas tomorrow."

"He wants you to call him Henry. Don't forget."

"Right. E-mail me everything. And, Annie?"

"Yes?"

"Thanks."

I yanked the Bluetooth and held the bottle against my warm cheek, the smooth, cool glass as soothing as finding the cold spot on my favorite pillow. Only one person knew my penchant for this particular red. And only one person knew what I did after drinking too much of it the night Celia was diagnosed.

Three months, the doctors had said.

For as much as they knew, they'd known nothing.

Celia had stayed with us for six. Fighting, laughing, dying.

I opened the wine with the waiting corkscrew. I filled a glass. This was just a bottle of wine, which happened to be from an Ohio winery. Nothing more than a nice gesture. A welcome gift. It had to be, because I was not ready to think it was a reminder, an ultimatum, or even a long-distance peace offering.

I opened a drawer where somehow I knew I'd find snacks, and pulled out a sleeve of Ritz crackers. I opened the mini fridge and saw the block of cream cheese. Someone had told the new owner about this classic Chance hors d'oeuvre. I lifted the basket to the table and something rattled. I reached inside and pulled out a small, unwrapped box and removed the lid. It didn't occur to me that I might not like what was inside until the lid was off. I shut my eyes. Celia had always loved my enthusiasm, so I opened one eye. Then the other.

A wispy silver chain lay on a pillow of cotton. A brightly polished charm. Half a heart. A zigzag edge. The word "Best."

Celia and I had exchanged necklaces like this for Hanukkah

when we were in sixth grade, except we'd had ours engraved at a mall kiosk. I looked at the heart, remembering my first "real" jewelry.

We hadn't wasted a moment that day. We tried on the necklaces right there and admired each other, and ourselves, in the mall's mirrored columns, before we set our necklaces back into their boxes so they could be properly wrapped and exchanged.

This necklace. The one in the basket. It couldn't be *the* necklace. Could it?

One. Two. Three.

I flipped over the charm and stared at the engraved letter *T*. For Teddi.

My fingers trembled. Before now I'd chosen my reminders. I wasn't used to having them presented to me, in a picnic basket no less.

Obviously that was changing.

This *was* Celia's necklace. I shut my eyes and traced the engraving with my finger, then peered inside the basket, ran my hand along the lining. No note. No clue. Nothing. Celia and I hadn't worn those necklaces since eighth grade, but it didn't surprise me that she would have kept hers. It had to be Miles who left it. An unsung good deed, or something to exacerbate the guilt he believed I should feel for staying away.

I dug into the front pocket of my camera bag and pulled out a small black pouch I always carried but hadn't opened in years. I poured out my necklace, which had tarnished.

Friends. I flipped it over. *C.*

I clasped both chains around my neck and the halves fell together, a heart complete, though the necklaces were never meant to be worn by one person. The charms overlapped and the delicate chains tangled. I looked into the mirror over the dresser. I closed my eyes and the necklaces felt just right. Their temperature on my décolletage, cool and soothing; their weight, light but present.

I poured more wine and stood to the side of the window in case the neighbors could see in, which I knew they could. I had looked in these windows many times, although never as a half-dressed traveler.

Townie.

The garden on the east side of the house, like the one at the house I grew up in, was filled this time of year with hundreds of black-eyed Susans and petunias. My mother hadn't been an inventive gardener, but she was always passionate, except when she wasn't. But in this garden were lilac bushes and zinnias, delphiniums, lilies, and rosebushes—so many rosebushes—all of them more lush than when I'd been in my teens and twenties and had looked out this window, counting the minutes until Celia and I would grab our pay (cash, under the table) and decide what to do next.

The stepping-stones placed through the garden led nowhere except back to one another. That had always frustrated me, but it had never seemed to bother Celia. She'd been happy to walk the stones and turn around and walk back. I was the one who had wanted to keep going.

I could see the corner of the inn's garage to the west, its side covered with purple clematis. I looked at the rooftops nearby, now knowing what stretched beyond the garden, beyond Chance, beyond Ohio. That was where my adventures were born, the ones I hadn't imagined existed for me.

I rubbed the charms as if they were Aladdin's lamp. I held up my glass for so long that my arm hurt. A drink sealed the deal, even when you were alone.

"I'm back," I said aloud, willing the words through the white blanket of clouds to whatever heaven existed.

Chapter 3

THE CELIA STILLMAN COOPER
MULTIPURPOSE ROOM

I DIDN'T KNOW THEY'D named a room after Celia. No one had posted *that* on Facebook. I could see why. Naming a multipurpose room after someone who had died way too young—that was just, well, strange. A park or just a tree would have been nice. A room in a library or a library book about art. Or a street lined with trees with a library at one end, or a gazebo, or a garden. But a "multipurpose room"? I'd never thought of Celia as generic.

But once I was over the threshold, the room popped to life with sculptures displayed on the floor, on tables, attached to walls. Papier-mâché, metal, wood, clay. Paintings and sketches hung on the walls. People filled the room, as did chatter and laughter.

Now her name fit.

"I'm going to find Vi and Shay," Miles said without turning toward me. "Look around. These kids are amazing."

THE BEST OF UNION TOWNSHIP said the sign. Well, if it was on a sign it had to be true.

I surveyed the scene. I could stand in one spot and look around the room, be finished in less than a minute, and just wait for Shay to show me around. Or I could start with the pieces closest to me, read the name of the artist, the age, and the name of the work and then study it. That was probably the better plan. I wasn't sure what was expected of me. Was I supposed to care about kids I didn't know?

I was here for Shay but I didn't want to appear rude and just look for her sculpture. Everyone else seemed to be *kvelling* and snapping smartphone photos of everyone and everything for social media bragging and cloud-based posterity. There were the duck face poses, and the head tilt poses, and the poses pointing to artwork like it was just revealed from behind Door Number 1 on *The Price Is Right*. There were also the ear-to-ear smile poses, parents hugging-the-kid-a-little-tighter-and-longer-than-she'd-have-liked poses.

My favorite photos to take were the quiet gotchas—someone staring out the window or at their phone or at someone else across the room. I loved freezing those moments—faces contorted from listening or laughing, bellies extended, foreheads scrunched. Those candids weren't the prettiest or most composed photos, but they were most real, capturing not just what someone was doing—but what they were feeling.

And that's why they paid me, as Simon liked to joke, "the big bucks."

There were dozens of photos like that of me and Celia—most tucked away in boxes, stored away in my memory.

My phone buzzed in the pocket of my dress. All my dresses had pockets, thanks to the seamstress at the Hester in New York. I was like a child the way I collected trinkets on my travels. Not to mention that I needed my hands free to hold my camera. After a second vibration, I slipped the phone only halfway out. *Simon.* I pressed a button to make him go away. For now.

Someone tapped me on the shoulder from behind. I turned

around faster than I should have, still woozy from the flights and their accompanying naps, not to mention the wine. As the girl came into focus, I looked into familiar green eyes and noticed dark lashes. The kind that didn't need mascara. The kind of lashes women envied, like Celia's.

"Aunt Teddi!"

Her giggle pierced through me. "Shay?" I stepped back to see her more clearly. Flat-ironed auburn hair down her back, a spray of freckles across her nose. I pulled her into a hug. "Shayna Rose!"

God, she was beautiful. Was it possible that she was more beautiful than her mother? And since when were there so many years between eleven and twelve? When I saw Shay in Chicago last summer she was a little girl. Now I detected the scent and shine of lip gloss. No, maybe ChapStick, maybe strawberry. Whatever it was, Shay was now one tube of liquid eyeliner away from being a teenager. I hugged her tighter and swayed. She hugged back, and didn't stop me from rocking.

"Should I say it?"

"Sure, Aunt Tee." Shay smirked.

"You look just like your mom did when she was twelve."

"I know."

My throat tightened and I squeezed my eyes closed. For one moment—maybe two—I pretended she was Celia, that I was twelve and hugging my best friend, that we had more than twenty years left together. But this was Shayna. I pulled back.

"You're so grown-up! I love your dress!" A mint-green skater dress floated around her slender frame.

Shay rolled her eyes and smiled. I chuckled. Celia had rolled her eyes in defiance as a teen—for effect as an adult.

"Show me your sculpture."

Shay and I linked arms as we walked across the room. Shay looked at me, and smiled. We were almost eye to eye. She didn't get her height from Celia, who tipped the growth charts at five foot one. I ached to lift Shay the way I had when she was two, when she'd hold on with her legs and let go with her arms, certain I wouldn't let her fall. How had we come so far and gone backwards at the same time?

We stopped in front of a metal structure that looked like an Erector Set pileup. And then I saw it. The slide. The swing perpetually ready to fall. "It's a playground!" I said as I glanced at the title that confirmed my vision. Thank goodness.

"You're darn right it's a playground."

Shay and I turned around.

"Uncle Beck!" She collapsed onto him, and he hugged her. "Do you like it?" Shay looked up at her uncle as if his answer was uncertain.

"Like it? It's the best one. I love it."

"It's for you! It's your backyard from when you and Mommy grew up. From the pictures you showed me."

"So it is!" Beck said.

I squinted. The slide and swings, the sandbox and playhouse I'd claimed as my own as a child. All artistically out of proportion and awkwardly, beautifully, close together and built from metal scraps and held together with nuts and bolts and imagination. And with hope.

"Nice to see you, Beck."

He nodded, as if I were a passerby in the grocery store he kind of sort of recognized. He glanced at everything except my eyes— my longer hair, the slight definition in my arms, the curve of my waist. Then he looked away. At least he didn't punch me like he had when we were kids, when he was the bratty little brother I never had but always wanted. Until we'd grown up and wanted more. My heart pounded in my chest and boomed in my ears, muting the sounds around me. Beck should not be happy to see me, and he wasn't.

"Teddi."

Then finally, for a moment, we looked right into each other's eyes.

I looked away first.

God, he looked good. Almost too good. Five-o'clock shadow and closely cropped hair (silver since his twenties) added a refined touch to his artsy veneer. I shuddered. He wore faded jeans (well worn, not bought that way) and a white button-down shirt. I diverted my eyes from his face, to the buttons. I stood close enough to see the cloth's weave. I looked back at the sculpture, but not before noticing how Beck's shoulders packed the inside of his black sport coat.

I wished he'd let himself go.

Beck was one of those annoying people without a substantial online footprint. I didn't really know much about him anymore, did I? There was a time I would have asked how he was, what was new, how he felt—and another time when I'd have just known.

Now I only knew what I saw.

Beck at thirty-five looked much older than Beck at twenty-nine. There was a seriousness to him, a heaviness, as if he couldn't be budged.

He wasn't the only one. I was weighted to the floor. Everything around me looked far away. I widened my stance so I wouldn't fall. I willed my voice not to shake, not to sound too happy, too terrified, too unsure. Too anything.

Before Celia became sick I'd have teased Beck. I might have

made fun of the gray or given him a noogie for old times' sake. But our shared sorrow had changed us. Brought us close. Kept us apart.

"I didn't expect to see you here," I said.

"Uncle Beck is here all the time!" Shay beamed.

I reached my arm around Beck's waist. He was six-four, so he bent sideways and reciprocated with a quick one-armed hug around my waist. He steadied me . . . and then pulled away. I wanted both arms. I closed my eyes, a fleeting wish for another scenario. But Beck stepped away and still had one hand in his jeans pocket. Casual and unaffected. Breezy Beck. Same as always. And not the same at all.

"Oh, I want you to meet someone," Shay said. "Be right back."

Shay scampered away, hair and dress bouncing with enthusiastic oblivion.

"I'm going to look around," Beck said as he turned.

"Wait, don't go . . . I'm not here to bother you." I couldn't even ask him if he'd left the wine. Considering this welcome, the gift didn't fit.

"I know why you're back." He shook his head. "What I still don't know is why you left."

Shay returned with two other girls and saved me. "This is Aunt Teddi, the one I told you about. She's a *photographer.*"

No one had ever said it with such pride.

Beck kissed the top of Shay's head and walked away.

"This is Chloe and Rebecca. Want to see their sculptures?"

I did not.

"Of course," I said. "Lead the way."

After my guided tour, I shrank into a chair in the corner of the multipurpose room as Shay and her friends rounded for the second and then third time. She waved at me with every lap, and I replied with a thumbs-up. Shay walked with her head up, shoulders back. She was a budding artist with a graceful air, who had time for school, art, and technology but not for toys. Or boys, from the looks of things. She stayed solely with Chloe and Rebecca. Celia and I had always existed within a cluster of girls and boys, living as if our roots were entangled, because they were. It was both the advantage and drawback of growing up in Chance—the infinite impact each person could have on you. And you on them.

Until you left.

Miles stood on the opposite side of the room with Beck and Violet, who I'd seen only in a few Facebook photos, along with assorted other parent-looking people. Miles, Violet, Shay, and Beck were the only people I recognized in the whole room. This was the rec center for the whole township—all eighteen thousand residents—and the classes were sixth through twelfth grades, or so I'd gathered from the artist bios that accompanied each piece.

The grown-ups in the room drank ginger ale out of plastic champagne flutes and tipped their heads back in laughter, waved their arms in animated conversation. The kids whispered and skipped, or stood, all serious brooding-artist-like, with arms crossed. Nobody—neither friend nor stranger—gestured for me to join them. This time, I was relieved when my phone vibrated in my pocket.

Annie: There's an issue with the meeting in Miami.

I typed back, only briefly glancing at the screen.

Me: What?

Annie: They want to reschedule for another weekend but your
     calendar says Portland. What's in Portland? Do we have a
     property in Portland I don't know about?

Me: Don't worry about Portland. Book Miami.

I had just finished typing when I saw Shay walking toward
me with—with Violet. I stood, ready with my excuses for staying on the other side of the room, antisocial, engaging with my
technology and not with the artwork or humans. The closer
they came, the taller Violet appeared. And wispy. Tall and wispy
like a single flower. She wore a pink linen sheath. Her hair was
short and tapered and offset by a pair of dangly earrings that
showcased her long neck. Her makeup was subtle, yet polished.
She wore it all well.

If I were working, I would refer to Violet as "the bride." I'd
grown accustomed to the billowy ease, and lofty expectations,
of born-to-privilege women, not to mention the high demands
that matched the high style of the ones who were self-made. I
knew just what to do. But Violet was no ordinary bride. She was
marrying my best friend's husband. And she had her arm around
my best friend's daughter.

"Thank you for coming, Teddi." Violet drew me into a hug.

Damn, she smelled like a flower, too.

I stood in the community center foyer, staring at the flyer-covered
bulletin board. The kids and grown-ups around here had plenty
to choose from these days: a slick, colorful poster announced
children's theater auditions; a black-and-white photocopied flyer
offered a Mandarin tutor; other brochures listed local contests,

craft fairs, and sporting events. Everything from acting to ukuleles.

No zoology? *Slackers.*

I expected Shay to be huddled with Chloe and Rebecca, or buzzing about the awards ceremony with a group from her class, but she was walking the perimeter of the room—alone. I stepped back to the bulletin board before she could see me, and this time, I read about the computer classes for seniors.

"Hey, Aunt Tee."

"Hey, Shay-Shay." I kept my gaze on the board while I put my arm around Shay's shoulder. "Tonight was great. Thank you for inviting me. One day I bet your art will be shown in a fancy gallery in New York." *No pressure. No expectations. No rush.* "If that's what you want. And I will be right there on your opening night if you do."

Shay shrugged. I turned and playfully pushed her shoulder. "Don't do that," I said. "I mean it. You're really talented. I'm glad you're doing what you love to do. Not everyone gets to, you know."

"Did my mom?"

I smoothed my dress to camouflage the fact I wasn't sure how to answer. "Did your mom what? Do what she loved? Of course she did. She loved kids and teaching art and making clothes and she loved being your mom. That was top of the list."

"Why didn't she just, you know, be an artist?"

"It's not always easy. You know that, right? But she really always wanted to teach."

Shay turned her head and looked at me, as if the side-eye would force me to reveal the truth. That was the truth. Celia always loved kids and always loved making art. When she realized she could be an artist and a teacher, she was sold. One night she mentioned moving to New York to try the starving-sidewalk-artist lifestyle, but when I brought it up again, she laughed, citing temporary insanity. I wasn't always sure why she had tucked away her dreams for a picket fence, but Celia had always promised me that Miles and Chance were enough. I only half believed her until Shay was born, then I knew she was telling the truth.

"How about you?" Shay asked.

"What did I always want to be? I always wanted to be a photographer. But you! You wanted to deliver pizza until you were five. You thought that was the best job ever. We saved pizza boxes and you wore a hat and went outside, rang the doorbell, and delivered pizza to your mom and me about fifty times one night. Lucky for us you thought a nickel was a great tip."

Shay opened her eyes wide and laughed. Then she pointed to a brochure tacked to the board. "OMG, look at this." She unpinned it and handed it to me.

Union County Art Council Photography Contest

I unfolded the page and looked at last year's winning entries. First place—a covered bridge at sunrise, half-bare trees, leaves scattered on the road, high grasses curved from a breeze. Cliché, perhaps, but beautiful. Second place—an outstretched arm and open hand poised to catch a twirling, blurry baton. Third place—I closed the pamphlet. Maybe this year Shay could win. I'd definitely come back for that. "I didn't know you were into photography too, Shay. That's awesome." My heart pattered with delight and I bent into Shay, our heads almost touching.

"Not me, Aunt Tee. *You*. My next class is on collage, anyway.

No offense, I'm really into multimedia stuff. You totally should do it though. I bet you'd win."

"Oh, that's not for me, sweetie."

"Why not?"

Where to start? "Well, I'm here to shoot the wedding, and I don't live here anymore, it's for residents of the township."

Shay grabbed the brochure and rifled through it, then pointed and tapped.

Ages 18 and up

Subject: My Ohio

"Look, it says it right here. The subject has to be Ohio. The photographer doesn't have to live in Ohio, just have ties to Ohio."

I had ties all right, and at the moment they felt like a noose.

"Oh. You're right. I don't have any pictures of Ohio."

Shay tapped me with her shoulder. "Just take something while you're here. You said I should do what I love. Don't *you* love taking pictures? Not the wedding ones. The other ones."

"What other ones?"

"The art ones."

I swallowed as if I'd been caught in a lie. "I do love taking those kinds of pictures." I did, didn't I? I knew I *had*.

"So what's the problem?"

"That's not why I'm here."

"You hate it here." Shay snatched back the brochure.

"I don't hate it here." I took back the paper.

"You haven't been here in years. I hear what people say, you know. That you took off during Mom's funeral."

I felt dizzy and touched the wall for balance. "It's more complicated than that."

Shay rolled her eyes. "Whatever."

"Not whatever. I'll tell you what happened, but not here. Not now. Okay?"

"Fine. But that doesn't have anything to do with the contest. Don't you think there's anything here besides a stupid wedding you could take pictures of? Is that why you left? Because there's nothing here?"

"*You're* here. I came back because you asked me to. You know that."

"So what's the big deal in entering a contest while you're here?"

"Shay, look. I'm a professional photographer. And if you believe the hype, I'm good at my job." I laughed as I said this, hoping she would laugh too. No such luck. "It wouldn't be fair for me to enter. Would it?"

"Nothing is fair."

"What are you talking about?" I knew damn well what, so I draped my arm around her. "You know what I mean."

She looked away, as if so disappointed in me she didn't know what to say, or did know. I wasn't sure which was worse.

"Honey, I wish I could do the contest, but the thing is—"

"Don't you think you could win? Because if that's the reason then that's lame."

"I don't know," I whispered, talking to myself more than to Shay. "I haven't thought about doing something like this for a long time."

I didn't want to be part of anything here except Shay's life—and the wedding, as its photographer. Because of Shay.

"Please say you'll think about it, Aunt Tee, okay? C'mon, *be brave*."

She may have been mocking me, I wasn't sure, but I gulped back a swell of emotions. That's exactly what Celia had said.

That time, I'd said no.

I'd been sitting on the edge of Celia's hospital bed and we were playing War, like we had when we were kids, the card piles resting on her lap. "I want you to be brave," Celia had said, lifting one of my hands and holding it between hers, gripping as hard as I knew she could, which wasn't hard at all. "And I want you to promise me something."

"This isn't a real war, you know, it's a game."

Even the joke hadn't warded off the chills that crept up my neck, urging me to shiver. I would promise her anything.

"I want you to promise me you'll leave," Celia had said.

"What are you talking about? I just got here."

"No, Tee, listen to me. I want you to follow your bliss, your dreams, forge your own path, dance like nobody's watching."

I'd rolled my eyes on purpose.

"Go ahead, roll your eyes." Celia laughed and then exhaled. "You deserve to be happier than you can be here. It was right for me, but it's not right for you. I want you to be brave and leave Chance."

"Hell no," I'd said.

Celia never knew that I'd done as she'd asked. But, running out on her funeral, abandoning my apartment, and driving away with my foot on the gas, ignoring the rearview mirror as if I were living inside a chart-topping country song, was anything but brave.

And here was Shay using that same damned word.

"I'll think about the contest," I said. "That's all I can promise." Shay grabbed my arm and jumped up and down like she wanted a dollar for the ice-cream truck. I felt like she'd just reached into my gut and ripped out an organ. Maybe two.

"What are you going to think about?"

It was Miles.

"Nothing," we said.

In the parking lot, Miles and Beck fist-bumped like fraternity brothers.

"See you soon," Beck said.

"Absolutely," Violet said.

"We're going for ice cream, Aunt Teddi."

"Oh sweetie, I'm exhausted. I've been up since yesterday, I think." I looked at Miles. "If it's not out of the way, would you mind just dropping me off?"

"I'll drive you. It'll give us time for some girl talk," Violet said. I must've gone pale. "About the wedding. I would love to talk to you about the wedding photos," she said.

"Yes, we need to do that, but if you don't mind . . ."

"You're tired, I'm sorry."

"Don't be. It's your big day. And that's why I'm here." I smiled at Shay.

"How about if *Daddy* drives Aunt Teddi, and you and me meet him at The Frosty Fox?"

"You and *I* . . ." Violet said.

Shay rolled her eyes. "I don't have class until noon tomorrow, Aunt Tee. Will you meet me for breakfast?"

"Just text me in the morning."

Shay hugged me and as she pulled away I held on to her arm. "Love you."

"Love you too."

But she was already walking away with Violet.

"I'll drive her home. I mean, to Nettie's on Lark," Beck said. "You go catch up with the girls. I'll meet you there."

"You sure?" Miles asked.

Beck nodded.

No one asked if I was sure.

"You'll be over tomorrow to talk wedding, right?" Miles asked.

"Right."

"Well, good night, then."

"Night," Beck and I said in unison.

"Which car is yours?"

Beck pushed a button on his key fob and the lights in his SUV flickered nearby. My heart pattered in time.

"You're still close to Miles."

Beck's eyes narrowed; the smile and light he had around Shay had left. *Please, Beck, say something. Don't make me do this alone.*

"I'm Miles's best man."

"Wow, I had no idea." The best man, who will be in all the wedding photos. My throat burned and my eyes stung as pressure built.

"Of course you didn't. How could you? Miles and Shay are still my family. And Violet's great."

So I'd heard. So I'd seen.

"It's not too hard for you? It's none of my business but—"

"You're damn right it's none of your business."

I jerked back.

"Don't look so surprised. You went away. Disappeared. The rest of us stayed and helped each other through everything. If anything, it made us all closer."

"I can see that. I just . . ."

"Just what?"

"I never stopped caring, you know."

Beck walked away and then turned around. "Bullshit!"

I stepped away.

"Don't yell at me. This isn't easy for me either." My voice cracked and the words sputtered through. "I'm sorry."

"You didn't behave like someone who's sorry."

"I know. But I am."

"You're sorry you left or you're sorry you left without saying good-bye to me?"

"Both."

"You expect me to believe you?"

"No." I patched the holes in my ego with the truth. "But it's true."

It was the longest ten minutes of my life.

"Why did you insist on driving me if you're not going to say one word?"

"So Miles could celebrate with Shay and Violet. This art class is a big deal. Shay had to submit a portfolio to get in and this was her first show."

"A portfolio? At twelve? I didn't know that. She's amazing."

"You're right. She is." Beck clamped his lips, then opened them. "So, you two were thick as thieves before we left."

"I suppose you could say that."

"Everything okay? With Shay I mean?"

I placed the brochure on the center console between us. "She wants me to do this."

"Why?"

"Because it's a photography contest and I'm a photographer?"

"You're a *wedding* photographer." His emphasis was condescending.

"What is that supposed to mean?"

"It's not supposed to mean anything. It's just what you are, right? Isn't that what's on your fancy business card?"

"Wow, Beck, I—"

"Do it if you want. Not like there's anyone stopping you, but don't you think the scales are unfairly tipped in your favor?"

"How so?" How was anything ever tipped in my favor, especially in the past five hours?

"You already get paid to do this. Isn't that enough recognition? How much attention do you need?"

"Oh my God! I wouldn't be doing it for me! I'd be doing it because Shay asked me to do it. Like the wedding." He thought so poorly of me. I'd earned that. "It doesn't matter. I'm sure she'll forget about it by the morning."

"I wouldn't count on it."

"Why not?"

"Did you stop to think it might not really be about the contest?"

I waited for him to say more.

"Of course you didn't. I'll spell it out for you, but only because I don't want Shay to get hurt. She wants you to have a reason to come back, or at least to care. But you're right, it was probably nothing. How could someone possibly think you feel a connection to here?"

"You don't live here either."

Beck sighed and shook his head. "No, I don't. I live a whole hour away. But I didn't shed this place like old skin the way you did."

Be brave.

"We need to talk."

"I don't want to talk, Teddi. Not now. I just want to get through the week. I'm happy for Miles, but you're not the only one who remembers that if Cee were here, none of this would be happening."

I turned away, my selfish veil falling between us. I opened the car door but stayed in my seat.

"I'll see you at the wedding rehearsal."

"I'm not going home until after the wedding, so you'll probably see me tomorrow."

"Tomorrow?"

"It won't be intentional, don't worry. You're back in Chance. If you walk around the block—"

"I know. You see everyone twice."

I sat on the porch swing, watching moths buzz around the lights, that flanked the front door. They bumped into each other to reach the glow. That's the way people were drawn to Celia. In good times and in bad, even fucking cancer bad.

After Celia had been diagnosed, it was never again just plain ordinary cancer, as if that was a thing. It was fucking cancer. The kind that couldn't be blasted or banished. The kind that didn't last long, except for eternal consequences that began when I went back to my apartment and climbed into a bottle of wine, before Beck arrived and pulled me out of it.

"We can't fall apart when Cee needs us the most," he'd said. "Pull yourself together."

Soon, "You'll be all right" had turned into "We'll be all right" and we'd moved next to each other on the couch. Over Chinese takeout and bubble tea, Beck and I became grown-up friends and confidantes, and had planned to see each other the next night. And then, the one after that. To talk about anything and nothing. To watch movies that made us laugh and forget. To eat food that Celia couldn't bear to smell. To cry when happiness was unbearable.

After a month, he kissed the top of my head.

Took you long enough, I'd thought.

He'd lingered, his nose pressed into my hair. My head was near his chest, and I smelled Irish Spring and a musky aftershave. After a childhood full of Celia's and my attempts to ditch her little brother at the playground—I didn't want him to move one single inch.

I looked up and examined his features. Forehead: smooth, his hair trimmed short. Eyes: blue-gray, almost translucent. Eyelashes: blond and blinking. Nose: straight and somewhat broad, but well proportioned. Upper lip: razor stubble. Mouth—

I kissed him. Without interruption he kissed me back. The sadness tried to wiggle its way through so Beck kissed harder. I didn't stop him, because that pushed away everything else. After minutes, or maybe it was hours, I stopped, but kept my hands on his chest. I unbuttoned one button on his shirt and he lifted my face with his hands and kissed my nose and chuckled, but not in a way that made me self-conscious—his voice deep in a way that steadied me, as if I were on a rocking ship that had just been towed into a calm port.

"Are you sure?" he asked.

"Yes."

I was sure. It didn't matter what we did or didn't do, Celia would still die.

That began the best and worst months of my life.

Chapter 4

TAP TAP TAP.

I heard it again. *Tap tap tap.* Then the sound of paper sliding under the door. I sat, my muscles sore the way they always were when I stowed away for a night or two on the couch/guest bed/kitchen of my parents' Winnebago. My jaw clenched from a dream I'd forgotten, or maybe it was from everything I remembered. *Chance, Shayna, art show, contest, Beck, wine.* The wine! On the counter sat my glass with a respectable—or shameful, depending on your point of view—amount missing from the bottle. My dress hung over the arm of the rocker.

I loved that dress, with its ribbons of vertical blues and contrasting orange stitching. Celia had always said blue was my best color, so when in doubt, I wore blue. A smile tugged at the sides of my mouth and I was grateful for the little moment of joy. I experienced them infrequently now, those specks of time where I forgot Celia was gone, that I couldn't talk to her later. Gone was a given.

After breakfast I would visit Celia's grave.

I'd never been there. Not after the funeral, when I should have been tossing a small shovelful of dirt into the earth. (I had been busy breaking my lease and packing my bags.) And not for the "unveiling" a year later, when I should have seen the headstone before retreating to Chance Hall for lox and bagels with Celia's family. (I was busy managing a photo shoot in Santa Monica.)

I blamed my job for keeping me away.

The note.

The note was scribbled in dark pencil on a torn piece of sketch pad paper.

Good morning Aunt Tee! ☆♡ :ü

When you wake up just text me and I'll meet you at the Fat Chance Café.
(Dad said to tell you it's where Chance Bakery used to be.)

Love,
Shay ♡⊕✿

(Your phone must be off so Dad said to let you sleep but I have something I want to show you so I hope you wake up soon.)

♡ ü ✿

I scampered back to the bed and dug under the blankets. I toggled the switch to turn my phone on. Beeps meant Annie. Chimes meant Shay. It was different, being with Shay on her home turf. When we met up each summer in Chicago, I'd whisk her around the Hester, arm in arm for our weekend adventure. The staff knew her as my niece and I'd never corrected them. Since the summer she turned seven, I'd flown to Chicago from wherever I was working, while Miles had driven to Chicago with Shay. Then he stepped back for forty-eight hours into his complimentary room (or so he thought), allowing me and Shay quality girl time in my suite and beyond.

In Chance, Shay was showing me things and showing me off, taking the lead in both good ways and bad. She'd planned our morning. I didn't know what would happen, who I would see, or what I would feel. A haze of worry unsteadied me. I grabbed on to the dresser. When these feelings had tapped me on the shoulder over the past six years, I'd shoved them into drawers in one city and moved on to the next, because everywhere and nowhere was my home.

I imagined that if Simon had it his way, I'd call San Francisco my home. I also imagined that if Simon had it his way, I'd call him my husband.

The early-morning air hinted of the humidity that would later stifle the county. I swore I could feel my hair frizzing at my scalp, but I left it down anyway. I tiptoed across the porch and down the four wide wooden steps, as if everyday footsteps would wake the neighborhood. I skittered to the other side of Lark Street like a car was zooming toward me, but the only sound was the whoosh and whirl of the automatic sprinklers next door.

I stared at the house, grand in its appearance, simple in its comforts. Looking through the viewfinder, I zoomed in. The white paint on the banister had tiny chips at the edges. Was that from use or from time? Was it an oversight? I moved the camera away from my face.

At work, I scrutinized everything. I captured images and then created perfection. I also stole morning moments like this one to experience the hotels' mountain views or beach sunrises without any filters, without making any adjustments. I *was* still taking pictures just for me, beauty stored on a memory card. I didn't *do* anything with them, but I held on to them. Like one of those harried parents who had given up on the grand idea of a scrapbook, I'd stopped saying *someday*.

In world-class cities, I sat in our hotel lobbies sipping coffee from a monogrammed paper cup, a folded newspaper in my lap, and watched as the world awoke in slow motion. I loved the way that high-heeled footsteps ticked on marble floors, the way rolling suitcases hummed or bumped along with a broken wheel. And I loved to watch men and women stride ahead, all purpose and intention, on their way to . . . somewhere.

Today it was my turn. I sashayed down Lark wearing my light blue sundress, as if I were the star of an elaborate tampon commercial. All that was missing was the voiceover. I seemed to be the only person outside. So much for walking around the block and seeing everyone twice.

At a Hester hotel, someone was always up and about and milling around, tidying up from one event, getting ready for the next retreat or wedding or bevy of families on vacation. There were always people around, yet I was almost always alone. This was different.

I turned right onto Main Street, stopped, and my mouth dropped open. "Close your mouth before you catch flies," my mother would say.

Main Street splayed in front of me as if in a Hallmark movie. I lifted my camera and watched through my lens where the world existed only within the frame. Men and women ran through Chance Square, doing laps on the perimeter, stopping to stretch, to chat, to guzzle water. Women with ponytails pushed strollers up and down both sides of the street, some with an extra mini-me trailing behind, wearing plastic sunglasses and carrying a sippy cup as if it were a latte. A yoga group was setting up just out of the way of a climbing wall.

I continued down Main, slowing my pace and my thoughts. I pushed away each bit of work that tried to wind its way through, although I tapped a few notes onto my phone for the sake of safekeeping—and sanity. I set a second reminder to call Mr. Thomas—Henry—and a third to confirm next week's appointments. I stood under an awning, looked up, and snapped a picture. No one even turned their head my way.

I sat on an iron bench before the sun could transform it into a frying pan. People milled about on the sidewalk in front of me. Behind me I captured the homespun scene from another angle. I didn't remember such bustle.

I turned back and as the last of the crowd dissipated, I saw my reflection in the window in front of me. I was more fit than I'd been in my early thirties; after two years of promising myself to use the gym three times a week, I had finally done it.

My shoulders and arms had never been flabby, but now they were slightly defined. I surreptitiously curled and uncurled one arm and watched my bicep expand and retreat. I stood straighter and shifted from left to right and my dress followed. I grabbed my pockets as if to curtsy, lifting my dress enough to see a few inches above my knees. Beck had called me Chicken Legs when we were kids, but my legs—and his opinion of them—had changed over the years. I let go of my skirt.

Shit. Was that someone on the other side of the glass? I stepped forward and squinted and beyond my image saw a tall table with carafes and containers. Shit. Shit. Shit. How had I not realized I was standing in front of—wasn't this the tailor, or had it been the shoe repair shop? I stepped back and saw the sign on the door as it opened.

PERK

HOT COFFEE FOR COOL CUSTOMERS

Two coffee-cup–toting hipsters walked out. I didn't know what was more unsettling: hipsters and small-batch roasted coffee, or being caught looking at my reflection by someone on the other side of the glass. I turned back to smile, to accept my embarrassment head on, but the man wearing the apron just continued with his work, placing a large pitcher in the center of a high top, and rearranging the smaller ones around it, as if they were an audience. I darted away from the window.

At least I hadn't picked my teeth.

I continued down Main and when I turned the corner, there was Miles standing by the light post, Shay standing by the wall next to him. She leapt toward me and grabbed my hand.

"Let's go!"

"Good morning to you, too."

Shay laughed. "Good morning, Aunt Tee. I thought you'd never get here."

"Good morning." I hadn't expected to see Miles. "I thought we were meeting at the bakery."

"Well, it's not really the bakery anymore."

We started walking, Shay holding my hand, being sweet. Being Shay.

"It's a reincarnation of Chance Bakery," Miles said. "Steel-cut oatmeal, organic muffins, gourmet sandwiches and salads. A smoothie bar. I'm sure you'll like it."

"It's called Fat Chance!" Shay said.

Of course it is.

I'd scrolled past the uploaded photos on Facebook and Instagram and had read through enough comments to know that a local woman bought Chance Bakery. From what I could gather, she hadn't concerned herself with politically correct business names and old-fashioned baked goods, it was all cost analysis, profit and loss statements, and whether gluten free was a fad or the new normal. The new owner was a CPA by training and an analyst by nature. I had a feeling she didn't give away free cookies. Chance Bakery had always given everyone a free cookie.

My phone buzzed and I stopped short, yanking my hand from Shay's, which startled me more than it did her. I was unaccustomed to being attached. I kissed the top of her head, grateful she was still a bit shorter than me. Miles kept walking. "One sec," I said as I thumb-tapped my home screen and then swiped away another text from Simon.

I slid my hand back into Shay's. "I'm hungry."

"Here we are," Miles said.

Bistro tables and chairs with primary-colored umbrellas had been arranged within a low white picket fence. Pots of drought-tolerant geraniums sat in the middle of each table. A few strollers crowded one corner, with toddlers sucking on straws and sippy cups and women I didn't recognize sipping from over-sized mugs. A mister was blowing a fine breeze. As if my hair wasn't frizzy enough. I looked away, feeling like an intruder, yet wanting to capture this moment I never imagined, never could have imagined. It would be creepy if I started taking pictures so I could remember the Americana. At work, no one questioned the constant clicks and snaps, because my name tag said TEDDI LERNER, HOUSE PHOTOGRAPHER. That title made me laugh and cringe, as if I walked around taking pictures of houses.

I held up my camera anyway. *Click click.* The colorful umbrellas against the light blue and cotton puff sky. Flower petals. Wheels. Cracks in the sidewalk—the only thing I recognized. Shay tugged at me and mouthed, *See?*

"Take a picture of me and Daddy!" Shay stepped in front of the camera and smashed her cheek against Miles's. He smiled. He'd done this before—posed with his daughter for an impromptu photo session. It was the thing to do. It just wasn't something I'd ever done.

Click.

"Now let me take one of you and Daddy."

"You don't have to do that," I said.

"I know. I want to."

I stepped next to Miles and folded my hands over my camera. He put his arm around me, tipped his head toward mine, and smiled. Perhaps Miles had forgotten I couldn't vote in Union County.

"Look at me, Aunt Tee." I did. Shay lifted her phone and tapped. "Done."

Everyone's a photographer these days.

I opened the door as Shay and Miles walked inside. I followed, and let the door close so close behind me that it tapped my behind and moved me forward. With that one step I felt as if I'd entered a hotel suite in a city I'd never been to, only to find it smelled of familiar perfume.

The space had been renovated from bland bakery to intentional vintage with mismatched chairs and patterned booths, checkered curtains and stainless steel countertops.

"Ta-dah," Shay said. "See why I wanted to come?"

"Yes, I love it!" I never thought I'd be able to get a smoothie with wheatgrass in Chance. I loved being wrong. I could also order egg-white quiche. And a gluten-free carrot muffin, if I went gluten free in the next week.

"No, look!" Shay pointed. "I designed the logo for Dad's campaign. There are signs in a lot of the store windows, too."

Attached to the front of the counter was a red, white, and blue banner draped with a COOPER FOR COUNTY COMMISSIONER logo. C-C-C. Shay dipped her head and looked up at me. I winked.

Shay blushed and then a smile spread across her face. Celia's smile. Wide and slightly open-mouthed. Genuine, unmistakable, infectious.

"Sculpture, collage, graphic design. What's next?"

"You'll see."

Miles glanced at his phone. "Shay, I've got to go. Walk home and Vi will drive you to class this afternoon, okay?"

"Fine," Shay said.

Miles looked at me. "I promised Vi I'd go over the seating chart with her. Again." He chuckled.

"Stupid," Shay whispered. She looked at Miles and said, "Sorry."

"I'll see you this afternoon, right, Teddi? Around two?" Miles asked.

"Sure thing."

Shay tugged away as Miles kissed her on the head. She turned to me and shrugged.

"Let's sit and order something," I said. "I'm starved."

Shay and I ordered, and waited, and ate. I still hadn't seen anyone I knew. Maybe I'd imagined my entire existence here. Maybe Chance had always been a beehive of small-town abundance and I somehow missed it, or worse, ignored it.

"So, I was thinking about the contest," I said with my mouthful of muffin.

"Uncle Beck said I have to apologize for that. For bugging you. That it's not your thing and I have to respect that. So you don't have to do it. You shouldn't do it. Forget I mentioned it."

"Maybe I want to do it."

"I promised Uncle Beck I'd apologize, and if you enter the contest he'll think I guilted you into it."

"No he won't."

"Yes he will."

"I'm a grown-up. If I want to enter that contest, I can. I just haven't decided whether I want to."

"I don't want to get into trouble."

"Oh my God, Shay, it's not like you could've forced me against my will." But she totally could have. I should have been relieved, but I didn't want anyone telling me what to do. Or not do—especially not Beck.

Shay sipped on the straw of her oversized chocolate milk and then blew into it, creating a crown of light brown bubbles. I didn't tell her to stop.

Shay rested her elbows on either side of her plate of challah French toast.

"They're going to make me move, you know. They think I don't know, but I heard them talking about selling the house. They can do what they want with the house but I'm not leaving."

I stabbed a piece of my omelet and chewed as many times as was possible, which wasn't very many.

"Maybe you didn't hear right. If you were moving, surely someone would have told you."

"I guess."

"Is there a For Sale sign in the yard? People coming through and looking at the house?"

"No."

"Did your dad make you clean out your closet?"

"No."

"Then it's not for sale."

"Not yet."

"Right, so don't worry about it yet. What do you want to do today?"

"I have to go home for a stupid dress fitting before art class."

"Nothing stupid about a dress fitting! I love dresses. Want me to come?"

"Daddy said you can't."

Really? I could fly across the country to take the pictures at the wedding but I couldn't watch Shay have her dress hemmed. "But I'll see you later, right? When I come over to talk about the wedding pictures?"

"Don't go back to Nettie's on Lark, Aunt Tee! Stay with us! Dad's always saying it's a shame that there's no nice hotel around here. Our house is better than a hotel anyway! You can stay in my room."

I would not, could not, sleep in Celia's house.

"I'll text him!"

"Shay! Stop!" I grabbed her phone. "Your dad and Violet need their privacy."

"They don't live alone. I live there too. And why shouldn't you be there, you were Mom's best friend."

"You're right, but it just wouldn't be comfortable."

"Why not?"

"Because things are different now."

"Obvi."

"Shay—"

"I just wanted you to be close since you're usually not around at all."

Called out by a twelve-year-old. Again. "I'll be around all week. We'll have lots of time together. How about we hit that mall you love? Tomorrow after art class, okay?"

Shay smirked. "Fine."

The door opened to a blast of giggles, and a group of girls walked in, no discernible space between them. I recognized only the idea of them. At that age, Celia and I had always wanted, needed, to be close enough to whisper and be heard.

I hoped Shay knew these girls. I wanted to meet her best friend, to see flashes of my and Celia's past in their private jokes and feel hope for the future in their rays of laughter. I wanted Shay to know, really know, how twelve-year-old promises could last a lifetime, to one day look back and know that twelve-year-old jokes could always be funny. Or that remembering them could be funny. I wanted to tell her that these friendships, the ones she had today, mattered in the scheme of her big, long life. Especially her best friendship. The simultaneous need and independence of a lifelong best top-tier friendship was unparalleled and irreplaceable. *That* was both the blessing and the curse. I couldn't tell if these girls knew Shay. She'd never mentioned a best friend before. I hadn't asked. Shay stared at her food, and I stared at her.

I focused my attention on the chattering of the girls, the pitch and cadence of their giggles, snaps, and foot taps. They read the chalkboard menus aloud, as if for the first time.

"That's a hideous banner," one girl said, pointing at the banner Shay had designed for Miles. "Stupid thing to hang in here."

"Hey . . ." I said.

The girls swiveled their bodies toward us, then back to the counter.

"Don't, Aunt Tee!" Shay whispered and shook her head.

"Do you know them?"

"Yeah," she said.

One girl surreptitiously pressed her foot on the banner, leaving the dusty print of a flip-flop.

"Holy—"

"Shit?" Shay whispered. "I know."

I should have said no, that holy moly was what I was going to say. I might not have been a perfect faux aunt, but I wasn't a liar. "Yes. Holy shit. Shouldn't we do something? Call the manager?"

Shay just shook her head.

The girls stood near the counter, collected bags and cups, and floated toward the door without a glance our way. I watched until each of them was outside and the door shut.

"What was that all about?"

"Leave it alone."

"Tell me."

"Can't we talk about something else?"

"What's going on?"

"Let it go, please!" Shay wasn't demanding, she was pleading.

"Fine." How was I supposed to follow what had just happened? Talk about the weather? "Chloe and Rebecca from last night seem nice."

"They are."

"Are they your best friends?"

55

"I just met them. In art class. Not everybody has to have a best friend, you know."

"I know, but . . ."

"Who's *your* best friend now?"

I swallowed. Celia had been the only person I'd ever called my best friend.

"See? You don't have one. Why should I?"

"Well . . . when your mom and I were your age we were inseparable."

"Well," Shay said. "I'm not my mother."

"Oh, you're just like her. You look like her, you even sound like her, and you're talented like she was—crazy talented. That sculpture? That banner? I bet you could sew too if you wanted to."

"I don't want to sew." Shay looked away from me, at the wall, then the table, then back to the wall.

"Well, that's okay, I just meant you were a lot like your mom. That's a good thing. A really good thing."

Shay shrugged, and tucked her hair behind her ears, but wisps of preteen insecurities remained.

I wondered how Shay would have been different if Celia were alive. Or was this Shay—a little uncertain, sometimes bold, and both serious and whimsical—predestined from the start?

It was irrelevant really, because Celia wasn't here. But Shay was, and she was fabulous, even when she ignored my questions or snapped at her dad.

"I'm sorry. I didn't mean to say you should want to be just like your mother. You're your own person. And that's exactly who you should be."

"It's not that I don't want to be like her," Shay said. "I'm just not."

Chapter 5

I STAYED AT THE Fat Chance Café answering e-mails and writing next week's to-do lists for an hour after Shay left. The waitress refilled my Royal Albert vintage teacup with hot water three times without being asked. I folded a ten-dollar bill and slid it all the way under the mismatched saucer before I left.

I headed away from Main Street and the town square, away from Lark Street, and toward the oldest part of town with the biggest trees, the smallest houses, and the most space that hadn't been filled in with something new. Here, the sidewalks rippled from overgrown roots. The houses were stone or brick, two- or three-bedroom family homes built when no one had en suite bathrooms or attached garages. The residents either stayed for decades or left for the newer east side of town when their second or third babies were born, aching for a little more space inside and a little more space outside between themselves and their neighbors. That's where I grew up, even though my parents never had that second baby. And now, even that part of town wasn't new anymore.

I stood in the middle of the road and stared through the tunnel of arching oaks. The small stone cottage on the corner sat atop a hill. I'd always thought that house belonged in a fairy tale, or had been stolen from one. I crouched and looked up. The cottage looked like a mansion from this angle, pinned onto a bulletin board made from a cumulous sky.

House photographer, indeed.

A woman pushing a double stroller passed me and smiled, as if she always passed a woman in a dress squatting and holding a camera.

"Good morning," I said. Maybe I'd seen her yesterday at the art show, or earlier on Main Street. If I hadn't, I'd probably see her tomorrow—so, win-win. The toddler twisted his body to look back at me. I baby-waved and he waved back.

Then I saw my cousin, Maggie Myers, standing outside her one-story redbrick bungalow, with a bucket at her feet, dragging a squeegee across her first-floor windows. Or at least the bottom half of the windows. Maggie was my mother's second cousin, but to me, she was always just Cousin Maggie. She had retired from her half century as head librarian at Chance Library, staying on even after the Union County Public Library had opened years before. She had e-mailed my mother that the whole town had thrown a surprise retirement party and announced the closing of Chance Library that very same day. I'd been convinced the town council kept it open just for her.

I turned my back to Maggie's house, embarrassed that I hadn't called her in years, guilty that I hadn't yet stopped by or at least let her know I was coming. I'd come back later, or another day, to say hello and catch up on family gossip I'd already heard from my mother.

"Yoo-hoo!"

Step, slide. Step, slide. Step, slide.

"Yoo-hoo!"

I turned around. "Hi, Cousin Maggie."

"Can you help me?" she asked.

"Sure." I walked up Maggie's steps and met her in front of the window.

"Can't reach that corner," she said.

I took the squeegee and maneuvered it into the upper right corner of the window. I twisted the handle and pulled, making it longer.

"Oh, I knew I forgot something."

"How are you?" I asked. I waited to be scolded for something. Cousin Maggie had always been very kind to me but was also known for being no-nonsense.

"I'm good now that I can reach the top of the window." Maggie looked at the window and ignored me. Then she turned to me and startled, as if I'd appeared out of nowhere. "You're here."

"I am. I'm . . ."

"Going to the wedding."

Miles and Violet's wedding was the event of the summer; everyone in town would know about it.

"You look well, dear."

"Thank you, so do you."

"Oh, don't be ridiculous. I look about as well as my windows here, and they're peeling and creaky and get stuck from the heat and then stuck from the cold."

My parents had always complained of the same thing.

"What's this I hear about you leaving?"

"I left six years ago and moved to Chicago. But I live mostly in San Francisco now, when I'm not traveling for work, that is."

"How does someone live somewhere mostly? You either live somewhere or you don't. And anyway, you and Lester have lived on Poppy Lane ever since the day you two got married. I don't know why you are taking off in that contraption of yours."

She thought I was my mother.

My thoughts shuffled. I didn't know if I was supposed to correct her. I looked back down the street in search of help. No one was coming from either direction.

"Is anyone home?" I asked.

"You know Melvin passed more than twenty years ago."

Okay, Cousin Melvin *had* died when I was in high school. Maybe Maggie was coming around to the present. With my arm around her, I led Cousin Maggie toward the front door, suddenly relieved it was me who she yoo-hooed to help her, and not some stranger.

"I'm not Joyce, Cousin Maggie. I'm Teddi, her daughter. My parents moved, remember? You were at their going-away party. You broke the bottle of champagne on the back of their Winnebago."

Cousin Maggie looked at me and blinked a few times as if snapping her own mental pictures, or perhaps, scrolling back through her memories. "The trailer. They drove off in that godawful trailer."

My mother preferred the term "mobile home."

"That's right."

"And you're Teddi."

"I am."

"I always thought that was a silly name."

Now I remembered why my mother didn't like Cousin Maggie very much.

To me, Cousin Maggie had been like a fairy godmother in sensible shoes. She seemed to know what I needed, and when I needed it. It was Cousin Maggie who handed me *Are You There*

God? It's Me, Margaret two months before I got my period when I was eleven. Cousin Maggie also gave me my first real camera for Hanukkah when I was fourteen.

"You can make the world look however you want it to look with this," she'd said.

Not sure that was the best advice, but it was the best gift.

Just then, a petite black woman stepped out of the front door. She was dressed in bright coral capris and a sleeveless white blouse, with a short scarf tied around her neck like she was a character in *Grease*. Her hair was wide and loose and bounced with each step. Cousin Maggie was wearing seersucker Bermuda shorts, a royal blue polo shirt, and a visor. They both were dressed for a day out, though it didn't seem as if they were going anywhere.

"You okay out here, Maggie? Who've we got here?" Her voice contained remnants of an island accent. She pursed her lips and stared at me.

"I'm Teddi Lerner, I grew up here. My mother is Maggie's cousin, I mean, I'm Maggie's cousin. I'm here—"

"For the wedding."

I sighed.

"Well, Cousin, I'm Maggie's friend." She looked at my hand, still on Maggie's shoulder.

"Should she really be out here on her own? Washing windows?" I touched Maggie's arm with my other hand.

"Oh, she's fine."

"I've known her my whole life. She doesn't seem fine to me." More words bubbled up but I swallowed them.

"When was the last time you saw her? When was the last time your mother saw her?"

I said nothing.

"When was the last time you talked to her?"

I said nothing.

"How about your mother?"

"I don't know."

"Well, I do know, and nowadays, *this* is how Maggie is, Cousin Teddi."

They walked into the house and the door slammed behind them. I stood there and pictured the Cousin Maggie I'd known, with a short bob and a little bounce, her feet slightly turned out like a duck's, wearing shoes that made her feet look like paddles. She'd always had a book in her hand and another under her arm, and had been the only relative my mother tolerated, even with the digs about my name and the Winnebago. Cousin Maggie never had children of her own. She had handed me an envelope with ten one-hundred-dollar bills the day I left for college.

"For your books," she'd said.

It was the only time I'd hugged her.

I turned, snapped a picture of the double-hung window, the bucket still on the ground, a squeegee beside it. I wished I'd asked that woman to take a photo of me and Cousin Maggie.

I sat on Maggie's steps and scrolled through e-mails. I didn't reply, I just read. It was time to let Annie steer the ship. If she needed help, she'd call.

When I finished, I stared at my home screen, at my favorite shot of the Golden Gate Bridge I'd taken from Hawk Hill. I hadn't even shared it on Instagram or Facebook. My social media was all work related, all the time. Sharing personal photos like this one would be too, well, personal. I held my breath at the thought of my worlds colliding and exhaled when I realized it wasn't possible for my two worlds to collide.

I was only part of one world.

The door behind me opened but I didn't turn around. I'd been reprimanded enough in the past twelve hours.

"I'm leaving." I flagged another e-mail and stood.

"Don't go on account of me." The woman sat on the steps. "She's asleep. Sit."

"I didn't mean to trouble her. Or you."

"You're not. And she might not even remember."

"No one visits her?"

"No."

"I'm surprised."

"Why? You're related and you don't. I'm not trying to be mean. If her family took care of her, I'd be out of a job."

"I thought you said you were her friend."

"I am. But I'm also being paid to 'watch her.'"

I bobbed my head, not knowing what to say.

"We have a copy of the *San Francisco* magazine you were in. Where they wrote that article on your boss."

"You do?"

"Absolutely. I showed it to Maggie online and she wanted a real one. So I ordered it from their Web site."

"It has been really good for business." There was just one part about how I'd photographed Gretchen Halliday's mountaintop wedding in Aspen, and our bookings tripled nationwide. Of course, Simon had failed to mention Gretchen's business manager was *his* cousin.

"That's in part to you, I bet."

"Well, the article was about Simon."

"Yes, but there was a whole sidebar on the weddings there. And a photo of you."

"I wasn't the only one in that photo."

"You might as well have been. At least to the people here."

"You're too kind. It was just part of my job."

"Would you autograph it?"

"Autograph what?"

"The magazine. I'll go get it."

"Me? No, that's silly."

"It absolutely is not silly. You should be proud of your accomplishments. Own them. And I can't think of a better way of owning something than to scribble your name right on top of it." The woman rose and walked into the house and right out again with the magazine and a pen. She sat and opened it to the page with my photo.

"I've never done this before."

"First time for everything."

Indeed. I clicked the pen. "I'm so embarrassed, I don't know your name. I'm sorry."

"My name is Lorraine, but sign it to Maggie."

"Nice to meet you, Lorraine."

"Likewise."

Dear Cousin Maggie,
All of this was made possible because of the Canon X40.
Love,
Teddi

Lorraine looked at it and smiled. "She'll love this. Sorry I barked at you earlier. I'm just protective of Maggie."

"Is Maggie the only person you're 'friends with'?"

"She's enough."

I laughed. "Seems like a hard way to spend your days. Have you always done this kind of work?"

"No. I just needed a change."

"I can relate to that."

"I think we all can at some time or another, don't you think?"

"Do you think she's happy? Maggie, I mean."

"I think so." Lorraine lifted the magazine from my lap and placed it on hers. "The doctor says the glitches in her memory are normal for someone her age. She's tired a lot, and ornery, but otherwise she's good company. She can still talk about books for hours. Or until she dozes off. I consider it an honor to spend time with her. With anyone this age, really. I don't have family of my own nearby, and neither does she. I hope I'm blessed enough to be washing windows when I'm her age."

"Me too."

For months after Celia died it was hard for me to look at any woman older than she would ever be, wondering what she would have been like at forty, at fifty, at eighty-two. I had envied those women and their families and friends with such fervor that sometimes I'd turned away and counted to ten, or one hundred, before I could turn back, tell them to smile, and fake my enthusiasm as I snapped their picture. I never thought about what these women's lives might have been like on an ordinary day.

"I should go. It was nice to meet you. Thank you for taking such good care of Cousin Maggie."

We stood, hesitated, and then hugged. "You're very easy to talk to," I said.

"So are you, Cousin Teddi."

I stepped away, still clutching my phone, then laid my other hand on Lorraine's arm.

"How about we take a selfie?"

I was heading back to Nettie's on Lark when my phone buzzed.

This is Violet. See you at 2? Would you like to stay for dinner?

I stared at the last part of the text.

Would you like to stay for dinner?

Celia's replacement was inviting me to eat dinner in Celia's house with Celia's husband and Celia's daughter. It was zero degrees of separation from all things Celia.

"Teddi?"

I jolted and looked toward the street. "Josie?"

She pulled out an earbud and bounced in place, jogged over to me, and continued bouncing. Her Lycra running shorts and top glistened from the sun. Or maybe from sweat.

"I heard you were back! You should've called me!" She hugged me tight, disregarding the fact that sweaty people shouldn't hug. She swayed from side to side as if she didn't want to let go. I hugged her back. I could shower off the sweat later.

"It's so good to see you," I said as I pulled back.

"It's amazing!" Josie hugged me again.

She looked the same as she had six years ago, and the same as she did in every online photo. Josie had one world too. Josie's World.

Her bright white teeth shone through an uncomplicated

smile. Josie was trim, but curvy, with big boobs and long, dark blond hair. She always looked good, which would have been annoying had it been anyone but Josie. She may have looked like one of the Real Housewives of Beverly Hills, but her big heart was all Chance, Ohio. You didn't see that in those photos but I remembered that now.

"You look great," I said.

"Have to stay fit. But obviously I don't have to tell you that. You look amazing, Teddi."

I shifted my gaze from Josie's glowing face and looked down the street, as if my finish line was in sight.

"What do you think?" Josie asked.

"Of?"

"Of Chance. It's changed, hasn't it?"

"It sure has. I can't believe how many people were out and about. And a coffee shop? And a trendy café."

"No more Manny's Luncheonette," Josie said.

"It's kind of sad."

"Really? I don't think it's sad. Why would you think it's sad?"

"I don't know. It's just different."

"The outside is different. Not the inside." Josie stopped bouncing and placed her hands on her hips. "We're attracting a lot of young families because of all the development in the county. The mall, the rec center, the pool. And the whole park around the pond has been redone."

"I read about that."

"I guess you know about Miles. What am I saying? Of course you know."

I grinned with my lips closed. That was my I-have-no-idea-what-to-say grin.

"Oh!" Josie yelled, and bounced faster.

"What?" I yelled too, and swiveled my head from side to side. Who did she see? What was the matter? Josie had always been a well-meaning alarmist.

"You have to come for book club at my house tonight. All the girls will be there!"

"Oh, that's so sweet but . . . I haven't read the book." It was the best excuse I could think of on the spot.

"Oh, none of us reads the book, silly. Well, maybe some of us. But that's not the point. The point is to have a set time to get together. It's more of an excuse than anything else. You'd be surprised how easy it is to lose touch with someone who's just around the corner." Bounce. Bounce. Bounce. "C'mon, it's just the girls. Casual. Good food. Better wine." Bounce. Bounce. Bounce.

"I can't impose."

"You're not imposing—you're invited. Come at seven. Once everyone knows you're back they'll want to see you."

All of a sudden six years didn't seem like enough time to get ready. "Tonight at seven. Got it. I'll definitely try." My voice shook.

"I won't take no for an answer."

I didn't think she would.

I held my camera away from my chest. "Well, I guess I'll see you later. I'm just off to take some pictures."

"Of course you are. Think of that! The same photographer Gretchen Halliday had for her wedding is taking pictures of our town. Could I come along? What are you taking pictures of while you're here? Besides the wedding, I mean? Are you scouting locations for a new hotel? For a destination wedding? I won't tell a soul, I promise. Maybe I could help."

"No, nothing like that. I just . . . it's just what I do."

I hated people watching me while I worked. Civilians always

chimed in with "helpful hints." *Don't you think you should move a little to the left? You'll see better from here.* Or they tried to see what I was looking at by nearly resting their chins on my shoulder for perspective. *I wish I had your eye.* I wished they'd take their chins off my shoulder. Take a picture *of this, of her, of him, of me!*

One minute I wanted to be a townie again, and the next I missed being on my own at a hotel, where I could nod and smile and keep on going to the beach or a deck or a pool, unencumbered by expectations, and unaware of exclusions. I'd been on my own for six years, without too many personal demands. Perhaps I'd forgotten how to be part of something.

Josie glanced at her Fitbit. "Got to fly!"

"I don't really . . ."

Josie held up one finger and I stopped talking, as directed. "Later, okay? We'll be expecting you tonight. It's casual, come as you are. You're welcome to bring your camera, of course." Josie winked. "Have to finish my run before the kids wake up. Although teenagers could sleep all day. Welcome home, Teddi. You were missed."

Josie didn't wait for a response. She waved, pivoted, and her bounce turned into a run.

I headed in the opposite direction from Josie and from Lark Street. That's when I realized I was running too.

West End Cemetery was at the west end of Chance. The town's founders had been nothing if not literal.

I paced back and forth in front of the closed iron gates. Then I walked to the far corner, toward the residential streets, and back to the cemetery gate. I shuffled my feet and looked down the street as if waiting for a ride, my heart pounding harder than it should have been for the walk/run I'd taken to get there. I exhaled to slow my pulse, then sipped lukewarm water from the bottle I'd bought at the Fat Chance Café.

"Tomorrow would probably be a better day," I said aloud to no one. "Cee wouldn't care either way."

I remembered Celia every day, but in third person. *She* would have liked, loved, or hated. (Although Celia didn't hate.) I never thought of her as or said "you." Maybe that was my problem. Maybe well-adjusted people fashioned invisible companions from their dead loved ones, talked to them aloud, set a place at the table, continued where they left off, at least inside their own minds. I saw my and Celia's friendship like a movie that ran on a loop and watched it as if I were an observer. Today, Celia would have been glad I was here at the cemetery, but only because I hadn't been coerced, because it was my idea. She never would have begrudged my absence; guilt wasn't her MO.

It was mine.

Without leaving the comfort of the sidewalk, I could see that the grass in the cemetery was audaciously green. Stones, pebble sized to golf ball sized, were layered atop the headstones and placed sporadically on the ground. Jews didn't leave flowers. Flowers died. Stones remained. Like memories.

I didn't subscribe to all the customs of my religion, but this one was dead on.

I chuckled and covered my mouth even though no one was around to hear me. Celia would have laughed too.

I felt the stone from my pocket, its ancient water-worn curves, smooth and cool. I'd chosen it with care more than five years before and carried it with me everywhere.

I was going to do it. I was counting to ten, and then going in. One.

Two.

Three.

Four . . .

I reached the gate.

"If you're waiting for someone to come out, you're going to wait a while."

I turned my hand into a visor and saw a tall man with a square, clean-shaven jaw. He wore khaki shorts and a blue T-shirt with a yellow bear silhouette I recognized as Oski, the Cal mascot. The man neither smiled nor frowned, but he did nod. His face said *I am being respectful because I am in a cemetery.* My face most likely said *I am a chicken shit.* He took a pen from his ear and scribbled into the notebook in the palm of his hand. Then he poked the pencil back through his brown hair that looked intentionally tousled. Or styled. He tucked the notebook into his sock.

"Sorry, I didn't know anyone was there." God, that was stupid. There are hundreds of people in there. Maybe thousands.

"Seems to me you wanted to come in, but thought if you stood there long enough someone might come and get you. Or, I could help you find who you're looking for."

This was a solo mission.

"No, I don't want to come in, but thanks for the offer." I spoke firmly while looking at the ground. Who was this gatekeeper anyway? Couldn't someone go to a cemetery unattended and uninterrupted? I reached into my pocket and rolled the stone between my fingers. The stone and the cemetery would still be here tomorrow. Hopefully the man would not. I raised my head to say good-bye.

He was gone.

Chapter 6

I HAD NO REASON to dislike Violet. I had no reason to dislike Violet. I had no reason to dislike Violet.

Say it enough times, Teddi, and you might believe it.

I stood on the porch in front of Nettie's and glanced at my phone. I hadn't responded to Violet's dinner invitation. My mother would cringe at my bad manners.

I walked down Lark, turned left onto Main, crossed Chance Square, and detoured down streets where my childhood friends had lived. I wandered a few blocks too far west, photographing lilac bushes and white picket fences, cracks in the sidewalk and more trellis-climbing clematis. Most houses in Chance were small, but they loomed large in my memory—trees I'd climbed, porches I'd sat on, sidewalks I'd scraped my knuckles on playing games of jacks. As I grew older there had been bar mitzvah brunches, sweet sixteen luncheons, graduation barbecues. The tables full of home-cooked food were a beloved Chance tradition, my mother's baked contributions a regrettable one. The images pushed through in a way they hadn't when I'd still lived there. My gait wobbled. I felt as if I'd been gone for decades.

I turned onto Grand Street—Celia's street—and looked up

through the tall oaks and let the leaves frame the summer-blue sky. *Click.* Was the sky better here? Brighter? Or did it just seem so because things on the ground seemed a little dark and daunting? I'd leave these scenes as my naked eye saw them and the lens captured them. No enhancements. No calibrations. No retouching. They'd be honest and imperfect. Maybe just right for a little contest? Or maybe, just right for me.

I switched to work mode and imagined the light, the best bench in Chance Square to take photos before the wedding ceremony, and how the sun would filter through the trees and dance atop the chuppah. I loved the art of my work. And I was beginning to like the management of it as well. Simon had encouraged me to become somewhat corporate in addition to being creative. He included me in planning meetings for all the hotel's marketing materials and Web sites. I'd started to compile a manual for new photographers. The hotels were known for their four-star restaurants and wine cellars, so I suggested we hire someone just to take food photos for social media. That wasn't my specialty.

But, noticing how the sky was an unbroken shade of blue, so wide and uninterrupted by clouds that it seemed right above me—that came naturally to me, as it always had. I held my breath for a moment and waited, as if it would float down and wrap itself around me. As if it should.

Minutes later, I stared at the numbers nailed next to the door: 304. I saw Celia at the window, the door, in the garden, with the stroller, wearing a big, floppy straw hat that hung past her shoulders as if she were Droopy Dog. God, we loved those old cartoons and spent many Saturday mornings watching them with my dad. I hadn't thought about that in years. We'd sit on the floor, much closer to the television than either of our mothers would have allowed, eating bowls of Rice Krispies. My dad always turned up the volume, playfully blaming Snap, Crackle, and Pop that he couldn't hear. When was the last time I'd eaten Rice Krispies not mixed with melted marshmallows and butter? The hotel chefs made monster-sized krispie squares dipped in chocolate, who could blame me?

Next thing I knew, I had grabbed the doorknob. *The doorknob.* I yanked back my hand as if I'd been burned. I couldn't move. Chills ran through me even though the temperature was likely high eighties, with ninety percent humidity. Then I started to sweat.

This was no longer Celia's front door.

I dropped my hand to my side and then grabbed my knees. My heart pounded in my chest. With the back of my hand I wiped the sweat from my forehead, but then everything started to tilt. I shut my eyes and blindly reached for the ground. I folded onto myself and inhaled as much air as I could hold. I couldn't pass out. I'd never passed out. I wouldn't cry.

Celia always left the door unlocked for me—the same door that now rattled and then opened with a swish. I glanced up to see a woman wearing crisp white cotton shorts with a belt and a pink Polo with the collar turned up. She aced the country-club-catalog vibe, which was in direct contrast to my crumpled-catalog-on-the-floor-of-the-car vibe.

I looked up and forced a smile. "Hi," I sang. "Just taking a little rest."

Violet reached out her hand toward me and helped me stand.

"Thank you."

"I told Miles he should have driven over to get you. It's hot out here."

"It's not his fault. I wanted to walk."

I followed Violet into the house and stood on the same Oriental rug that had been there since Celia had found it at a thrift shop halfway between Chance and Columbus. The air smelled like Thanksgiving, or maybe like a lit pumpkin spice candle. The house smelled the way I felt—out of sync, out of sorts, and out of touch.

"I know this must be hard for you," Violet said. "Do you want to sit down?"

I nodded.

Violet half stepped into the powder room and emerged with a box of tissues. I plucked two, unsure of what to do with them, as the sweat ran down my back and inside my bra.

"Are you going to be okay?"

"I'm fine." I dabbed my face and the back of my neck. Evaporation would take care of the rest. Now it was my turn to extend a hand. "Let's get down to business, shall we?"

Clearly, someone had been reading bridal magazines. Dog-eared copies stacked two feet high sat on a corner chair under a folded sheath of ivory satin. Someone had also been playing table-dress-up. The dining room table and chairs were adorned in Tiffany blue and chocolate brown. I guessed Vera Wang place settings and Waterford crystal. The flatware was sterling. Tall vases filled with a blue-colored gel held curly willow branches, white orchids, and balls of moss.

"I had them set it up here so we could just make sure. Live with it a bit. You don't think it's too much, do you?"

"No. It's lovely." And it was. "Do you want to look through the photos? I can get an idea of what you and Miles like, and how you envision *your special day.*"

I said the last three words with my Hester Hotel lilt firmly attached to the lump in my throat.

"Let's wait for Miles."

I didn't want to remind Violet that he'd been through this already—he'd stood under a chuppah, a wedding canopy; he'd broken the glass. He'd had a wife. I had no doubt Miles loved Violet, but the bridal bedlam—chair covers, for instance—didn't seem to fit the guy I'd known. When Celia and Miles had married, it was casual to the point of embarrassing their mothers. The couple had preferred a picnic at the Jasper Pond Pavilion to the typical Jewish wedding at one of the local synagogues with a live band, passed hors d'oeuvres, and a crushed rendition of the *hora*.

Shay bounded into the room, earbuds draped around her neck, which I assumed was not a choking hazard for a twelve-year-old. One day Celia and I replaced all mini-blind cords with wands, when Shay was a toddler, after Celia had read about an eighteen-month-old who had died after getting caught up in the cords.

Shay's hair was pulled to a loose ponytail over one shoulder. She stood with her feet apart, hands on hips, reminding me of Peter Pan.

"How was class?" Violet asked.

"Fine," Shay said without looking at her. "Aunt Tee!" She threw her long arms around me and hugged.

"Dad and I are going to talk with Teddi about all the wedding photos. Do you want to stay?"

"No, my shoes are ready! The store just called while we were in the car. Can we go get them? Please?"

"You want me to take you? I should really stay here with your Aunt Teddi."

"Daddy can stay here with Aunt Tee and you and I can go get the shoes. Don't you want to see them? What if they didn't dye them the right shade of Tiffany blue?"

Miles stepped inside the room. He looked like the other half of Violet's catalog page, wearing khaki chinos and an untucked Oxford-cloth shirt with rolled-up sleeves, not the suit he'd worn this morning. "What if what's not the right shade of blue? Because we can't have that now, can we? You know, I'm thinking of getting *my* shoes dyed. Periwinkle would match my eyes. Don't you think?" Miles batted his just-about-periwinkle eyes at Violet.

I'd only ever seen him fuss and flirt with Celia. I hated that for that second, his happiness pinched my heart.

"Daddy!" Shay tried to sound annoyed, but the hint of a grin gave her away momentarily. "I told Violet my shoes are ready. We need to get them. The store's only open till five today. Shouldn't Vi take me to get them? Please? We'll be right back! She doesn't want to leave Aunt Tee, but you'll be here."

"We can do this another time," I said. Maybe next time I could avoid a panic attack. "I just thought if we got it out of the way now, you wouldn't have to worry about the lists and the details, but we have until the end of the week. I'm not going anywhere." Just a reminder.

"No, I was looking forward to it. And you walked all the way here. Plus, my parents are coming in a few days, and cousins, and my college friends," Violet said. "I was hoping—I mean— you're such an expert on weddings and we did all this ourselves without a planner. I'd just love your professional opinion—if it's not too much to ask."

Shay fiddled with the tablecloth, smoothed a napkin, and

ran her finger round and round the rim of a goblet. If it had been filled with water, she'd have played a song.

"Sure, not a problem," I said. "I'm happy to help."

"So you'll wait here? With Daddy? We won't be long," Shay said. "Promise you won't leave?"

"I promise."

Miles exhaled with a sigh. "I'm sure Teddi has other things to do today."

Had he meant to insult me? You should always be nice to the person serving your food, and you should always be nice to the person taking your photograph. Especially when she's doing it for free.

"Nope, I don't have anything else going on for the next few hours." Miles would just have to deal with me on his own.

"It's settled then," Violet said. "We'll be back in a flash." Violet kissed Miles on the cheek. She lingered—just for a second, but it was a loving linger nonetheless. "Ha. Back in a flash to talk about photography. Get it?"

I did.

Shay hugged me again and kissed her dad before following Violet through the house toward the garage.

"Have fun while we're gone!" she shouted as they left.

Without talking, Miles and I moved into the kitchen, where the table was set with cotton placemats dotted with embroidered pineapples.

"Shay said you had a nice breakfast."

"It's a nice little café."

"That it is."

"Can I ask you something?"

Miles looked at me, in want of more information.

"A group of girls walked in and made fun of your banner."

"I'm sure you're overreacting," Miles said.

"No, it was like they knew Shay and were being mean because she was there. I don't know, and Shay wouldn't talk about it . . ."

"She's a teenager."

"She's twelve!"

"Well, you know what they say, twelve is the new sixteen."

"I don't know what they say, actually. And I don't know what that means, Mi."

"It means she's not spending her days playing with dolls anymore."

"I didn't think she played with dolls. How did the fitting go?"

"For my tux? How did you know about that?"

"No. Shay's dress fitting? For the wedding?"

"Vi and Shay's dresses have been ready to go and in the upstairs closet for weeks. Vi is amazingly organized."

"Oh," I said. "I guess I misunderstood."

Miles pulled out a box of saltines and pressed two into his mouth. "Cracker?" he mumbled, crumbs escaping.

"No thanks."

He nodded. "Did you sleep okay?"

"I did."

"Is it strange to be back?"

"It is."

"Do you miss the fancy hotel digs?"

"Sort of."

"Teddi, are you going to ever answer with more than two words?"

"Perhaps."

I wanted to ask him about the necklace and the wine. I wanted to ask about the nonexistent dress fitting and if they were selling the house. I wanted to ask if Miles almost fainted when *he* turned the doorknob.

But today was about Miles and Violet. And Shay. It wasn't about me and it wasn't about Celia. How I longed for the distance and detachment I felt from my usual wedding couples, their history and lives revealed only in reenacted sweetness and photo montage videos.

I sat in what had been Celia's chair at the table. I didn't know who sat there now, or if no one did. I pulled my tablet out of my bag, turned it on, and slid it toward Miles. "Why don't you look at these photos and show me which ones you like, and which ones you think Violet would like."

Miles scrolled through the photos with hardly a glance, as if swiping away losers on a dating app. He stopped on a photo of a couple under a tree. His eyes traced the couples in the next few photos as well. Was he thinking about himself and Celia standing amidst the trees at Jasper Pond? About the wedding where he was the groom and I was the maid of honor? About his life with Violet where I was an interloper? Maybe he was not really looking or thinking anything at all. Most likely.

"Will you be on the hook with Simon Hester for doing a side job?"

"No."

"Do you want me to pay you? Will Hester be mad? We're not exactly 'high profile' here."

"Don't be ridiculous. I do not want you to pay me. And who do you think Simon is? The godfather of the hotel mafia or something?"

"I just know he's a serious businessman."

"He's a really nice guy."

"Nice guys don't build mini empires. And they're not named eligible bachelors in national magazines."

Miles was wrong again.

"You stopped at a photo back there. What caught your eye?"

"Nothing, but I think this is really Violet's area of expertise. I'm in charge of the bar."

"Great, because I could really use a drink."

"Nice."

"I was only kidding, Miles. Did you have to pack up your sense of humor to hit the campaign trail?"

He grimaced and pushed the tablet toward me. "It's not easy raising a daughter alone, Teddi. And working full time. And trying to have a life. And planning a wedding."

Or having me here.

"Sometimes it's all just a lot. Can't you just take the pictures? Do we really have to discuss it?"

"It's protocol."

He cocked his head and lifted one eyebrow.

"Okay, so it's usually protocol to have the bride and groom look through photos and let me know what they like, what they don't like, what they want their photos to be like. Violet wants to do this, I can tell. And I think Shay would like it too."

"I know. Can you just make sure the three of you do it together? No one gets left out, okay?"

"Sure." I tapped the tablet and opened another online photo album. This one was headshots for Hester executives, all except for Simon. "I can take some headshots while I'm here. If you want. For your campaign, or just for work. I have a lot of time between now and the wedding."

Miles stared at the tablet.

"We don't have to."

"Let me think about it?"

"Sure. What made you want to run for office anyway? I don't remember you ever having political aspirations."

"Things change. Now I just want to make a difference. Leave a mark. Improve what goes on in the county for future generations. Bring in more commerce, attract tourists."

"To Union County?"

"Why not?"

I rolled my eyes.

"A hotel by the outlets would be perfect. It's near the airport and close enough to Chance to attract some shoppers and history buffs. West End Cemetery is the oldest in the county, did you know that? Real estate is doing well because of the jobs in the area." And with that he changed the subject.

"You don't like San Francisco?"

"I love it. But I'm not there for more than a few days at a time. And when I'm there I'm living out of a suitcase." Or one drawer at Simon's.

"So rent an apartment. Or buy a house. You must make enough money. You don't—"

Miles stopped.

"What? I don't have any responsibilities? Attachments? Yes, I know. I also travel all the time."

He tucked the box of crackers back onto the shelf. He closed the cabinet door without making a sound, as if a baby were sleeping nearby. Then he lowered his voice, certain not to wake the nonexistent baby. "You should have a place to call home, Teddi. Even if it's not Chance. Especially if it's not Chance."

I clamped my lips to hold everything inside. Miles turned away, unable, unwilling, uninterested to know more. I watched as he puttered, wiping the counter, turning on the dishwasher, watering a windowsill plant in a painted terracotta pot I recognized from a Web chat with Shay. I envisioned Simon, and how his condo with the waterfront view could be the home where I could putter and water plants. My clothes would hang in a walk-in closet as big as a hotel room, but without dry cleaner bags. Nothing would stay folded indefinitely inside the Samsonite suitcases my parents had given me for college graduation. Simon's condo that could be "our condo" had four bedrooms—each one with a view of the Bay Bridge.

I would have it all.

"Teddi, did you hear me?"

"Huh? Oh. Sorry."

"Are you staying for dinner?"

"Do you think Shay could visit me in San Francisco instead of us meeting in Chicago? I mean, if I ever did end up making that a more permanent home? Like one with a guest room?"

"I guess. Is this something we have to decide right now?"

"No."

"Are you staying for dinner?"

"Is that something we have to decide right now?"

Miles smiled. "I guess not."

"Let's have some photos ready to show Violet when she gets back."

"I think she'd like to see Gretchen Halliday's photos, but I don't think she'd ask you."

Everyone wanted to see the photos of the actress's wedding to the Olympic skier. And then to mimic them.

"I'm not really supposed to but . . . I can show her a few." I meant it to sound more secret-spy-like than it did. "Can you at least give me a list of the wedding party? Or tell me how many tables you're going to have so I can put that into my notes?"

Miles picked up the tablet again and scrolled back through the photos, stopping at one with the bride and groom sitting on a tree swing. "Do you ever wonder if people are as happy as they seem in your pictures?"

"They're usually happy that day. After that I never see them again, so it doesn't matter." I stammered. "Of course, it won't be that way with you and Violet. And it does matter to me if you're happy. I haven't forgotten all the fun times we had. All those years we were the Three Amigos even when you would have rather been alone with Celia. You did that for her. I always appreciated how you included me."

"I considered you my friend, too, you know. Not just Celia's."

"Me too." It was all I could say. "So, you and Violet met again at a reunion or some event she came back for?" I had shifted into work mode again. It was useful to know just a little about the couples I photographed so I could make them laugh, or tear up, on cue. I knew too much about Miles, but nothing about Miles and Violet.

"We met at a grief support group actually—"

There was a loud knock at the door. Miles pushed back his chair and left the kitchen, likely relieved not to have to answer me. I looked out the window at the backyard to the idle wooden swing set with its covered sandbox. I didn't remember it being so big, or so still. I resisted the urge to crane my neck to see who was at the door.

I didn't have to wonder for long. I recognized the bearing of the footsteps, the low roll of the muffled conversation. Beck stood in the doorway and looked past me as if the most interesting thing in the room was beyond and above me, as if I didn't exist at all. Then he opened the door and stepped outside, taking his Irish Spring with him.

Chapter 7

I WALKED TOWARD THE corner of the yard and examined the patches of yellow coleus tucked into a bed of mulch and rocks. Beck appeared in my peripheral vision as I knelt and pinched off a handful of blossoms. They would fit nicely into a vacant wineglass and brighten my room. I grabbed a small rock and pushed it into my pocket as I stood.

"Why did you tell Shay to apologize to me about the contest?"

"Because it's not her place to make demands of you."

"I can take care of myself, make my own decisions."

"Obviously."

"What is that supposed to mean? Look, can we just talk? I—"

"You're not the center of attention here, Teddi. This is about Miles and Violet and Shay. So just step back and let them have the spotlight."

"I don't want a spotlight." I never had the spotlight. I never wanted a spotlight. I looked at Beck straight on. "I just don't want you to pretend I don't matter. *There's a difference.*"

"You matter to Shay because she still sees you as a link to Celia."

"I *am* a link to Celia."

"No, *we're* the links. You're just a reminder."

"Why would you say something so mean?"

"People change." Beck shoved a hand into his jeans pocket.

"Not fundamentally."

"Yes, fundamentally. People change. You don't think you're a different person than you were before Cee died? I know I am."

I wanted to argue but I didn't want to fight, and that's what this would become.

"What do you mean, you're different?"

"It doesn't matter."

"It matters to me."

Beck chortled. "You don't know what went on here after you left, and I'm sure as hell not going to be the one to give you a history lesson. You saw Shay once a year at some fancy hotel. I'm glad you didn't abandon her completely, believe me, but now you come back and we're all supposed to be grateful and let the great Teddi Lerner slip back into place in our lives? Maybe you bring back bad memories. Maybe nobody wants you here."

" 'Nobody' being you."

"You said it, not me."

"We were good together."

"You were not good for me, Teddi. Not after you left. I . . ." he said, and then stopped.

That's when I saw that look in Beck's eyes, the squinty look, the one where he glanced away because he was calculating what to say next. Beck didn't do anything spur of the moment; even when it seemed like he was being spontaneous, he'd thought it all through. His jawline softened as he pulled his hand out of his jeans pocket.

My phone beeped.

"You might as well answer it."

"What were you going to say?"

"It's too late to play catch-up and pretend everyone here is important, Ted. You went away. You outgrew Chance and everyone in it."

"That's not true."

Beep.

"I don't have anything else to say. Just do what you're here to do and then go home. And do not hurt Shay."

"Do you really think I would do something to hurt her? *I love her.*"

Beep. After this, the call would go to voicemail.

I assumed it was Mr. Thomas. His company, Titan Industries, would be a new client and all his retreats would be booked at our properties around the country. I'd be the one snapping photos to showcase on their Web site, arranging for formal portraits, and hiring photographers to shoot each corporate event. If I didn't answer, the deal might fall through. Hester wasn't as big as hotel conglomerates, but we offered more personal service—and part of that service was answering the phone.

Beep. "I've got to get this."

"Of course you do."

I swiveled around and plugged a finger into one ear. "Hello, Mr. Thomas. I mean, Henry. Nice to hear back from you so soon."

Beck walked behind me, through the yard, up onto the deck, and into the house. I didn't need to look or stop talking to know. The ground shook with every step.

Violet led me by the hand. She looked as unfazed and fresh as she had when I'd arrived. She pulled two chairs out and patted one. I sat. Violet tapped my shoulder with hers.

"I hope Beck wasn't too hard on you."

"What do you mean?"

"Nothing."

Not again. "Tell me, really."

"He didn't want Shay to ask you to come."

My shoulders shook and I rubbed away the ache, pretending it was a chill. "Oh. Well, we have a history."

"I should say! You've known him since he was born. I'm sure it's just because you remind him of Celia."

Shay stomped in wearing her dyed shoes.

"These are awful! Do I really have to wear them?"

"You wanted the same shoes as the bridesmaids," Violet said. "You were excited to have them match the dress!"

"I changed my mind."

I clamped my lips.

"Can't I just wear sandals or something?"

"Or something? Really, Shay? This is your dad and Violet's wedding," I said. "They're not that bad."

"Thank you," Violet said.

"Are you kidding me? You're on her side?"

"I'm not on anyone's side. I just think if the bridal party is wearing dyed shoes that you should too."

"I know it's a little old-fashioned," Violet said. "But it's what I always pictured, you know?"

I did not. I did not dream about weddings or gowns or dyed pumps. Well, I didn't dream about my own.

Shay harrumphed. "Fine. Where's Uncle Beck? I want to show him something."

"He's in the kitchen with your dad."

Shay clomped away as if trying to fling her shoes off with each step.

"I'm not used to seeing Shay like that," I said.

"She's a teenager."

"What is it with twelve being a teenager? Where did 'tween' go? Isn't tween a thing?"

"You're not around too many kids, are you?"

"Well, no . . ."

"The tween years lasted about a week."

"You're not kidding, are you?"

"I wish I was, but middle school is like another planet. They start sixth grade like Lindsay Lohan in *Parent Trap,* and end up like, well, like Lindsay Lohan."

Violet hummed as she scrolled through my photos with a flourish of her index finger. I pointed to updos and headpieces, to silk mermaid dresses and knee-length taffeta. We discussed skylines and sunsets, cities and mountains. I described San Francisco, Bozeman, and Miami. Violet chatted about Chance, and she swayed a little any time she mentioned Miles. She sat up a little straighter any time she mentioned Shay.

I showed Violet a few of Gretchen Halliday's wedding photos that I'd kept on my tablet for this purpose, as well as blooper photos of just about every bride, all stored in a password-protected file. Violet studied the photos of Gretchen, the Oscar-nominated bombshell, and I wondered if Violet thought she wasn't as pretty as the movie star. She was. After the first photo of a bride pulling at her gown, in, let's say, an unladylike pose, Violet bellowed a deep, resonant, powerful laugh, and then covered her mouth. I laughed at the difference between her looks and her sound, and it encouraged us both to ride out our giggles. Violet's crossed leg swung like a pendulum timed to her heartbeat.

"This is really fun, Teddi. And I don't just mean because I'm a Gretchen groupie. Thank you."

"No problem." I meant it.

Everything about Violet was as smooth as her skin and as eager as her laugh, and all without pretense or malice. She was the kind of woman who glistened and didn't sweat.

And who I started to like anyway.

Violet skittered around the table adjusting the silverware and plates, moving them a millimeter, stepping back to assure herself of the change, clasping her hands as if asking for approval. I wasn't used to insecure brides. The privileged women who married at Hester properties had entourages and expectations. Violet got the giggles any time she mentioned anything remotely opulent, like cascading hydrangeas and the chocolate fountain. She looked at me straight on, but not as a challenge. With Violet, I felt welcome, a sweet and sad welcome.

"Can I come in?" It was Shay.

"Do I really have to wear these shoes? They hurt."

"Nice try," Violet said.

"I have an idea." I glanced at Violet, not meaning to interfere but interfering all the same. "You could wear these shoes for the pictures and wear them down the aisle and then change into something else for the party. The best people are doing it," I said. Violet turned to me and I nodded. "It's true. We could even bedazzle a pair of flip-flops."

Shay scrunched her face and pulled back her head. "Huh?"

"Glue sparkly things to them."

Shay smiled. "Can we do that?"

"Of course," Violet and I said together. Then I realized Shay hadn't been talking to me.

Shay pulled out the chair next to me and sat. With Violet on one side and Shay on the other we studied more photos and went off on tangents about shoes and hair that had nothing to do with weddings. Shay doodled in a small notepad the whole time.

"What did you and Daddy talk about while we were gone?"

"Pictures." I tapped the tablet. "And then Uncle Beck came."

"What did the three of you talk about?"

"Nothing really, sweetie."

"You didn't talk about my mom?"

"Just wedding talk going on here, nothing else, Shay." Violet's voice was stern but kind, like she knew what Shay was talking about.

"Anything else you can think of, Shay?" I asked. "About the wedding? The pictures?"

"That seems like a lot," she said. "Of pictures, I mean."

"I usually take a few hundred pictures, because although you look good in every shot, Shay-Shay, that's not true of everyone. I want your dad and Violet to have a lot of choices."

Violet smiled.

"But if you're taking that many pictures—during the party, I mean—how are you going to have a good time?"

"I love my work. I always have a good time at weddings. There's music, beautiful clothes, and happy people. And you'll be there. That will make it a wonderful day for me."

"What table does Aunt Tee sit at, Vi?"

"Aunt Tee will be *working*, Shay." Violet looked at me.

Maybe she wasn't as nice as I'd thought.

At Hester Hotel weddings the chef always saved a perfect plate of food and had it waiting for me in the kitchen. A perk of being on staff. A perk of being thought of as Simon Hester's girlfriend, even though I wasn't officially anything. Not yet.

"I'll eat in the kitchen and sit when I can. I promise. It'll be fine. I do this all the time."

"Well then you have to stay and eat with us tonight."

"I can't, sweetie, but thank you."

"But Uncle Beck is here!" *Exactly.*

"Who's talking about me?"

We three turned in tandem and saw Beck step into the dining room.

"I want Aunt Tee to stay for dinner, but she says she has to go."

"Well, if Aunt Teddi wants to go, nobody can stop her."

"Tell Aunt Tee you want her to stay, Dad."

"I think Aunt Teddi is tired."

Shay slumped and rolled her eyes.

"Shay, show me those shoes you just picked up," Beck said. "And your newest drawings. Let these guys talk wedding."

"Fine."

Beck followed Shay out of the room and I heard them walk upstairs.

"I wish you'd stay," Violet whispered. "Beck will ease up on you. He's a sweetheart."

"I think we're good to go," I said. "With the pictures, I mean."

"Fabulous."

Violet flitted around the table, as if she would be responsible for each place setting at the reception.

I gathered my tablet, my papers, pens, and bag, checked the time. That's when I realized I had nothing to eat and no one to eat with. The idea of Josie's book club was looking better by the moment.

"I guess I'll be going . . ."

"Thank you so much for everything."

"Let Miles drive you back to Nettie's."

"It's okay, I'd like to walk."

"Are you sure?"

"Absolutely. I like the alone time." It's what I'd grown accustomed to. "I'd like to say good-bye to Shay."

"Of course," Violet said.

I also wanted to say good-bye to Beck. Maybe he *was* different. Maybe I was different too. But different didn't have to mean indifferent. Not anymore. I knew Beck when he was born, when Celia got the little brother I'd always wanted and said she'd share him with me. I'm not sure she meant it the way I eventually took it. No matter the hurt, Beck and I had known each other our whole lives—Before, During, and After Celia's death. Well, not so much after. I had to say good-bye this time.

Even if he didn't say it back.

I walked up the steps sure-footed but without sound, as Violet watched. I didn't want to surprise Shay or Beck, but I also didn't want Beck to hide in the bathroom. I wanted Shay to sense that we all got along. Even if we didn't.

Once on the landing I noticed the master bedroom door was closed. That was good. I didn't want to see a new bed, or new curtains, or rearranged furniture. The guest room door was partially open. Celia had spent weeks in that room on a hospital bed, so I certainly wouldn't be going in there, but I could see new shiny dark wood furniture and taupe walls. Violet's touch, perhaps?

I walked to Shay's door. "Knock knock," I said, and pressed my cheek to the doorframe.

Shay looked up and smiled, her hands tearing pieces of paper into small random shapes. "Sorry Uncle Beck was early and you couldn't just do the photos with Dad."

"That's okay." It was more than okay. "So, where is Uncle Beck?"

"In the attic looking for something."

"I'll see you tomorrow, right? We have a date at the mall after class? It ends at noon tomorrow, right? See? I remember everything you tell me."

"Yeah." Shay smiled and continued with busy hands. "Dad said he'd drive us on his way to a meeting. And then pick us up. Maybe the three of us can have lunch."

I walked to Shay and kissed the top of her head. "We'll see." She had stacks of paper in shades of every color around her on the floor, surrounding a piece of poster board arranged with torn pieces. It looked like—it looked like Miles. "Are you making a portrait of your dad?" She held up a small photo of Miles, Celia, and herself. I remembered that photo. Shay was three and had cut her own bangs. They were almost straight. "She'll be an artist," Celia had said. It made no sense to me then, but Celia's intuition had been spot on, as usual.

"It's my collage." Then I saw it. The snapshot had been duplicated in a pencil outline, with numbers and words scribbled in each section, like a paint-by-number. Celia's likeness was still empty, white, untouched. Was that how Celia felt to Shay? Like a pale outline of a mother for whom she worked to fill in the color? I felt sad, but Shay's deliberate movements, her intentions—those felt brave.

"I'll see you tomorrow, okay?"

Shay nodded. I left the door open just a crack, then walked down the hall. That's when I heard the creaking of the floorboards above me. Yes, Beck and I were waiting each other out. Or at least I was waiting out Beck. How long could I stay before Miles and Violet realized I was upstairs? How long until Beck returned and I could apologize for hurting him, for leaving without saying good-bye? I wouldn't apologize for leaving. I wasn't sorry I left.

By doing so, I'd honored Celia's last wish for me.

But ignoring calls and texts from Beck for months?

That genius had been all mine.

I played with words that might ease the tension when I heard stomps down the attic stairs. Then, the shift of the door handle. Carpeted floors absorbed Beck's footsteps but they came closer and closer. I felt him stand behind me, close enough to be touching, but not. I closed my eyes and tipped my head toward the floor, dwarfed by Beck's presence, ashamed of my own. My neck shivered and my shoulders lifted to abate the chill. Beck could have stopped it, but he wouldn't. I wanted him to say something but I wouldn't ask him to talk. I wanted him to hug me but I wouldn't reach back for his hands. I used the last of the wishes I'd saved, or pretended to; I used a little prayer not knowing if I believed in anything. What I really wanted was to open my eyes and see Celia there. Even dying Celia. Any Celia. Just one more time.

It had been stupid to think that tying a knot in the past would stop it from fraying into the future. Everything ran together here. It was messy.

I opened my eyes and looked up and into the mirror on the far wall. Beck glared back at me. It was the faraway Beck I longed for, the kind Beck, the loving Beck, not the one behind me with a piercing glare and deep scowl. I stared through the wall he'd built to when he'd been like a younger brother to me—laughing, teasing, cracking jokes—until everything changed. I glanced away. I felt naked, but not in the good way.

Beck placed his hands on my shoulders and leaned in. I felt his breath on the side of my neck. A quiver ran down my spine. Everything tumbled back. I smelled the soap mingled with aftershave, felt the stubble, tasted the leftover Thai he'd tried to mask with toothpaste, the morning coffee. I prayed for words of forgiveness, understanding, or even reparation. For one second I wished that we could start over, catch up, reminisce. Move forward.

Then he whispered in my ear. "Just leave."

Chapter 8

BECK HELD A GRUDGE. I didn't blame him, but for a moment I'd allowed myself to believe that he would forgive me.

I looked back in the direction I'd come from. Maybe Beck had decided to follow me, to make sure I was okay, to apologize for the way he dismissed me. Because that's what he'd done, dismissed me as if he were king and I were his subject.

How dare he.

Beck had always been moody—turbulent, even. Now he was mean. Still, when he pressed into my shoulders I'd recalled his physical strength and how I'd always thought of him as steadfast. Beck was the boy who'd mowed everyone's lawn and shoveled all the neighbors' steps. He grew into the man who everyone turned to for advice. Beck always told you the truth, before someone else did. If the ground shook Beck hung on to you so you didn't fall.

Unless you flung yourself so far away that he couldn't reach. Then there was Simon.

Even-tempered and analytical Simon with impeccable taste in everything. Simon was kind and generous. He hired kids out of high school as part of a "Learn & Work" program that subsidized college tuition, and instructed HR to hire women returning to the workforce after staying home with children. The assistant front desk manager of the Santa Fe hotel had started as a busboy. Simon offered many people opportunities to join him on the way to—and for his stay at—the top. But make no mistake—if you couldn't cut it, he was going anyway.

These men were so different, but I'd lied to them both.

Before I knew it, I was standing in front of the house where I grew up. Seems my subconscious had guided me, dropped me off, and then peeled away.

White siding still covered the house. Its pitched roof covered an attic not even I could stand up in, so the pull-down stairs led only to the idea of a second floor. My mother had such plans for that space. Raise the roof! A sewing room. (She'd learn to sew!) A craft room. (She'd take up crafts!) A guest room. (She'd welcome guests!) The shutters were the same ones my parents had replaced before they moved, the first thing they ever did that surprised me, but not the last. The yard was stark but neat. What happened to my father's flowering bushes? There was no porch (how I had coveted a porch), just a few steps leading to the front door that we'd lined with terracotta pots overflowing with bright pink geraniums by the end of every summer. It had been my job to water the flowers and to deadhead the blooms. One summer Celia sketched the flowers in various stages of blossoming, and I'd photographed them. Since then I'd always photographed things that grew. Babies, kids, flowers, relationships. Those things also died. I realized that too late to change careers.

After a minute or two, or maybe twenty, I nodded once to my house as if not to hurt its feelings, and then ran across the street to the house that would always be Celia's. The Stillman family house had been my shelter, my family, my fairy tale. The wide steps were swept bare. There was no car in the driveway, no one driving down the quiet, narrow, two-way street, so I sat on the second step, set my camera bag on the first, and wrapped my arms around my myself so that I didn't budge, so that my memories stayed close after years of my keeping them so far away.

What I loved most was behind me, literally and metaphorically. I longed to feel as much value in the present as I did in the past. It was easier to stay away; it would be easier when I went back.

I'd forgotten what it was like to be with people who knew things about me besides what I'd chosen to tell them. People who looked at me and *just knew*. I was friends with Annie, but to her, my life began the day I started with Hester Hotels. With Simon, it was the same. I'd always said I didn't want to talk about my past. He never pressed. Neither did Annie.

It wasn't that I didn't know what true friendships and deep relationships meant.

I knew exactly what they meant—letting someone in, maybe letting her down, and possibly, letting her go.

Or him.

I reached into my bag and pulled out my phone. I would text Simon. No, I'd call him. Talk to him. Tell him things I'd never told him before. Simon was kind and considerate. Simon was handsome and interesting. I could convince him to feature some of my landscape photos in hotel rooms, or the lobbies, or the business centers. I'd explain how much taking those kinds of photographs once meant to me, about the little contest that was looming large.

How could he understand that when I didn't?

Simon hired me six years ago when I had the good fortune to walk into the Hester on Michigan Avenue the day his photographer had come down with food poisoning—three hours before a big wedding. A quick look at my portfolio got me the gig. Praise from the bride's father got me a full-time job.

But the one time I told Simon my dream—it took four glasses of Beaujolais Nouveau—well, let's just say he wasn't impressed by my ambition.

"I want to have my photos hanging in a gallery one day."

"Your photos hang in homes all over the country."

"I know."

Simon hugged me. "That's not enough?"

"Maybe not. Don't know. Won't know until I give it a whirl again. You know. Artistic stuff."

I stood from the couch and twirled around until I almost threw up, which didn't take long.

"Do you know how hard it is to make a living as an artist?" Simon asked. "Do you know how hard it is to be valued as an artist and not even make a living at it?"

Why did he have to be so sensible when my head was spinning?

"I think the fact that I'm taking pictures of rich people's weddings proves that I know very well."

I sat on the couch again. "I'm sorry. I am happy here. With this work. With you."

"The best is yet to come," he'd said.

Deep down, I was choosing to believe that.

"Well, if it isn't Teddi Lerner." I jolted and turned around.

"Excuse me?" I stood and stepped back and away. "Do I know you?"

"You did."

I recognized the voice, but more so, the T-shirt. Cemetery man. He was tall and slim, with hair long enough for him to comb his fingers through to push it back from his forehead, revealing a faint tan line. I hadn't noticed this morning that his hair was dark blond, but he'd been wearing a hat, which had also made him look older. Maybe cemeteries just made people look old.

He walked down two steps and I stepped back again, then he held out his hand.

"I'm Cameron Davis."

I put my hands behind my back, and realized I'd left my camera bag on the step. He picked it up and handed it to me. "How did you know my name?"

"You used to live across the street."

"How do you know that?"

"I lived here too. Over there, I mean." He pointed to the house next to the one that had been mine. "Until I was eight, that is. Then we moved to California."

"Oh my God! Cameron Davis! Look at you! All grown up."

"You are too."

"Well, Cammy, I took the blame for those muddy footprints you left all over my front steps, you know. My mother made me scrub them off. You were such a brat." I laughed.

"No one has called me that in a long time. Cammy, that is. Brat I'm kind of used to."

"I can't believe you're back in Chance. Why didn't you tell me this morning?" I pictured myself as he'd seen me, mumbling, stumbling, ridiculous.

"It didn't seem like a good time. You seemed a little preoccupied."

"Yeah, sorry about that. How did you recognize me anyway?

I'd never have known who you were if you hadn't told me." He opened his mouth but I raised my hand to stop him from talking. "You know about the wedding."

"Well, it is a small town, and I saw the camera bag, and then you looked up and I just recognized you. You look the same as when you were ten. All eyes and all hair."

My cheeks warmed. Facts filtered back. He was two years older than Beck and two years younger than me and Celia. We never knew where he belonged.

"You were always really nice to me," he said.

"I knew what it was like to be an only child. I think I always wished you were my brother."

"Story of my life." He sat on the step and I sat next to him. "I had such a crush on you."

"You were in third grade!"

"Good taste in women knows no age limitations." He bumped me with his shoulder and it felt like I'd been tapped with a brick. A brick radiating heat. "So, what are you doing here?"

"You know, I'm here because of the wedding."

"No, I mean here. Sitting on the step, not even knowing who lived here."

"I was just . . ."

"Thinking about Celia?"

I shrugged. Most of the truth wasn't up for discussion. "I guess I was just reminiscing."

"I was so sorry to hear about what happened to her. She was always nice to me, always a happy kid. This was a happy house. It still is, if that helps at all."

A lump lodged in my throat. I nodded. "It does."

New families brought their own goodness and craziness into

a house and made it their home. I just carried my craziness with me from place to place.

"Want to sit on the swing? I mean, if you don't have anywhere you need to be? You can do all the thinking about Celia and other things you want. I won't bother you."

"You're not bothering me. I'm the one who seems to keep intruding on your space." I didn't ask who he'd been visiting at the cemetery. I didn't have the energy or the emotional space.

I held the porch railing and my hand fit over the whole wooden rail, but I saw a small hand when I looked, a little-girl hand, and how I reached the other out to Celia the first time I had admitted I needed a place to get away. I was six.

"All this must seem a little weird," I said.

"A little."

I followed Cameron up the steps. He sat on one end of the porch swing, pushing himself to and fro the way Celia, Beck, and I had as children and teenagers. Cameron may have swung here as well, I didn't remember. He'd lived next door to me for a year, and had floated in and out of my life without consequence or thought, the way things and people do when you're ten. I sat at the other end of the wooden swing.

"What brought *you* back to Chance?"

The screen door opened and a girl poked out her head. Her long brown hair and freckled face looked familiar, which was impossible, except all kids sort of looked the same to me. A hazard of wedding and bar mitzvah photography.

"Mom said to bring these out." She held out a paper plate piled with pale cookies dusted in powdered sugar.

"Thanks, Morgan."

Of course. Cameron had come back with a wife and child.

Maybe children. No ghosts for him, only happy, welcoming memories.

"Hi, Morgan. I'm Teddi Lerner."

"I know who you are." Morgan's husky voice didn't fit her frame, and her tentative smile seemed suspicious. She was one of the girls from the café.

Cameron lifted his index finger and Morgan closed her mouth. "That's not polite," he said.

"I saw you at the Fat Chance Café. I'm sorry I didn't recognize you just now. You're about the same age as my—you're the same age as Shayna Cooper."

Shay wasn't my anything. Not officially.

"Yeah, I am," Morgan said.

Morgan disappeared inside without a glance or a good-bye. I really needed to work on my tween communication skills, but Morgan might have also needed to work on her manners.

I pulled a crumpled tissue from my pocket and wiped my mouth, politely depositing my gum inside. Cameron and I had played hide-and-seek almost thirty years before. There was no need to hide now.

"May I have one?" I asked. "It's been a long day. I'm starved."

Cameron held out the plate. I lifted a cookie and bit into it. My stomach rumbled its approval and gratitude. I patted it as if to say *be patient*.

"Sorry about Morgan," Cameron said.

"Please don't apologize. You've been nothing but nice—this morning and now—and Morgan was sweet." I took another cookie from the plate.

"She has her moments of sweetness, that's true, but I don't get credit for any of that. That's all Deanna."

"Your wife? I'd love to meet her."

"No, Deanna's my sister."

"You don't have a sister, Cammy." I grazed his thigh with a tap of my fist, then drew back my hand. Beneath the khaki shorts hid rock-hard quads. I wanted to crawl into one of the backyard holes we'd dug decades ago.

Cameron chuckled. "I didn't have a sister until I was nine, then along came Deanna. We lived in Sausalito by then." He swept invisible cookie crumbs from his hands. "Morgan's my niece."

Chapter 9

I KNEW ONE THING for sure. I was humidity-challenged.

Back at the inn, I pulled my sweaty dress over my head and stood in front of the air conditioner, held up my hair with both hands, thereby drying my face, neck, and armpits simultaneously. I turned around to dry my back.

I should've rented a car. Although if I'd had a car, I'd have sat on Poppy Lane in cool-air bliss and never ended up on the Stillmans'—Cameron's—porch. I'd smiled the whole way back as I'd eaten the cookie I'd swiped "for the road." It was fun hanging out without fear of being reprimanded. The longer Cameron and I talked, the more we both remembered. We'd built forts with webbed lawn chairs and drank from the garden hose; we'd eaten my mother's blondies that were supposed to be brownies (she'd forgotten the cocoa), and Cameron had even helped Celia and me during our tulip bulb–planting binge for my mother one fall.

I'd asked nothing about his life today so that he'd ask nothing about mine. I'd have only given him my canned answer about my creative job, posh hotels, gourmet food, frequent travel—and depending on the direction of the conversation, might have mentioned dating a nice man.

I cringed. All I could muster was "nice man." I moved away from the air conditioner, frozen through.

How I missed Celia at moments like this. She'd held the key to my steamer trunk full of emotional backstory. She'd have known what to say.

But I knew the upside to marrying Simon. He was financially secure, handsome, and smart but not snobby. He recycled, he biked, he ate locally sourced foods, he offered his employees parental leave and health insurance. He opened doors, pulled out my chair, gave me the remote, and asked my opinion.

And there *was* chemistry. It wasn't heart-pounding, belly-laughing, can't-catch-your-breath chemistry. It was quiet chemistry. It was B-minus instead of A-plus chemistry.

Coupled with a view of the Golden Gate Bridge, I'd negotiate some freedom to explore the world with my camera, and with Simon—that could be enough. I was thirty-nine, for God's sake, and Simon was almost fifty.

I could call him right now and tell him about Chance. Nettie's on Lark was a landmark historical property, that would interest him. And that plot out by the mall. Maybe—no. He wouldn't care that I was back in my hometown for a wedding, or that I didn't ask him to accompany me. I could tell him about Celia and Shay and spending time with her every summer at his Chicago hotel (which I properly paid for).

A barrage of questions I'd never even thought to ask Simon piled into my brain and landed on top of one another. We spent our time together as if we'd landed on large stones in a rushing river, then we skipped to the next one without falling into the water below. Or even acknowledging it was there.

Inside my thoughts, the view outside of Simon's window grew

dark, the landscape no longer in full view, as if someone had activated their remote control from afar. Again, I was in my underwear, making a phone call. I sat on the bed and scrolled through my contacts.

So many numbers and so few people I could talk to. I called Annie.

"What's wrong?"

Right at this moment, everything. I inhaled and exhaled. "Why does something have to be wrong?"

"You're on vacation, remember?"

"Oh, right. I just wanted to say hi."

"You are not a 'hi' person."

"Maybe I am now."

"And this metamorphosis happened because . . ."

"Fine, I need your advice." What should I do about Simon? "What do I wear to a book club?"

"You're going to a book club?"

"Yes."

"Since when do you read?"

"An old friend invited me and I want to make a good impression. And I'll have you know I used to read all the time. And I'm going to start again."

"Wear your blue dress."

"Very funny."

"Don't worry about it. You always make a good impression."

"You're no help."

"Always glad to be of service!" Annie said. I rifled through the dresses and chose three, put back two, chose another one. "I read your e-mail about Mr. Thomas but I didn't reply because, you know, you're on vacation. I knew you could close that deal.

I'll tell Simon tomorrow. If he has any questions he'll call you and—"

"No."

"What do you mean, no?"

"I don't want him to call me."

"Okay, I'll tell him to text you. Or e-mail you."

"I need time away, Annie. From everything." I hadn't realized how much.

"He's your boss. I mean, I know he's more than that but—"

"Can't I have a break?"

"Yes, I suppose you can. And this one sounds *exotic*, let me tell you! You're going to a book club. A book club! What's tomorrow? A trip to the mall or a game of canasta?"

If she only knew.

"Everything else going okay?" I asked. How well the work hat fit when I was avoiding the real-life hat. "The Halsted-Tyler wedding? The Pierson retreat? The Bella Dolce photo shoot? What about the—"

"Make up your mind. Do you want to talk about work or not? Because I can go over twenty minutes' worth of notes from this morning's staff meeting if you want."

"I do," I said. Then I shivered.

If I didn't pick a dress and head out for Josie's in five minutes, I'd be late for book club. I shimmied into my turquoise and coral Lilly Pulitzer sheath, then dropped it and stepped out, leaving it on the floor. I settled on an indigo silk shirtdress with a subtle stamped lemon print that I'd bought in Miami at a trunk show. I pulled my hair into a ponytail and added a faux-tortoiseshell headband, but left the heart necklaces on the dresser. I didn't want to answer any questions. The bottle of wine winked at me as if asking to come along.

That's right! I should bring something to Josie's besides myself. My mother was a stickler for manners and all things socially acceptable. Hostess gifts were at the top of my mother's must-do list. Had anyone ever invited us over, they'd likely have been wowed.

What did I have, what did I have, what did I have? I twirled with each inquest and fell back on the bed.

Wrinkled silk be damned.

"What did I have to show you" had been a game Celia and I played since the first time she came home from overnight camp the summer we were nine. Camp Shamash was somewhere I never wanted to go and my mother never would have agreed to anyway. Celia and I walked around my bedroom that August day, and I showed her every and any bit that I'd accumulated in the three weeks she'd been gone. Later we'd done this in our dorm rooms, our apartments, and her house, simply finding things to share that the other hadn't seen, holding them out, describing them as if willing the other into its origin. We knew each other's life by heart and by tchotchke.

What did I have to take to Josie's tonight? A half sleeve of Ritz. Cinnamon Altoids. Half a bottle of Ohio Pinot.

My camera.

And good intentions.

I closed the door and locked it. I jiggled and twisted the brass embossed doorknob twice, even though I knew I'd done it right from a lifetime ago of practice. I traced the swirl of the banister and looked at my finger for dust, but there was none. I heard movement upstairs—not footsteps exactly, but someone was on the second floor. I wasn't alone. It was as comforting as it was disconcerting. I turned back to yell hello, but I was already pushing my book club luck.

I stepped out onto the porch and a horn beeped. I headed down the steps and the passenger-side window of a black SUV disappeared down into its crevice.

Josie waved. "I figured you'd want a ride but wouldn't ask. Get in!"

I opened my mouth in protest, but the truth was, I didn't want to walk. I also didn't want to be a burden, or burden myself with expectations.

"You didn't have to." I buckled my seat belt and set my camera bag at my feet.

"No big deal. Just figured you could use a little help getting where you needed to go."

Josie's house stood like a castle at the end of a solar lamp runway. It was bright white brick with black shutters and a second-story Palladian window revealing a chandelier that I knew loomed over the foyer, *Phantom of the Opera* style. Josie style. The other houses on Rose Court were either two-story colonials rehabbed in the seventies, or 1940s bungalows that had never been face-lifted. There was one modest folk Victorian on the corner. The wannabe, my mother had called it. If there was ever a kettle-calling pot, it was Joyce Lerner. She also said you shouldn't have the biggest house on the block (likely because ours was not). Josie needed hers to be. As we parked in the three-car garage I pictured Josie's childhood home not far from mine, nor far from here, with its sagging-roof carport and gray-painted siding. I hadn't wanted Josie's house but I had wanted her sisters, the two younger ones with whom she shared a bedroom.

"I always loved your house," I said.

"I love it too, thanks. It's a work in progress."

"I mean the one you grew up in."

"Really?" Josie turned to me as the SUV hatch opened. "I always wanted your house. That's why I went with white brick for this house. It always looks so clean and uncomplicated. Of course with a husband and three boys what's inside is neither clean nor uncomplicated, but what are you going to do?" Josie chuckled and motioned to the door with her chin. That door led to the mudroom, something I'd never heard of until one was on Celia's must-have list when she was house shopping with Miles. Must-haves could be moot in Chance, but Celia had gotten what she'd wanted. Josie had built what she wanted. "I have something in the back of the car," she said. "Go ahead in."

I turned the knob and pushed open the door, letting go and waiting, almost counting to three before stepping inside.

The laundry room looked like a newfangled Maytag commercial, bright and uncluttered with glistening stainless steel appliances, but no evidence dirty laundry had ever been there. The boot racks had been abandoned for summer and the cubbies were bare, save for some dangling goggles and headphones. To the right, the family room was neutral and calm with a sectional sofa that looked like a chunky toddler puzzle. Warmth emanated from the room, with its decorative pillows and chenille throws, its oversized chair and nearby stacks of books. The outside of the house was stark, yet alluring. The inside was pristine yet cozy.

Just a few steps up and to the left and I knew I'd land in Josie's kitchen. Voices and footsteps drifted toward me and kept me at bay. I'd expected an empty house, and to help Josie set up whatever one sets up for a book club—unread books, themed snacks, kitschy cocktails. I thought I'd help her greet the guests, and ease myself into a comfortable spot within the group.

Josie bounded in with a swish of shopping bags and slipped her hand into mine. She swung our arms back and forth as if we were grade-school chums again.

"It's like riding a bike," she said. "Let's go."

"Everybody might not be as excited to see me as you were."

"Don't be ridiculous. You're Teddi Lerner."

Josie tugged me right into the kitchen and launched me at a crowd of women I hadn't seen in years. The women buzzed with enthusiasm, moving en masse like a hive of busy bees.

"Look who's here," someone said. "It's Teddi!"

"I'm sorry I'm late," I said.

"Oh, nonsense!" The voice seemed to emanate from the group. "You know how we operate . . . if it's the same day, you're not late."

Everyone hushed, inhaled a collective deep breath, and then broke out in a litany of *Teddi*s and *welcome*s and hugs. I'd grown accustomed to crowds, but not to being the focus of their attention.

My racing heart slowed, my shoulders eased. I released Josie's hand to offer a hug.

These women were the friends I'd left behind.

I knew everyone used the word "friends" indiscriminately these days. I tried not to, always arranging people into sections in my head and roping them off. But these women *were* more than acquaintances. Much more. We'd grown up together. We knew the names of each other's childhood pets and signed our high school yearbooks with secret symbols and *X*'s and *O*'s. We shared milestones (their weddings, their children) and had a common history.

But now these were women whom I followed on social media but rarely checked in on with a phone call or personal e-mail. I liked them. I was interested in what they said when they said it, but didn't necessarily need or want details. Was that a friend? A friendly acquaintance? An old friend? A former friend? A potential friend?

The difference was critical to me.

I never craved minutiae, except from Celia. With Annie everything circled around work. For me and Simon, our banter was pointed and precise.

"You're doing great," Josie whispered. "It's just us. Relax."

All I had to do was step in and take my place, so, I breathed deep. I helloed and hugged. I smiled and nodded. I behaved as if this was normal. Fake it till you make it. I wasn't faking it, exactly; I was making it real. Because that's what Celia would have done. I could only see her, feel her, know her, this way, here. In Chance. *And I'd left and stayed away.* Maybe the particles of healing existed here alongside pain, not separate from it, with these women and in this town. With Shay. With Miles. And with Beck, if I was being honest. Even in the dashes of memories shared with Cameron on the swing.

Celia hadn't thought about that when she insisted I leave, so I couldn't blame her.

Yet sometimes I did.

Chapter 10

CHANCE HAD NOT HEARD of the "small plates" culinary movement, so I loaded up: mini sandwiches piled with corned beef and
coleslaw, tuna, and egg salad; kugel, sweet and firm (no raisins);
apricot rugelach, flakey and firm, but soft to bite.

Try this. Try that. Not enough. Save room for more.

Chance residents shared a proud heritage of overfeeding.
Today, these women, the Wagoneers as they were lovingly called,
were upholding grand tradition. The Chance Women's Welcome
Wagon started over a hundred years ago, when its job was to welcome new Jewish families to town. Nowadays, there weren't
many new families in Chance, so the Wagoneers showed up at
every shiva and simcha with appropriate amounts of food, armed
with either sympathy or celebration. Thankfully, my visit seemed
to fall into the joy category. But it was strange to see that the
Wagoneers were now my age and not my mother's.

Somewhere between my greeting and dessert, I was no
longer an outsider. Lydia was talking about her master's thesis.
Ellen told us about her husband's health scare. Katie's daughter
had started medical school. Josie showed us Instagram photos

of her son's summer travels, and, slowly at first, Samantha admitted she and her husband were in counseling. We all listened.

I had always wanted the best for these women, for their husbands and children, their careers and dreams. But I hadn't wondered much about them. When I traveled I didn't see tchotchkes that would make them laugh or jewelry that could make them tear up. Not the way I still did with Celia, my parents, Shay—even Beck.

But these women were shedding my defenses faster than I could gather them.

"When do you talk about the book?" I asked.

Everyone laughed.

"Next time, we'll talk about the book," Josie said.

"That's what we always say." The words came from each person at different intervals, in different tones.

"So, what's it like living in fancy hotels?"

"It's nice," I said. "Lots of perks." Like not paying a mortgage or rent.

"Like a laundry service."

"And room service."

"And cabana boys!"

"Cabana boys call me 'ma'am,'" I said.

The women laughed.

"I read the article."

"Is your boss as hot as he is in those pictures?"

"He *is* very handsome." I stuffed my mouth with a forkful of chopped liver, then swallowed. "He has a reputation of being a bit of a recluse, but he's not. He's very friendly to his staff and the guests. He's very hands-on." A smile pressed against the inside of my cheeks.

"Hands-on what exactly?"

Everyone giggled.

"Have you spent a lot of time with him?"

"Of course she has, she's like, in charge of everything."

"Not everything. Just event photography."

"And Simon photography."

I laughed. "I suppose."

"So how well do you know him? My sister just got divorced," Katie said.

"I'll be sure to tell him." I left the table and helped myself to another mini tuna sandwich.

After that, the conversation drifted away from me and on to the food, frantic summer schedules, and the latest episodes of *Real Housewives of Anywhere*.

"Any more photos of him you can show us?"

"I might have a few." I pulled my phone out of my pocket, wanting to give my friends at least some of what they wanted. My worlds were overlapping. Right here, right now, I liked it.

They waited as if I were about to read winning lottery numbers. I scrolled past photos I'd taken of the tulips at Butchart Gardens. I'd imagined enlarging a few, framing them, and hanging them up in my someday house. Maybe I still would.

When I saw photos of Simon, I passed the phone to Josie.

"There's Simon at his desk." As my phone was passed down the line, I hoped they wouldn't help themselves to any more photos.

"It's so formal."

"He's so handsome."

"Did I mention my sister is divorced?"

"You did," I said.

"Nice smile."

It was. In that photo the women saw Simon seated behind his

mahogany desk in an oversized leather chair, oversized smart-phone to his ear. It was one of a dozen I'd taken with my phone as test shots for the company newsletter. Simon was camera shy. At first he didn't like this one because his elbow was on his desk—but really it was because he looked relaxed. And that was exactly why I did like it.

"Does he always look so—serious?"

"He's leaning on his elbow, looking out the window. That's not serious. That's—pensive."

"Okay, does he always look so pensive?"

Fair enough. "Yes," I said.

"How could he not? He owns like fifty boutique hotels."

"Thirty-two," I said.

"Does he ever stay in one place?"

"I don't think my sister would mind traveling. He goes first class, right? I'll text you her profile photo from JDate. You re-member Marni, don't you, Teddi? She lives in Atlanta now, and sells Shakely. She's doing very well . . ." Lydia elbowed Katie and she stopped talking.

"Good for her," I said, and I meant it, as long as she stayed in Atlanta.

"So . . . where does he live?"

"He travels a lot but San Francisco is his home. It's the only place he doesn't live at one of the hotels. He has a condo on—" I was already saying more than Simon would have approved for public consumption. And more than I wanted anyone to know that I knew.

"Okay, enough about Simon, let's talk about you! Ellen, I saw your Facebook photos of your bathroom renovation. Looks luxurious."

Ellen opened her mouth to speak but had no such luck.

"Ooh, it's Simon, is it? You don't have to call him Mr. Hester?"

"Knock it off." Josie stood as she said it. The mayor of Book-clubville had spoken. She nodded at me as she sat, as if she knew more than I'd already said. Gratitude filled me.

"We *all* call each other by first names. It's company policy. We also all wear name tags when we're on property." I hated that part of my job.

"Why haven't you snagged him for yourself?"

"Teddi's a career girl, no time for love, right, Teddi?"

"Don't put words in Teddi's mouth," Josie said.

"I don't know why you are all so interested in Simon Hester's love life, you're all married!"

"We're not interested in his. We're interested in yours."

"Nothing to tell you at the moment," I said.

"Even with those fancy weddings you shoot? There must be love in the air."

"That's work," I said. "They mean nothing." Just like the staged brunches, choreographed beach volleyball games, and precision lobby scenes. They were all creations, usually mine, with the help of willing participants and picturesque sunsets. And Photoshop. I looked at Josie.

"I have an idea," I said.

I slipped into the laundry room to get my camera. I'd forgotten what it was like to be encircled by a group of women who could whisk me off to places I wasn't sure I wanted to go.

I stood close to the row of cubbies near the garage door, un-zipped my bag, and inhaled a momentary reprieve. I'd take a few photos of everyone together for social media posterity. I could look at the pictures and remember the present part of my past.

I could show the photos to Annie. The pictures were what I could give them of myself, enough but not too much.

I heard shuffling and movement in the family room a few yards away. I almost said hello, but heard whispering, which attracted my attention and forced my silence more than screaming would have. I kept my head down, as if searching for the bottom of Mary Poppins's carpetbag. I closed my eyes to help open my ears.

"She looks good."

"I'd look good too if I were living at luxury hotels and sleeping with a millionaire."

"Do you think she knows about Shayna? What about Beck?"

"She must know. Don't you think?"

"Did you find your lipstick? Let's go back."

I opened my eyes and lifted my head, but stayed behind the cubbies. I couldn't move. I couldn't talk. I couldn't think straight.

"Let's go, ladies."

I listened as Josie herded her flock.

"We were just getting our lipstick."

I heard rustling, cajoling, and tapering taps of footsteps.

"You can come out now," Josie said.

I stepped into the middle of the room. Josie walked in from the family room. I was flummoxed; any words would spew out as gibberish. I completely lacked an eloquent way to explain what happened or how I felt. "They were talking about me! And about Shay! And Beck."

"I heard the end of it. I'm sorry."

"They were talking about my job and my clothes and—and— Simon. It was a big deal for me to show you all that picture of him. He wouldn't have liked that but I did it because— Oh hell,

I don't know why I did it. And what am I supposed to know about Shay, because I don't know anything about her! Or Beck."

"Calm down, you know a lot about Shay, and about Beck, I'm sure. Think for a minute. They probably are just talking about the wedding. It's got to be a little hard for everyone, right?"

"I guess."

"And you showed us the pictures because we're your friends and you share things with your friends."

"I didn't come back here for friends; I came back for Shay. Then I saw you today, and my cousin Maggie." I thought about Cameron and Beck, but I didn't say anything. "I remembered what it was like—you know—before."

"It can be like that again, you know. No matter where you live. Or with whom. You can just be yourself here."

Until yesterday I'd known just who that was. Or thought I did.

I slipped my camera bag onto my shoulder. I wasn't letting go of it again. "Shay's off-limits. They wouldn't like anyone talking about their kids."

"Don't listen. I'm sure it's nothing."

"Tell me if there's anything that I should know about."

"I'm sure if there's something you should know, someone will tell you."

"I don't know about that."

"Then ask."

"Ask who? And what do I ask? What if it's bad . . . like really, really bad?" I remembered the whispers when Celia had been diagnosed, but after that came offers of help and displays of compassion. Chance had good people. Really good people. Mostly. "I don't know. I don't have time for this, Josie. I don't have the energy for this. Not now. Do you know what it did to me just to see . . ."

"Who?"

"My old house. And Celia's." Beck was a secret I'd always keep. I rested against the washing machine, as tired as if I'd run on the beach or away from the cemetery. "You know what? It doesn't matter. If there's something I should know, someone will tell me. I'll be gone soon enough."

"Don't talk like that."

"What am I supposed to do? I can't say anything."

"Why not?"

"'Excuse me, bitches, I heard you talking about me.'"

"Why not?"

Josie rubbed my arm and my emotions swelled. I wanted to hug her then turn and leave.

"Are you two coming?" The voice drifted in from the kitchen. "We have a bunch of women here who tell me they've found their good sides."

"I can't believe *Teddi Lerner* is going to take our picture."

I ignored the third-person reference and peeked out the window of the family room to study the sunlight, but mostly to waste time. I pinpointed a good spot in Josie's backyard for confronting the gossipers. Maybe I should just ask them. My stomach flip-flopped. I didn't know if I was afraid to ask or afraid to know. And I wasn't sure which was worse.

"Where should we stand?"

I feigned artistic and flailed my arms. "Maybe by the wall, over here. In front of the chairs. The lighting is divine." No one laughed at the exaggeration.

"Work your magic, Teddi."

"Make us all look thin and young."

"I wish we were at one of Teddi's fancy hotels."

"They're not mine." No one acknowledged me. The women buzzed around the room. These were college-educated, professional women. Some were educated women who chose to stay home with their children—the children they were acting like, just because I took pictures of celebrities. Sometimes. And my photos were online and in magazines. Sometimes.

"I need to stand on the right, that's my good side."

"Let me go fix my makeup."

"You all look great, really. And we can fix anything afterward. Just get a little closer. Okay, ready . . ."

"You have to be in the picture, Teddi." I wanted to ask everyone to whisper so I could figure out who had been in the room with me.

And then I just knew. Josie had seated herself between them on the sofa. She looked at me wide-eyed. She had them under her spell, at least for now.

As would I when I colored their teeth yellow in Photoshop before posting to Facebook and Instagram. And tagging them.

"Everybody look over here!"

"We can use it for the Welcome Wagon page on Chance's Web site."

"I want to be able to say Teddi Lerner took my picture."

"I want to make sure it's printed in the *Gazette*."

Most of these women were sincere and excited, so I set the camera on an open shelf and set the timer. "You have ten seconds!" I said, and took my place across the room from Josie, scrunched on the end of the arm of the couch. After the flash went off, I clapped twice. "Let's do it again, just in case." But my voice trailed off as everyone stood and puttered, headed back to the food and the dining room, suggesting all the places this group photo would be appropriate. Even for me.

"You can put it in your office as a reminder of home." Others suggested my living room, my bedroom, my kitchen—as if my life were a Mad Lib and they were filling in "place in one's home."

Fact was, I didn't have a "my." Not a mantel, dresser, nightstand, nor a coffee table. Not any that belonged to just me.

The women had appeared in a bundle, and they seemed to leave as one too, with waves and hugs and a few air-kisses, affection penetrating the needed space between us. We agreed to "do it again soon." Some said "see you at the wedding."

The gossipy duo waved from across the room. I waved and smirked with a closed mouth. I wasn't ready for a confrontation.

"Sit and relax. I'll be ready in a few," Josie said.

The hum of the dishwasher soothed me and I snuggled into the corner of the couch in the family room. Books packed the built-in shelves. I wondered if Josie had read any of them, or if they, like the book club, were for show.

Josie plopped down near me. "Did you have a good time?"

"I did. I'm glad you invited me. But . . ."

"Don't worry about them. Not now. You have time to ask them what they were talking about or figure it out for yourself. Or figure out if you care."

"But Shay—"

"Don't think about it."

"How can I not? Now I'm worried."

"That will get you nowhere fast. But tell me—is there anything to what they said about you and Simon?"

"You mean that I'm sleeping with him?"

"Are you?"

"Yes, but it's more than that, actually . . ."

"Well, there you go! They just got a vibe when you were talking about him. I didn't pick up on it—that you liked him, yes, but nothing more than that. My radar must be off tonight." Josie adjusted invisible antennas on her head. "So—you and Simon Hester, the eligible rich bachelor, huh? Is it serious?"

"Not really. Well, maybe it could be."

"How long have you been seeing him?"

"A few years."

"A few years! You can't be involved with someone for a few years and not be serious!"

"It's not, though. We have fun. I've learned a lot about the business. He's interesting."

"Uh-huh."

"It's difficult to explain."

"I'm not going anywhere . . ."

"I don't want to talk about him, okay? Not right now. I'm trying to figure things out."

Josie touched my knee with her hand. "I have a favor to ask you."

I sighed inside, disappointed because I hadn't thought Josie wanted anything from me. What could it be? Family photos? Glamour shots? A free room upgrade? With her other hand Josie held out a small, black, rectangular key and pressed it into my hand.

"I want you to drive Jason's Prius while you're here. He's traveling for the rest of July."

"How is this *me* doing *you* a favor?"

"The car can't just sit in the garage for three weeks, and the other boys don't drive yet. It's better if the car is driven. You don't leave until after the wedding, right?"

"I can't." I laid the key on the couch in between us.

"Yes, you can, and you will." She pushed the key back to me.

"This is too much." I pushed the key back to Josie.

"I'm not giving you the car, I'm lending it to you for a week. You can't expect me to just show up and drive you everywhere you need to go, you know."

I shook my head and chuckled. "I guess not." I reached out and took her hand. "I didn't expect you to be there waiting for me. You know that, right?"

"Of course I know that. And you wouldn't have asked." She picked up the key and closed her hand around it as if imparting a spell. "You just didn't think this through. I mean, what it would really be like to be here."

I shook my head. I hadn't thought any of it through.

"It's settled then."

"Wait. Jason won't mind?"

"You saw the pictures. He's studying coastal conservation in Costa Rica. He won't even know. And it wouldn't matter. Evan and I bought the car and pay the insurance."

"And you're sure?"

"I'm sure. I know this is small-town America but do you really want to walk everywhere?"

"I wouldn't mind."

"I might run every morning, but after that, it's all A/C and four-wheel drive, baby." She held up the key. "I am not as eco-logically minded as my seventeen-year-old. Plus, we're not in high school anymore!"

"Then what am I going to do with all the shoulder pads I

packed?" Josie laughed and I relaxed back into the cushions. "What can I do to thank you?"

"Meet me at Perk in the morning. It's on Main Street, and the scones are to die for."

"Are you sure that's all you want me to do? No portraits of you and Evan? The house? Anything?"

"Nope. That's all. Is eight too early?"

"I'll be there."

Josie started to stand and I pulled her back.

"What if something's really wrong with Shay? What if she's sick?"

"Stop it! You're jumping to conclusions." She placed the key in my hand and stared with a dare in her eyes. I didn't hand it back. "Now, drive over there and tell Miles you overheard something and want to know if Shay is okay."

A faint light-headedness caused me to sway. I exhaled a long breath as sweat gathered at my temple and hairline. "I can't interfere."

But for the first time in years, I wished I could.

Chapter 11

I AWOKE WITH THE same thought that had lulled me to sleep. Shay was fine. If she wasn't, Miles wouldn't be getting married on Sunday and Shay wouldn't be enrolled in a summer art class, or clomping around in dyed pumps and rolling her eyes.

A morning moon sat high in the sky to the south. I reached for my camera, always nearby, and bent my waist slightly over the railing, positioning myself to get a clear shot, one that captured the full awakening day. This was the moon I'd stared at from my bedroom window when I was a little girl, the one Celia stared at as well. It was the moon we'd walked home under as teenagers breaking curfew, and the one we'd sat out under on summer nights in Celia's parents' backyard as we'd all planned her wedding. This was the moon I'd stood under for my first kiss and the one that had lit the way as Beck left my apartment before dawn. And, this was the same moon that hung over San Francisco, the one Simon could see from the deck off the master bedroom. But it didn't feel like I was standing under the same moon.

Maybe it wasn't the moon that was different.

With the viewfinder crushed to my face, I loosened my grip,

lightened my touch, and focused again on what was above and beyond me, to capture it and take it with me wherever I might go.

I had agreed to a coffee klatch and had no idea what that meant. Not anymore. For me, coffee was room service on a balcony or a quick swig from a paper cup on my way to an early-morning shoot.

I yawned. Thwarted anonymity, an unreconciled past, and re-imagined friendships exhausted me. In less than a day and a half Chance had seeped back into my bones. Or it had seeped out of them.

Back in my room, I stepped out of the robe and in front of the closet, again. My habit from living alone. The first time I un-dressed and walked around at Simon's, he was taken aback, then turned on. It hadn't been an invitation; I'd just wanted to choose a dress from a few I'd hung in his closet.

I'd forgotten what it was like to see the same people every day, how someone might notice a repeating wardrobe. Rifling through my dresses I knew I wanted a new look for coffee and for the mall.

I tugged the lone yellow sundress out off a hanger and waved it like a flag.

I pulled open the door to Perk. People sauntered out, thanked me, and dispersed as I scooted inside. The room was paneled in rustic wood; the floor was stained concrete. Copper lanterns hung from the ceiling and burlap sacks stamped COFFEE lined the floor under shelves displaying vintage kitchenware. A row of distressed leather couches ran the length of the room. I stepped into line. The worn décor was on-trend and continued to chal-lenge my preconceptions of home.

"Hey," Josie said. She sidled up to me when there I was two customers away from the counter. "Sorry I'm late. I'll grab a table—get me a soy latte?" She handed me a five, which I pushed away. "Great! Then I want a lemon blueberry scone too, since you're paying. Get one for yourself, I don't share." She walked away.

I approached the hip-high counter. The barista turned around.

"Cameron?"

"Teddi?"

We laughed. "You work here?" That was a stupid question; he was behind the counter wearing a black apron with PERK UP embroidered in tan across his chest.

"I do, a few mornings a week in the summer. What can I get for you?"

"I'll have a skim latte and my friend wants a soy latte and a lemon blueberry scone."

"You should get your own scone," he said. "Sharing is discouraged by the town—guests."

He was going to say "townies."

I watched him pull the espresso shots, steam the skim milk and then the soy, and pour them into oversized matching Perk mugs.

He set the cups and Josie's scone on the counter in front of me. Then he held up one finger and bent his head slightly as he reached back into the glass case filled with morning sweets. On the top of his hat was an embroidered emoticon smiley face. He looked up at me and grinned, his expression almost matching his cap's. My left leg swayed as if someone had kicked it. I'd seen that cap before. But how?

No!

Cameron had been the one on the other side of the window, the one smirking as I'd pulled my hair into a ponytail and almost curtsied.

He plated a scone and placed it in front of me.

"A pink scone? Truly?"

"Strawberry," he said. "It matches your cheeks."

"The barista's hot," Josie said.

I sputtered into my steaming latte and placed it on the low table in front of us. Then I smacked her knee.

"Do you know him? He lived next door to me when we were kids and now he lives with his sister in the Stillman house."

"That's Deanna Davis's brother?"

"You know her?"

"She teaches at Chance Elementary. Moved here a few years ago with her daughter. Where's she been hiding *him*?"

"You don't know him?"

"Contrary to popular belief, I do not know everyone in town. I know our friends." Josie drew a circle with hands. "Our friends, my boys' friends' families, Evan's friends from work. I know a lot of people but not everyone. Oh, and I know you if you want to buy a house. That's how I met Deanna."

"So, she bought the house or Cameron bought the house?"

"Cameron, is it?"

"I told you, we played together when we were kids, then he moved away."

"What did you play? Doctor, I hope!"

I smacked her knee again.

"And now you're both back. How convenient!"

"I'm just curious about the house, that's all."

"Not about Cameron at all?"

"Not like that."

"I know you don't want to talk about Simon, but 'not serious' must be something special if you're not interested in him." Josie tipped her head toward the counter and wiggled her eyebrows.

I gritted my teeth. "Stop."

"Fine. I know, you don't want to talk about it."

"Not now, if that's okay. So, do you remember who bought the house?"

"Well, if memory serves me . . ." She tapped her chin. "Deanna bought the house on her own. I would remember seeing *him* come into the office."

I stretched my arm over the back of the sofa and surreptitiously turned as if inspecting the stitching in the leather.

A lanky teenage boy with blue-streaked hair cleared tables nearby. He had multiple earrings and black eyeliner. He hummed a melody that matched the warmth of Perk, belying his harsh appearance.

I turned back to Josie and pointed to the name clipped to the waist of her linen pants. "Tell me about your job. When did you start selling real estate?" I would have to beef up my social media surveillance in the future.

"I'm the receptionist. I was really bored all day with all three boys in high school, so I went to Kay Kaplan and asked her for a job. Been three years now."

"Do you know who bought Nettie's on Lark? I've heard some footsteps upstairs, but I haven't seen anyone. I don't know if it's a guest or the owner."

"Does it matter?"

"I'm just curious. Plus, it's a little creepy to think I'm in that big house all by myself."

"You can stay with me!"

"Next time?" I said it before I realized the implications.

"I'll hold you to it."

"You don't know who bought Nettie's?"

"Trade secret."

"Are you kidding me?" I'd had to sign confidentiality agreements with some of my higher-profile clients, but for the most part, publicity was part of their plan.

"So? Did you talk to Miles?"

"No. I decided if there was a problem with Shay he wouldn't be getting married, and it's not my place to ask too many questions." Miles had made that clear. "I'm taking her to the mall this afternoon, so I'll know if something is wrong. I mean—if she were sick or something he wouldn't let her go to the mall, right?"

"Absolutely."

"Tell me more about Evan and the boys."

Josie chugged the last of her latte and glanced at her phone. "Tomorrow. Same time, same place? Or we can meet for lunch at the Fat Chance. Either one, but I won't take no for an answer. I've got to fly. Have fun with Shay today."

Josie walked over to the cool-dude busboy. I thought she'd hand him a tip, or tell him to get a haircut. Instead, she put her hand on his shoulder, stood on tiptoes, and kissed him on the cheek. He shook his head and looked around the room.

"No one cares if I kiss you." Josie smoothed his hair and looked at me. She pointed to him as he collected more mugs, plates, and newspapers and walked toward the back of Perk.

"Jonathan," she said. Her smile widened. "My musician."

And her middle son.

I skimmed last week's *Chance Gazette* and this morning's *Columbus Dispatch,* but my thoughts wandered back to San Francisco and down to San Diego, over to Dallas and then Savannah, and up to Alexandria, the site of the newest Hester property. My heart pounded. I should have gone to Virginia. Maybe the week of training wasn't enough for the new photographers. Maybe their portfolios were bogus. What if I missed an e-mail? If someone quit? I pulled out my phone. The ringer was at full blast. No missed texts or urgent e-mails.

I reached into my pocket and pulled out the tissue-wrapped necklaces. I'd wanted to have them with me, but wasn't ready to wear them in public. As I laid the chains over my hand, the hearts caught the light and glistened.

"A gift?"

I looked up and saw Cameron, without his apron and with a little bit of hat hair. I dropped the necklaces into the tissue and folded it. "No."

"Sorry, I just thought . . ."

"No, I'm sorry. That was rude. Want to sit?"

"Thanks, but no. I'm done for the day and getting out of here."

"At nine in the morning?"

"I just work the earliest shift, then I have the whole day."

"For what?" I covered my mouth with my hand and talked through it. "Sorry. None of my business."

"Not a problem. I'm just meeting my sister before she heads off to teach summer school."

I placed my hands in my lap. "I heard your sister is a teacher here. Is that why she moved back here? For a job?"

"Why don't you ask her? She's outside. I'm sure she'd like to meet you. She's heard about our Poppy Lane antics. Just don't give away any of our secret hiding places. I need to maintain my big-brother mystique."

I lifted my plate and cup and looked around for a place to deliver them.

"Jonathan will get it. It's his job. Great kid, by the way. That was his mom with the soy latte and blueberry scone, right?"

"Right." I remembered my apparent blushing and my cheeks grew warm. I ignored it and hoped Cameron would do the same.

With the necklaces back in my pocket I walked to the front of Perk. Cameron pointed out the same window I'd looked in yesterday. I thought I was about to get busted.

"That's Deanna."

Sitting on the bench facing Perk was a woman with a long sleek bob and aviator sunglasses. Standing facing her was a tall man with one hand in his jeans pocket. Prickles traveled from my fingertips to my neck.

"I have to go." I stepped backwards. "Is there another door?"

"The service door in the back. Where are you going?"

I looked Cameron square in the eye and whispered, "That's Beck Stillman."

"I know who it is. Wait. You don't want to see Beck?"

"No, I don't. Please, Cameron."

Cameron touched my elbow and led me through the maze of Perk's storage room to a back door. He pressed the lever, pushed open the door, and I stepped outside into the alley behind the Main Street shops. He stood against the door, keeping it open.

"Thanks," I said. "You're a good friend."

Cameron stepped out into the alley and the door closed with a thud and a click. "Then tell me what the hell is going on."

"So, you're uncomfortable around him. How are you going to *get* comfortable if you avoid him the whole time you're here?"

"Believe me, he would rather I stay far away from him, from here, from everything."

"You've been away for what? Six years? You're really going to let him dictate where you go and who you see when you come home? What did he do to you?"

"Nothing, it's not like that. I'm the one who hurt him. And I don't think I realized how much."

"That doesn't sound like the Teddi I know."

By this time, I was pumping my arms. "But you don't know me very well, do you?"

Cameron stopped. I stomped a few more times and then stopped, turned, and looked around at him even though I wanted to keep moving until I was going, going, gone. "Please don't make assumptions about me. Especially if they make me out to be the good guy." I spit my words and wiped my mouth with the back of my hand even though I had tissues in my pocket.

"I'm not assuming anything. You asked me for help and then you told me there's tension between you and Beck because you left. You leaving here is really kind of sad, I think. It certainly doesn't make you the bad guy."

"I ran out in the middle of Celia's funeral."

"You were upset."

"I didn't go back. That was the last time I saw Beck. Until yesterday, that is."

"Oh."

I paused and fiddled with the edge of my pockets.

"It must've been awful," Cameron said. He touched my elbow, but I wasn't sure if it was to draw me closer or to keep me at a distance. "Who was there with you?"

"The place was packed. But I was alone."

Celia and I had always attended funerals together, or at least knew the other was there. Synagogue, funeral home, graveside. Grandparents, townspeople, two kids our age during high school. That day, I was alone; I didn't know where to look. Up or down, in or out?

At least at a wedding there were drinks and hors d'oeuvres. When alone as a wedding guest, I talked to the bartender, sipped cocktails, nibbled my way through the mashed potato bar. Maybe funerals should have cocktail hours too.

Mini latkes with applesauce.

Kosher wine to drown your sorrows.

Monogrammed tissues.

I'd draw the line at funeral favors.

Celia would have taken that tangent to town. Our irreverence was legendary and soothing—at least to us. And now, to me.

"I'm sorry it was so hard for you," Cameron said.

"You have nothing to be sorry about."

"As far as I can see, neither do you."

"How can you say that? I left all these people behind to deal with the fallout without me. I went off to Chicago, moved in with a friend from college, and didn't look back. Literally."

"You were in pain."

"For six years?"

"Apologize then. Explain everything to Beck. Everyone makes mistakes."

"I can't. It's complicated. And it wasn't a mistake. That's the problem."

"Look, I remember you and Celia and Beck as kids. I remember a lot of fun times. Those don't get erased with one bad decision."

Oh, if it had been only one.

"You're assuming I'm the person I was when I was ten. I'm not. And I doubt you are either."

"You chased me and Beck around the backyard until all of our sides hurt from running and laughing. You climbed trees and built forts with Celia and then went inside and did whatever other things girls did back then. Played with dolls? I didn't know you very long but I remember someone who was brave and adventurous and fun. That's part of your DNA. I can't believe you're that different."

"Things change. Celia's gone. That changed everything for me. And for me and Beck." I gasped and turned away, the truth tugging on me like I'd been tangled up in a fishing line and was being dragged out to sea, where I'd drown.

Cameron stayed quiet, but I knew he was there. His shadow overlapped mine on the ground.

"I didn't know." He said it in a soft, yet full and deep voice, without any hint of surprise or sarcasm.

I shrugged and turned around. "No one did." My eyes were filled but had not overflowed.

"Was it serious?"

Why did people always ask if a relationship was serious?

"No. I mean, I don't know. But it doesn't matter, because he hates me for leaving."

"I don't think he hates you. He didn't say anything either way."

"You talked to Beck about me?"

"Not about you, but he came over last night to see Deanna and I mentioned you'd been there and he didn't say anything."

My heart twisted, released, and then twisted again. "Beck and Deanna?"

"She took him out for dinner to thank him because he fixed her fence. He wouldn't let her pay for any of the materials and he's always stopping by to help out. I think he feels responsible for the house, even though she owns it. And I'm better with an espresso machine than a hammer."

"They're not dating?"

"Does it matter?"

I shrugged.

"Deanna said the word in Chance is that he hasn't dated anyone in years. I think she'd like to be the one to change that. But, you know, he had some trouble after Celia died."

"What do you mean he hasn't dated anyone? Wait. What trouble?"

"You don't know?"

"Know what?"

"Oh." Cameron shook his head. "It's not my place to say anything. Sorry I mentioned it. I just figured—" Cameron's phone dinged. "It's Deanna. I'm going to tell her to walk home without me." He tapped his phone and pressed it against his thigh.

"You don't have to do that."

"I am not leaving you in the alley in this . . ." Cameron scrunched up his face. "In this condition," he said, waggling his finger at me.

I laughed, though I wished I hadn't.

"See? I do know you. Hey, what are you doing right now?"

"Nothing for another hour. I'm picking Shay up after her class and taking her to the mall."

"Come with me to the cemetery."

I fanned myself with my hand, strangely lightened by the morbid suggestion. Then I borrowed a hint of the Southern accent I'd picked up at our hotel in Atlanta. "Why, Cameron Davis, you do know how to make a lady feel special, bless your heart, but no thank you."

"I gave you a scone."

"I *bought* the scone."

"Details, Teddi Lerner, details."

"What is your fascination with that cemetery?"

"I like history."

"There are these things called movies, you know—or even books."

"Yes, I know about books, I'm a teacher. AP History. But there are other reasons I go there."

My chest felt heavy, my heart so exposed I wanted to zip it up. "I am so sorry. I didn't mean . . . I didn't know . . ."

"No, nothing like that. It's that I like to write stories so I look at the headstones and think of the people's lives and what they might have been like. What happened in their dash."

"Their dash?"

"Between the day they were born and the day they died, there's always a dash. Sometimes there's a list of labels, and that can help, but the ones that just have dates and a dash, I feel sorry for them. I wonder if there was nothing at all or just so much that no one could pare it down for a marble slab."

"That's kind of sad."

"I don't think of it that way. I look at it as an opportunity, and I'm kind of obsessed with it. Maybe I could give someone life again with a story or a novel. Sounds pompous, I know. I don't have a God complex or anything. I just think that the future sort of lies in the past. No pun intended."

"Have you ever written one?"

"One what?"

"A story inspired by a headstone."

Cameron bent his arm and held it out so that I could link mine with it, and I did. "Walk there with me and I'll tell you."

I shook my head. "Sorry, the next walk I'm taking today is

around an air-conditioned mall. But you be sure to tell your friends I said hello."

Cameron shook his head and laughed as I slipped my arm from his. He held on to my hand for just a second. "See you around, Teddi Lerner."

I had a feeling he would.

Chapter 12

I LOVED HAVING A car.

Me: I'm here.
Shay: Want to show you something. Back door open.

I stepped over the moss-grown cracks in the slate path that led around the house and toward the deck. Purple clematis climbed a wooden trellis we'd hung on the house before Shay was born, the new plantings offering hope, but a long-range plan that had not turned out as beautifully as the flowers.

I turned and stood in front of the trellis. I'd left my camera at Nettie's but I could come back when the light would land on the flowers and make them sparkle without Photoshop. Maybe flowers that Celia and I had planted would be the right photo for the contest that I hadn't yet decided if I'd enter. I watched my feet as I walked. Pro, con, pro, con, pro, con. I wasn't sure why it mattered. I shook my shoulders and waggled my arms to reset my thoughts.

Then, I saw a worn brown leather duffel bag to the side of the back door—Beck's duffel bag, the one he'd carried in and out of my apartment after dark and before dawn dozens of times. Where was his car?

I shoved my hands into my pockets and palmed my stone. I looked around the backyard as if I were a detective, looking for any unusual movement in the bushes or unlikely shadows on the ground. Nothing besides a squirrel kept me company, and even he hopped along the top of the fence and out of view. I hoped I'd maintain my balance so easily, if need be.

I stood outside the duffel bag's force field. Clouds provided a shield from direct southern sun, so I saw inside the house without squinting. Shay's back was to the door and she stood at the kitchen counter with Beck. She nodded and Beck stretched out his arm behind her and drew her in with a squeeze and kept her close. He nodded. Maybe they were talking about the wedding, or Celia, or me. Maybe she was trying to wrangle him out of a few shopping dollars. Then Beck kissed the top of Shay's head.

I stepped back, almost onto the duffel, my fist releasing my stone, my heart pounding. I picked up the stone and shoved it back into place and breathed. The guy who hugged and nodded and pulled his niece in close—that was the Beck I knew. *That* was the Beck I missed. The Beck I'd forgotten about on purpose.

I turned and tiptoe-ran across the path, stepping on any moss or plants in my way. I needed to get around to the front of the house. I was panting but moving in slow motion, the small Cape Cod somehow reminding me of the new, sprawling Hester property in Scottsdale.

Made it.

I lifted my hand, kept it far from the doorknob, and knocked.

Shay opened the door right away. "Why are you all sweaty? And why didn't you come in the back?"

"I'm just anxious to go, sweetie."

"I want to show you my collage. It's in the kitchen."

She pulled me inside and through the house at a clip.

"You here alone?"

"I'm not a baby, Aunt Tee." Shay's voice was course, impatient.

"No, you're not." The collage lay on the counter. I pushed my hair off my forehead and behind my shoulders. There was no one else in the room. I looked outside. No Beck. No duffle bag. Shay lifted the paper and turned it around. She inhaled as if she were about to reveal a long-held secret.

"Hey, Aunt Tee! Look!"

I stared and as I blinked, shades of color and bits of paper morphed into one seamless and cohesive family portrait of Miles, Shay, and Celia. "That's amazing."

"Thanks." Shay looked at her creation, and a tentative grin grew into a wide smile that rivaled Celia's. I flinched to stop myself from looking for my best friend.

How I wished that bittersweet was still a term best left for chocolate.

"The collage is due tomorrow but I didn't want to have to cancel our plans, so Uncle Beck stayed up late with me last night while I finished it."

"That was nice of him. So, Uncle Beck went home?"

"Uh-huh."

"He still lives in Columbus, right?" This was wrong. I should not be asking Shay about Beck. If that had been my MO, I would've been asking her about him when we FaceTimed and texted, but I never did. Maybe I should have.

"Most of the time he's in Columbus. Sometimes he's here."

"He visits you and your dad and stays with you? That's nice."

Shay tipped her head back and laughed as if I had just told her the funniest joke she'd ever heard. "Why would he live here when he owns Nettie's on Lark? He lives *there*."

"Sure. Right. Of course. Silly me."

My thoughts swirled.

The basket. The wine. The footsteps. The necklace!

A thoughtful and thought-provoking gesture, out of character for this Beck. I tried not to think of how he'd been upstairs as I paraded around my room in my underwear, bathed for an hour in the claw-foot tub, and when I'd snuck outside late at night in my robe with just a T-shirt underneath. He'd been there all night, right upstairs. So close but yet so far—and so cliché it backed up into my throat and made me queasy, yet my pulse quickened.

I'd managed to dodge him once again.

"No more about Uncle Beck, okay?" I focused my gaze on Shay, searching for her unique features. The ones that made her Shay, separated her from Celia.

"It's time for our girls' day out. You, me, and the mall. Ready? Aren't you glad I have a car now?"

"Yep! And oh yeah—Daddy's meeting us for lunch."

We tried on feathers in our hair, rings on our toes, and scarves around our necks. I told Shay no, I could not give her permission for a second hole pierced in one of her ears.

"Do you remember when you had your ears pierced?"

"No, do you?"

"Of course I do. You were five, the summer before you started kindergarten. You wanted so badly to wear big-girl earrings and your mom and dad thought, fine, babies get their ears pierced. Shay's five. It's fine."

"It was fine," Shay said.

"You cried for three hours. Nonstop."

"I did?"

"Yes. But you also couldn't stop staring in the mirror, first at one ear, then the other, shrieking. But every time your mom asked if you wanted to take the earrings out, you screamed louder and said no, you loved your big-girl earrings."

Shay laughed and touched her earlobes.

"C'mon," I said. "We have time before your dad gets here. Let's go buy you a new pair of big-girl earrings."

I yearned to hug her but figured that was not what she'd want in the middle of the mall.

We headed toward Claire's boutique and saw the same group of girls that had walked into the café. Or at least I thought so. I hadn't realized how all tweens—teens—look the same to me.

"There are those girls again."

"Oh crap," Shay whispered.

It didn't matter that I didn't understand the "oh crap." She wasn't happy to see them and that's all that mattered.

"You just stand here with me when they walk by." I pulled Shay to the nearest kiosk and pointed to a pair of faux designer sunglasses. "Just ignore them."

"Let's go home." I could barely hear her. "I can't stand them." That I heard just fine.

The girls moved toward us in a heap, arms flailing with shopping excitement, voices raised in glee. When they reached the kiosk they went silent for two beats that seemed to last an hour.

Morgan turned back and looked at us. I flared my nostrils and peered, activating my *into-your-soul* X-ray vision.

I didn't mean to.

Yes, I did.

I looked at Shay. "Those are not nice girls. Tell me what's going on. I knew Morgan's uncle growing up and he's a nice man and I'm going to say something to him about that behavior."

"No, Aunt Teddi, you can't."

"I saw Uncle Beck with Morgan's mother, so we're going to have to talk to him and your parents—to your dad and Violet."

"No!"

I ached to chase after the girls, to yank them by their earlobes, pull them into the corner, and give them a what-for. I didn't know anything about most of them, but I couldn't blame Morgan's behavior on her having a single mom. Miles had raised Shay for the past six years and she was sweet, contemplative, and creative. Maybe that was why Cameron was hanging around this summer. Maybe he and Deanna needed to reel in the mean-girl behavior before middle school turned into high school and all hormone hell broke loose.

We walked in the opposite direction from the girls, toward the food court, away from our big-girl-earring destination and toward—I had no idea what.

I thought of book club and the whispering, of how gossip and hearsay runs through a small town like a river runs to a waterfall.

"Please tell me what's going on."

Shay looked straight ahead and kept walking.

Miles arrived at the food court wearing a suit.

"Hi, honey." He kissed the top of Shay's head. "My meeting was moved up but I have time to treat you to a quick lunch. What do you want today?" He reached into his pocket and pulled out a few bills.

"Aunt Teddi too?"

Miles looked at me. "Aunt Teddi too. The pad Thai isn't bad if you like that kind of thing."

"I'm just going to get a cookie." I wasn't hungry, but I didn't have to be hungry to want a chocolate chip cookie.

Shay plucked a ten from her dad and walked the perimeter of the food court. I hadn't promised Shay I wouldn't say anything to Miles. But I could make Miles promise.

"Something happened, but don't tell Shay I told you."

"Now you're telling me how to parent?"

"Really, Miles. She doesn't want you to know. Promise."

"Fine, I promise. What happened?"

"Those girls were here. The ones I mentioned."

"What happened?" He looked around the food court and over the hedge of fake boxwoods.

"Nothing happened, that's the point."

"I don't understand the problem, Ted."

"Neither do I. Maybe I can help if you tell me."

"It's not that simple."

"Doesn't the middle school have a no-tolerance policy for this kind of thing?"

"What kind of thing?"

"Bullying."

"Those girls are not bullying Shay."

"It's emotional bullying if they're making fun of her work and intimidating her into clamming up whenever they're around."

"No offense, but you need to mind your own business."

"Shay is my business."

"Since when? Since two days ago?" Miles looked at the table and back at me. "Look, I know you love her, but you're here at a really busy and stressful time."

Miles didn't say busy and joyful. Miles didn't say busy and exciting.

"Just enjoy her, and then go back to your life, okay? Next summer I'll bring her to Chicago. And things can go back to normal."

"What if I don't want things to go back to normal? What if I want to change what's normal?" I heard my voice outside myself—it was strained, almost begging.

Shay arrived at the table with a loaded baked potato, thereby negating any health benefits of baked potatoes—just like a twelve-year-old should.

"Did you ask her, Daddy?" Shay sat on a molded plastic chair.

"Ask me what?" I glared at Miles. *We're not finished yet*. He glanced away.

"Ask her, Daddy. Go ahead."

"Shay thought it would be a good idea to take some headshots I can use for the campaign."

I'd read the *Gazette*. There were two spots on the council and two people were running.

"I need new headshots anyway so I can update my Web site and my business cards. Can't keep looking like it's 2012." Miles looked up toward his receding hairline and smiled. How did he go from possessive to pleasant? Maybe that was the mark of a true politician. Or of someone skilled at avoidance.

"C'mon, Aunt Teddi, this is easy for you, right? It's part of your regular job. You take pictures of businessmen in suits, right? Dad looks good in a suit."

"He does indeed."

Celia and I had dubbed it the Suit Factor. Most men looked good in suits. The structure of the garment lent even a coward some credibility and charm, at least at first.

Simon *killed* suits. Suits fit Simon's tall and slim physique without bulging or creasing. A suited exterior matched his inner strength of character. He was always meticulously groomed, with weekly haircuts and straight-edge-razor shaves. My favorite suit was his navy double-breasted, but he looked at ease in all his custom-tailored garments, as if he'd dressed without a thought. I knew that each night he chose the next day's clothing with precision and a hand-held steamer. I grew wistful for his certainty and meticulousness. I would call Simon later.

"I'll take headshots for you before I leave, sure."

"Tonight?" Shay asked.

"I don't know, sweetie . . ."

"Vi's visiting her sister for the matron of honor dress fitting. I was just going to order a pizza for us," Miles said. "I'm not much of a cook."

"I remember."

"Okay, your dad's gone. Tell me what's going on."

"You were always around when Mom was . . . weren't you?"

"You promised you would tell me what is going on with those girls."

"I will, I swear. But you were, weren't you? Always around?"

"I was."

"Don't you miss us? Me and Dad, I mean."

"We're here together. Your dad just left."

"I mean the rest of the time."

I knew what Shay meant. "I think about you and your mom every day. And I love our texts and when we FaceTime and the times we've spent in Chicago. I know it hasn't been enough and I'm sorry. I'm going to be around a lot more from now on, okay?"

"I wish you lived here."

"I will come back to visit, I promise, but my job—"

"You can take pictures anywhere. I know you used to do it when you lived here. Daddy told me. He said you were away sometimes but you lived here and spent lots of time with Mommy and him and me. So you can do that again."

"I can't. I have a job—"

"Jobs can be anywhere."

Simon was not anywhere. This was so cliché it was a song. I'd left my heart in San Francisco. At least a part of it. "It's more complicated than that," I said.

"Grown-ups always make things complicated," Shay said.

We really did.

Chapter 13

SHAY HELD EARRINGS TO her ears and looked into a three-way mirror for the next twenty minutes. She pivoted and turned, pursed her lips, and flipped her long ponytail. Exactly like a teenager trying to make a buy-one-get-one-free decision and avoid my question about what was really going on in her life. Finally, she dropped earrings into her basket.

"Let's go find a new dress," Shay said. "That's not complicated, right?"

"Right." I slid the basket off her arm and headed to the register. We'd go to one of those trendy teen stores and I'd cross my fingers we'd find something age appropriate and agreeable. "A new dress after we find flip-flops, okay?"

"Okay."

"What kind of dress do you want?"

"Not for me, Aunt Tee. For you."

Complicated.

"You should see the closet in my room at the inn. And my closets in San Francisco. If there's one thing I have enough of, it's dresses. And I have them stashed all over the country. All I wear are dresses, if you haven't noticed. I am not a pants girl.

Except to work, and in the winter. Although I try to stay away from winter."

"I thought maybe we could pick out something for you to wear to the wedding. Your dresses are kind of *casual*."

"Is that so?" How was it that Shay thought she wasn't like her mother? That was such a Celia thing to say.

"The wedding is fancy."

"Yes, Miss Flip-Flops, the wedding is fancy." I playfully poked Shay in the side and she giggled, the sound cradling my heart. I'd been there the first time Celia heard Shay laugh out loud. She was about four months old and Celia had just nuzzled her belly. Then she looked at me.

"Did you hear that?"

I nodded. "Do it again."

She did and Shay had laughed. And then we laughed. So it went for the next half hour. It all happened in the days before moments like those were saved in perpetuity on smartphones, before the world could share your private joy with a viral video.

"I wear the same thing to every wedding." I swung my arm over Shay's shoulder and steered her toward the discount shoe warehouse that anchored the mall.

"Wearing the same thing is boring."

"It's work, so I wear sort of a uniform. I wear black pants and a white shirt."

"Like a waiter?"

"No, I have cameras hanging around my neck so I look like the photographer."

"Aw, c'mon, Aunt Teddi, let's get you something new."

"We can shop more if you want, sweetie, but your dad and Violet's wedding is a work day for me. I will be your friendly photographer who looks like a waiter. But I'm happy to buy you something new. Besides earrings and flip-flops, that is."

I heard yammering and laughter. Shay's eyes widened. She'd heard it too. The group of girls was heading our way again.

"Let's just get out of here," Shay said.

I took Shay's hand and led her back to a table at the food court, away from the oncoming foot traffic.

We sat and I reached into my bag and pulled out the necklaces. We'd appear engrossed and engaged. I didn't want Shay to talk. There was time for the truth, for her truth. Now I just wanted to share more of mine.

The necklaces had managed to stay untangled in the tissue. I laid them out side by side.

"These belonged to your mom and me. You wouldn't remember, we were a little bit younger than you when we bought them."

"I know."

"You do?"

"My dad gave me that one when he and Vi got engaged." Shay pointed to the *T* necklace. "I kept it in my jewelry box and figured I'd give it to you in Chicago. But then I realized you should be here for the wedding and asked Dad if it would be okay. And then I asked Uncle Beck to leave it in your room. And Vi gave him a basket of snacks for you too."

My pulse simmered with disappointment. Beck had been just the deliveryman. I looked back at the necklaces. "Why haven't you worn it? It's yours now."

"Because you gave it to my mom, not to me. You could give the other one to another friend. Your new best friend."

"I don't really have one."

"You don't?"

"Not really." I shook my head. "Not a best *best* friend."

"Me either."

I lifted the *T* heart from the table and walked behind Shay. I reached around and clasped it behind her neck. Back in my seat, I held out the *C* necklace. Shay walked around me and clasped it behind my neck.

"There. The tradition continues." I looked up at Shay, connected to me in this one small way just as Celia had been. "Friends forever?"

Shay smiled. "Better than friends."

My heart tightened, even more than it had the whole day, but as I looked at her, my heart didn't break. It filled.

No one told me a child could do that. That a child could burrow into a space inside me I didn't even know had the possibility of existing, take up permanent residence, and then split me open.

Someone should have told me.

"Can I ask you something?"

"Sure," I said.

Shay sat in the chair next to mine. "Do you mind not having a best friend?"

"Sometimes," I said.

"Yeah, me too."

Shay and I proclaimed we'd had enough of the mall—so we headed to the car with earrings, flip-flops, and a bag of by-the-pound gummy bears, just as Cousin Maggie and Lorraine were walking into the mall. This time, Cousin Maggie used a walker. I hugged her and then Lorraine.

"Shay, this is my cousin, Maggie. Maggie, this is my best friend's daughter, Shayna Cooper."

"Shay and I know each other," Lorraine said.

"Oh, you do?"

"Uh-huh," Shay said. "From—"

"From being around town," Lorraine said.

"Doing a little shopping today, Cousin Maggie?"

"No, I'm at the mall because I want to play hockey. Of course I'm doing a little shopping."

Shay chuckled and then clamped her hand over her mouth.

Good luck, I mouthed to Lorraine.

"No luck needed. The sun is shining and we've got pockets with a little spending money. Don't we, Maggie?"

"Quarters," she said. "I like the slots."

Shay and I stayed silent.

"Maggie . . ." Lorraine said.

"Lighten up. I know there's no gambling at the mall. I like to be prepared. Just in case."

That was our cue to go.

I drove without talking. Shay stared out the window and fingered the necklace every minute or so, then sank against the window. "If you don't want a new best friend and I don't want a new mom, why does my dad want a new wife?"

Damn. Grown-up things *were* complicated. But why was she asking me? I was less like a grown-up than any other grown-up I knew.

"What did your dad say when you asked him?" They had surely talked about this before Miles and Violet got engaged.

"I didn't ask him."

"Why not?"

"He seems happy."

"You're a big part of why your dad's happy."

"No, not really."

"Really."

Shay clasped her hands and then fidgeted and sat on them. Now I'd find out about the girls, maybe what the gossip at Josie's was about. Small-town rivalries ran for decades and mean girls were always at the bottom of it. "It's those girls, isn't it? That's been really stressful for you and your dad." Shay nodded. "And probably Violet too." Shay just shrugged. "Tell me the short version— you don't have to go into detail. What's going on?"

"Do you want me to be honest?"

"Absolutely. Tell me the truth."

"Morgan used to be my best friend. Now she's not."

"Why?"

"Because they're all weird."

I was expecting mean, nasty, cruel. Not—weird. I kept looking at Shay then back to the road. Shay. Road. Shay. Road. Shay.

"What?" Shay's sarcasm was laced with clichéd teenage hostility. "You said you wanted the truth."

Shay said nothing else until I pulled into her driveway. I wanted to ask her what "weird" meant, but I wasn't sure I wanted to know. The few words that trickled from my brain stayed lodged in my throat. I couldn't even come up with a reprimand, or a piece of passé advice.

I was in over my head.

"Will you pick me up from art class tomorrow?"

"I think we should talk about—"

"No, we shouldn't. You're coming back tonight, though, right?"

Shay's jawline softened. Pizza and pictures. And weird. "I'll be over about six."

"Dad's not usually home until about seven."

"That's okay. You and I can have some more girl time."

Shay looked at me, eyes wide. I mimicked her and stared back, daring her to bar me from the house, her life, and whatever was going on.

I parked at the end of Grand Street and called Annie.

"This is getting to be a habit. I like it," she said. "How's Mayberry?"

Today the small-town jab cut deep. "Not good."

"What's wrong?"

"Do you know anything about preteen girls?"

"Aren't you in the land of maternal overlords?"

"I guess. Well, would you do me a favor? It's a biggie. Actually, it's two favors."

"Sure."

"First, I need you to go to Simon's and get my dry cleaning out of the closet in the blue guest room and send it to me. Second, don't tell him what you're doing."

"You want me to steal your own clothes for you and keep it a secret. Can I ask why?"

"I need my work clothes and they're in there."

"You're in your hometown and the bride wants you to wear your penguin outfit? I thought these were friends of yours. Maybe it's time you transitioned out of your uniform phase of life, and this would be a good time to start. Go buy yourself something. They have a mall there, right?"

"Maybe another time. Just do this for me, please?"

"Why don't you just ask Simon to send it all to you? He *is* capable of calling FedEx, you know. He could probably even put it in a box himself." Annie laughed. "He keeps asking if you've called. Maybe you're right. He'd probably shove himself into the box if I told him."

"I'll call him, I promise. I just don't want to involve him in this, that's all. It's like old home week for me. Old friends . . ."

"I don't know, if I had someone like Simon in my life, I'd want to show him where I grew up."

"I can't, Annie. Not yet."

"I think you're crazy, but I'd do anything for you."

"Oh, thank you! Just get the black pants, and two white tops to me before the wedding on Sunday. Tell Simon I asked you to put the clothes in the office closet."

"Leave the details to me."

"I always do! What would I do without you?"

"End up staying in Mayberry."

"Annie!"

"Yes, I know. Chance, Ohio. Now, I need your address."

"Thanks, I owe you."

"You're right, you owe me." Annie sometimes blurred the friend/boss line, but then again, so did I. With her and with Simon. "Now, with that taken care of, I have to tell you about this possible client who called today," she said. "You are not going to believe—"

"No, Annie, I can't. Not now."

"Thanks for letting me come over."

"You're always welcome here. You sounded stressed."

I followed behind Josie, who'd changed from her work clothes into a short—maybe just a little too short—denim skirt and a fitted scoop-neck white T-shirt that showed off her tan along with everything else. We walked through the kitchen, which looked as if it had never been used, when it had been filled with food and friends fewer than twenty-four hours earlier.

"You need a drink," Josie said. "It's Tanqueray and Tonic Tuesday, you know!"

"Just water or iced tea for me."

"I think you need something stronger, but okay."

What I needed was a way to get Shay to open up. I didn't want to be on the perimeter anymore, not now that I'd seen—been invited—inside her life. Or at least part of it. That would require a clear head and some assistance.

I carried two glasses filled with ice, and Josie carried a pitcher of tea through the house and into the formal living room, which had a Southern flair.

"It was inspired by our trip to Charleston," Josie said as if she'd been reading my mind.

I felt as if I'd stepped into a preppy kaleidoscope. The walls were either hand painted or wallpapered in shamrock green with flecks of white, which upon closer inspection were tiny hand-painted pineapples. Gold-framed artwork and photos covered one wall as if it were a gallery. The couch and chairs were covered in soft white linen (with three boys!) while the accent pillows and one meticulously placed throw were a combination of green, bright pink, and multihued plaids. A hotel-size bouquet of color-coordinated tropical flowers graced the white marble fireplace mantel in front of an oversized mirror.

Josie pulled open a set of triple doors and left them ajar.

"This is the piazza," she said.

It reminded me of Savannah—though Josie said Charleston. The South. Same to me, although I knew that was geographically incorrect, as was the architecture of the house. But the details were on point, with the low wicker wrap-around furniture, the columns, and the slow-moving ceiling fans that almost insisted I slow down and sit. So I did.

Josie set the pitcher on a low table and I poured our glasses full. Then I sat on the chaise, the tufted cushion making way for me. It was soft, yet supportive. When I lifted my legs I felt relief, as if I was weightless and could drift away in the nonexistent sea.

"I almost forgot I'm in Chance." I snuggled into the corner among the mountain of pillows, and closed my eyes.

I heard Josie drop onto the sofa to my right. "I love it here, but I'll tell you a secret. That's the point."

"She said 'weird,' huh?" Josie sipped her drink and looked off into the yard. "Kind of un-PC, these days, don't you think?"

"I told her to be honest."

"Yeah, that's always a wide-open door you're sorry you walked through, isn't it? And before that Miles didn't seem surprised when you mentioned those other girls?"

"No, but it was before that comment, just when Shay was avoiding them at the mall."

"Maybe it's really just none of your business."

"How is it none of my business? I'm here. I saw what happened. First at Fat Chance Café and then at the mall. How can I ignore that?"

"Maybe you have to. They invited you to the wedding, not into their family problems."

"No, they asked me to take pictures at their wedding, which I'm doing because of our history. Because of Celia and because of Shay. The same reason someone should tell me what's going on." I rolled an ice cube around in my mouth and spit it back into my glass.

"Well, it's pretty hard to keep a secret around here. You know what they say! Someone in Chance always knows."

"I knew you were going to say that. You know what? That's not true. People around here have a disproportionate number of secrets. They just pretend they don't. And then they leave. Or die. With their secrets intact."

Josie scrunched her eyebrows together as if rummaging through her own secrets—or those of others.

"I think that when it comes to kids, things aren't so much secret as just private. Parents aren't always willing to discuss what's going on. Even if everyone knows."

"I'm not everyone. I love Shay, and I care about Miles. And I owe it to Celia. If something is going on, I want to help. I think it's a defense mechanism. She's such a sweet kid; if they're doing something to bother her, of course she's going to put up a wall . . ."

"Now you're a therapist?"

"No, but . . ."

"Maybe they don't want your help. Maybe your help is taking pictures. And taking Shay to the mall."

"Thanks a lot."

"I'm just being honest. Kid stuff is hard and—"

"And what? I don't understand because I don't have kids. You're right. I don't understand any of it. But I want to. I want to help her. I want to be there for her. How can I do that if nobody will talk to me?"

"Get Shay to tell you herself what's going on."

"I tried that. I'm no good at it. I'm good at the fun stuff."

"Today wasn't all fun, though, was it? And you did it. We end up doing a lot of things we never thought we'd do for the kids we love. Just give it time."

"I don't have time. The wedding is Sunday. I leave Monday. It's not just that I want to know, I know I can help her. Whatever it is."

"Well, since you're not a therapist, I know one in town you can talk to."

"You want me to go to therapy?"

"No, I want you to talk to someone who can help you talk to Shay, so both of you are okay when you leave again. I'm thinking about you too, Teddi. She really helped with Jonathan. Well, really, she helped *us*."

I thought of Josie's musician and wondered what had happened. According to Josie, even if I'd lived here, or been better at keeping in touch, Shay still might not have shared her struggles with me.

"I don't think I could talk to a counselor. I'm not really comfortable telling a stranger my personal problems."

"But you want Shay and Miles to tell you theirs."

"I'm not a stranger."

Josie cocked her head. She waited. I could wait her out. I crossed my arms. She wavered and I won. Although, not really.

"Deny it all you want, but once you left Ohio, you stepped onto the outside of Shay's real life."

I relaxed back into the chaise. "How do I get to the inside before Sunday?"

"I'll give you the counselor's card. Or just talk through the whole thing with someone who knows *you* really well."

"That's what I thought we were doing."

"We don't know each other like we used to."

My throat tightened. What was I doing here then? "I'm sorry, I didn't mean to bother you with all this. I shouldn't have assumed."

Josie sat on the edge of the chaise. I moved my legs and she scooted toward me. "Knock it off, you're not bothering me. I like it that we're friends again. Real-life friends. We're connected. I feel it too. I'm trying to help you. If it were me, I'd go to my husband. And I did. But Evan didn't know what to do either. So we got some help. Just think of who knows your heart, Teddi, who knows how you think. Start there."

I felt a stab in my side and my breath quickened, as if I'd been running. "I couldn't do that!"

"Is Simon really too busy to talk to you about something *this* important?"

I wasn't thinking about Simon.

Chapter 14

"PICTURES BEFORE OR AFTER pizza?" Miles asked. He fiddled with the knot in his tie.

"Before." I unpacked my camera and an extra flash onto the kitchen table. "Unless you're sure you won't get any sauce on your shirt."

"I'm going to work on my art project," Shay said.

I wanted Shay nearby so I could watch her with my newfound perspective. Problem was, she knew it. "You're not going to help?"

Shay cackled. It sounded more sinister than sweet. "You can handle Daddy on your own!" She headed for the stairs. "I'll come down when the pizza's here."

I said nothing to change her mind, fearful of what she might say, what Miles might hear. The right words were needed at a time like this, and I didn't possess them.

Or I was a coward.

"Where would you like the pictures taken, Mi?" I spun around as if I'd never been there before, as if I didn't know which room had the best natural light, the warmest wood, was least likely to allow my voice to travel up the stairs.

"Isn't it your job to tell me?"

I shook my head, but walked toward the living room, and Miles followed. I pointed to the piano bench, so Miles sat.

I felt accused by every syllable Miles spoke. I motioned to the piano keys. "Does Shay play?"

"No. She says she's an artist, not a musician."

I laid my hands on Miles's shoulders and rotated them a few degrees toward me. Then I opened a worn piece of sheet music on the piano. The theme to *Somewhere in Time*. I shuddered. Celia and I had discovered this 1980 Christopher Reeve and Jane Seymour movie more than ten years after it had come out, during a rainy Friday-night excursion to the Video-Rama during the summer between our freshman and sophomore years in college. It became Celia's all-time favorite movie, and then, her favorite piece of music to play. It wasn't until years later that I embraced the notion of the film—that a simple keepsake could keep someone tethered to the past, whether real or imaginary. I tapped my pocket to feel the stone I knew was there.

"You still have this?"

I thrust the paper at Miles, daring him to tell me it was a coincidence, willing him to say it was intentional. He set the music back on the piano and smoothed it open, as if it hadn't been anything more than a prop.

With the camera to my face I focused on the composition and the light, nothing more. *Tip your head, turn your chin, look over my shoulder, into the camera, off into the distance. Stand, sit, turn, smile. Hand in your pocket, behind your back, under your chin.* For a few minutes I forgot Miles was the Miles of Miles and Celia. He transformed into a shape I saw only through my lens from a comfortable distance with shadows and colors. Miles was right, it did feel like work, but in the best possible way, the way that made time fly as I made images stand still.

I moved the camera away and stared at Miles until he didn't look like Miles anymore, the way you can look at a word and after a while it starts to look different, even though you know it's the same word. Perhaps if you look at anything, or anyone, long enough and hard enough, it begins to change. Scrutiny was transformative.

"I think we're done."

Miles rose and loosened his tie. I looked at the mantel, arranged with new trinkets since the last time I'd looked, or taken inventory, probably many years before. A small wedding portrait of Miles and Celia in a simple black metal frame perched on an end table alone. I didn't know if it was set in a place of honor or if Violet didn't want her own belongings to intermingle and catch Celia cooties.

I picked up the frame and held it. I stared at the eyes of my friend like I hadn't in years.

"I'd like to talk about Shay before she comes down," I said.

"I'm not sure what you want to talk about."

"She thinks you're moving."

"No she doesn't."

"Yes, she does."

"We've talked about this, and yes, one day we'll probably move. But not now. And I promise you, she knows that."

I hadn't reached out to Beck in six years. And now, back in the room that he owned, my attempt went right to voicemail.

"Hi, it's me. I mean—it's Teddi. Can I— I would like to talk to you about Shay. Would you call me back? Please call me back."

Over the next ten minutes I held my phone to my ear, checked the Wi-Fi connection, restarted the phone, and texted Annie and asked her to call me. My phone worked fine.

Finally, I heard the default tone for texts.

Beck: I'm busy right now.
Me: Are you available later?
Beck: I'll let you know.
Me: You'll let me know WHEN you're available or you'll let me
     know IF you're available?

No reply.

I opened my door and listened for a creak, a footstep, a cough. If I heard evidence that Beck was upstairs, I'd just tiptoe up before he had the sense to escape out a window and shimmy down the chimney. Or, I could sit on the steps and wait. He didn't know that I knew I was sleeping in his house. His guard would be down. Then I realized Beck's guard was likely never down when it came to me.

Back inside the room, I drew the curtains, but left on the light. I climbed under the covers so as not to disturb half the bed. Knowing the bedding had been chosen and purchased by Beck made me want to wrap myself in it as if it were intended just for me. It felt intimate, even revealing, like anything I thought would be left in the room for Beck to find. The sheets were smooth, cool, and a high thread count. The comforter was light but thick, warm but not suffocating. The pillows were supportive and soft and had just enough give.

An hour later I awoke disoriented. I didn't know if it was late or early or somewhere in between. My mouth was open and dry on the inside, drool-drenched on the outside. My lashes were tacky with the mascara I hadn't removed.

I picked up my phone.

Beck: I'm around if you want to talk.

Damn. It had come through twenty minutes earlier. I hadn't even heard the beep.

Me: I fell asleep, sorry. Are you still awake?
Beck: Yes. I can meet you on the porch.
Me: Now?
Beck: Yes.
Me: Be out in a few.

I was wrinkled and rumpled and it didn't matter. This wasn't about me. Still, I wiped the mascara from under my eyes with a tissue. No need to resemble a raccoon; not that Beck hadn't seen that look on me before and teased me mercilessly. I trembled as I tied my hair into a loose ponytail and then took it out, turned my head upside down and ran my fingers through my hair. Beck had always liked my hair down.

When I quietly opened the front door, I saw Beck sitting on the porch, on the floor, with his back to the street. He faced the door and I readied myself for a verbal firing squad.

"I didn't realize you'd be out here already."

"But you know I own this place."

I sat against the railing with enough space for a linebacker between me and Beck. "Shay told me."

"I know."

"What made you buy it?" We both stared ahead.

"I needed something to keep me busy. And I knew how much Cee loved it."

I nodded.

"I thought if you knew I was the owner, then you wouldn't come for the wedding because you'd have no place to stay. I was against it—as you probably figured. But Shay seemed legitimately thrilled you were coming and I didn't want anything to get in the way. I should've been honest. I'm sorry about that. And I apologized to Shay too, for making things more complicated for her. I didn't realize at first . . ."

"I don't think this is what is making her life complicated," I said.

"Very true."

"I know something's not right. I think I know what it is but I'm not sure. In texts and on FaceTime she's sweet and funny and adorable—and not that she's not all of those things, but there's more. More I can see but don't know."

Beck laughed but the sound was shaded with knowing and sadness.

"Please tell me what's going on so I can help her!"

Beck had the answers but I didn't let him talk. Not yet. Whether he wanted to admit it or not, *he knew me*. He knew I wanted to help. He knew I wasn't leaving without knowing everything. That was likely the problem.

I told Beck about the Fat Chance Café, meeting Morgan, the mall, the ride home, Shay's comment about the other girls, and how Miles ignored that I wanted to know, to help, to be there. Lastly, I told Beck how Miles, Shay, and I ate pizza and talked about art, with not one word about the mean girls or the wedding or Celia.

"I'm pretty sure those girls are bullying her, or they bullied her this year, because she pretty much hides when she sees them. And then she called them weird, like she didn't want to admit how hurt she was. How can you all just sit by and let Shay get bullied by these mean girls is what I don't understand. Look what it's doing to her. She has no close friends. A girl needs friends! Cee and I always had each other and Shay has no one like that. I can help her—I know what it's like. My parents were never like the other parents, so maybe Shay's artistic and different—"

"Stop! I need you to listen to me." Beck sat with his knees bent and his arms propped up on them. Finally, he looked at me.

I folded my hands in my lap. "I'm listening." I mocked him.

"I mean it. Don't say anything, and let me talk, okay? I asked Miles if I could tell you the whole story."

"And?"

"He said okay. But you have to let me talk."

"You're scaring me, Beck. Just tell me already!"

"Shay is the mean girl."

"What?"

"She used to be best friends with Morgan. Like you and Cee best friends. Since Deanna moved here. Then together they started making fun of some of the other girls, but Morgan stopped. Deanna intervened faster than Miles did. But Shay didn't stop, and she turned on Morgan too. Teased her. Embarrassed her in front of other kids for being in lower-level classes—they call it grade-shaming. She was really demeaning and she even started a fistfight. It was awful. She was awful." Beck looked away. "And the school did do something. They suspended her for a week. And the rest of the girls, including Morgan? They chose not to be friends with the mean girl."

"I—"

Beck held up his hand. "Let me finish."

I covered my mouth to hold everything in but wondered if I'd have the strength.

As Beck spoke his eyes filled. He stretched out his legs and crossed his arms over his broad chest, as if keeping his heart in its place. He drew deep breaths between each scene he relayed to me in detail. And how it all started when Miles and Violet got engaged.

My thoughts banged together.

A lump formed in my throat.

"Counseling has helped and she's doing much better now. She's coping. Sometimes she even seems like the old Shay. I won't get into it all. That's for Shay to talk about. But those girls don't want to be friends with her, and no one blames them."

"That's how you met Deanna." I thought I'd said it inside my head. "Isn't it awkward?"

"Not at all. We're adults." I kept forgetting.

"And that's why Cameron's living with them."

Beck nodded. "For backup. And moral support."

"Why didn't anyone tell me?"

"You're like an apparition, Teddi Bear."

It was the first time he'd said my nickname; the sound of his voice traveled inside my head and settled there, soothing the wounds he'd just inflicted with his words about Shay, and just then, about me.

"I know no one wanted me to know. I know no one but Shay wanted me here. But I am here, Beck. I can't just pretend things are fine when they're not fine. I just can't turn around and leave without trying to help." I swallowed the irony and looked right at Beck. He gulped as hard as I did. "A lot of time has passed— you said it the other night. We're not who we used to be. I don't want to be the person who pops in and out of Shay's life. Or yours. Please, help me."

"Just like that?"

"Yes. Just like that. Forget you hate me. Forget I fucked up. Give me a break, B. For old times' sake. Oh hell, don't do it for me. Do it for Celia." I turned away, looked as far off into the night as I could. Emotional blackmail wasn't usually my style.

"Okay," he whispered. "But there's one thing I have to say first." I heard Beck slide across the floor. He touched my shoulder and left his hand there, heat transferring through my blouse. "I don't hate you."

He removed his hand and my temperature seemed to drop.

"Shay launched a full-out FaceTime campaign to get me here to photograph the wedding," I said. "Why did she do that if all this was going on and no one was going to tell me?"

"She wanted you to come because she has this crazy idea that her life would be perfect if *you* married Miles."

I turned around quickly. Beck lurched back.

"Excuse me?"

"She wishes you were the one marrying Miles."

"Don't be silly," I said. Then I thought of the times in the past few days when Miles had been there with me and Shay, when I'd thought it would be just me and her. When she wanted Violet to take her for her shoes, when she disappeared upstairs during our portrait session, when she apologized for Beck showing up early.

"Damn," I said.

"I'm just telling you what she said."

"She thinks he's replacing her mother, for God's sake. She doesn't understand that losing someone you love that much doesn't take away your ability to love someone else just as much."

"She's learning. It takes time, Teddi. It all takes time."

I looked at Beck and placed my hand on the ground. He laid his hand on top of mine. But it was different from before. His eyes were the same blue with specks of brown and his eyelashes were blond, almost invisible. As his nostrils flared, his breathing tempered. Neither of us moved closer together or farther away. After all this time it felt somehow taboo.

Simon.

I glanced away from Beck and then back.

"I should call the counselor Josie told me about, shouldn't I?"

"You should."

"Do you want to come in and have a glass of wine? I mean, just to relax."

"No thanks."

"We can talk more. Catch up. For real."

"We have time." Beck ran the back of his hand from the front of my neck to the back, and under my hair, pushing it behind my shoulder. I shivered. "I like your hair down," he said. "But you knew that."

Inside, Beck walked up a few steps, and then his footsteps stopped. I was partway down the hall leading to my room, and stopped as well.

"I know you ran out the back of Perk when you saw me with Deanna," he said.

"I just couldn't . . ."

"I'm not *with* Deanna, you know. We're just friends. But even if I was, you don't have to run away from me, Teddi. You never did."

I turned as he continued up the stairs. Without a light, he was shrouded in the safety of darkness. As was I.

"If you weren't with Deanna when I called, where were you?"

So much for not overstepping boundaries. Old habits had a way of feeling comfortable, even when they shouldn't.

Without stopping his climb, Beck answered me.

"A meeting."

Chapter 15

"AND THEN HE JUST walked upstairs," I said.

"Did you go after him?" Josie swirled a fry in a dollop of ketchup.

"No, I didn't go after him."

"Why not?"

"Because—I don't know. I'm not going to chase him, Jos. He doesn't have to tell me anything about his life. We were in a good place last night after talking about Shay and I didn't want to ruin it any more than I already have."

Josie sipped her iced tea and shrugged. "Men. Can't live with 'em, can't shoot 'em." She laughed as if she'd come up with that herself.

As the Fat Chance Café chimes clanged their now-familiar tune, I lifted my empty teacup and turned it over. Muddled voices trickled by and colorful streaks skirted my peripheral vision. Drips of lemon verbena landed on the saucer next to the mesh teabag. The words on the china didn't register so I replaced the cup. All I could see was that I had missed big things in Chance, and hadn't even recognized that possibility. Like everything important had happened right outside my reach. I'd spent six years toting around Celia's memory when people I loved might have needed me.

My throat filled.

"I have to go." I pushed back my chair and stood. I pulled a twenty out of the front pocket of my camera bag that dangled over the back of my chair and handed the money to Josie. "My treat. I've got to get out of here."

"Oh no," she said. "No more running away." Josie grabbed my camera bag and placed it on her lap. I sat.

"I'm not running away." I exhaled more air than I knew I could hold in. "I'm expecting a package and thought I'd check the post office." I knew full well that Annie would ship FedEx.

"Really? You know they'll deliver right to your door? We're fancy here that way," Josie said. "Why don't you calm down? Then, you can go find Beck."

"What makes you think I'm going to look for Beck? Actually, I need to go call Simon." I'd never called Simon. Shit. "I think he's going to propose when I get back to San Francisco."

"Are you kidding me? That's fantastic!" Josie whispered.

"It's not official. He only said he had *something* to propose when I came back."

"And you left this out of every single conversation? I didn't realize it was that serious."

"Neither did I."

"Didn't realize *what* was so serious?" a voice said.

Josie and I jolted and looked up from our huddle. The two book club gossip girls pulled out the empty chairs at our table and sat.

"We're waiting for takeout for the swim moms."

"You look great today, Teddi."

I'd worn my sleeveless denim shirtdress and a pair of flip-flops. I had my half of the heart necklace around my neck and my hair in a ponytail. My beauty routine had consisted of tinted moisturizer. There was nothing great about any of it but hell if I'd give them that.

"Thanks!"

"So, what'd we miss?"

"That's what I want to know," I said. These women were *chazzers*. Gluttons for gossip that they could parcel out for any takers. I wouldn't peck. "Not here," Josie said.

I raised my hands, but not in an act of surrender. "Sorry, Jos." I drew a deep breath. "I heard you talking about me when we were at Josie's."

"What are you talking about?"

"We were with you the whole night."

"I was in the laundry room." Recognition flooded their faces. Their jaws tightened. "I said—I heard you talking about me."

"I don't know what you're talking about."

"Me either."

I slid forward on my chair. "Ladies . . ." I reached out and touched their hands. "If you want to know something about me, ask me. But don't talk about someone's kid. It's really, you know, unattractive."

"We would never—"

"I'm just trying to help you out here, make sure you don't get yourself into an unsightly predicament."

"What are you implying, Teddi?"

"That in the future you mind your own business while you're hunting for your lipstick."

"Well, we just thought . . . you know."

"No, I don't know."

"That you knew about the wedding, and we were surprised you were here for it."

A bell rang twice and three large paper bags were placed on the counter. "Debbi? Order for Debbi! Debbi or Meredith? Six chopped salads, two hummus plates, one tuna platter, and one vegan BLT hold the T!"

"That's us," Debbi said.

"If I don't see you again, have a good trip back to— Where is that you're jetting off to after the wedding?" Meredith asked.

"Give it a rest, girls." Josie stepped lightly, once, on my foot under the table.

As the women left Fat Chance Café with their boxed-up mom fare, I pulled off the crust of my congealed grilled cheese, folded it accordion-style, and stuck it into my mouth. The buttery, crisp, and salty bread had just the resistance to need ample chewing, and I needed that to stop me from saying something I shouldn't say. Something *else* I shouldn't say. Because even in moments like this, my mother was in my ear reminding me not to talk while I was eating. I shoved in another piece.

"Forget them," Josie said. "They're not worth it."

"No, they're not." I swallowed.

"I can't believe what you said to them."

"I know. It was good, wasn't it?"

"You didn't really get any answers."

"That's okay, Beck really told me everything I needed to know about Shay. What he didn't tell me was anything about himself. I don't feel like I'm being nosy, I'm thinking about all the things I don't know. Like when he bought Nettie's on Lark, how he fixed it up, how his graphic design business is doing, if he's eating right . . ."

"If he's dating anyone?"

"I—"

"Don't even try to lie to me. You should see your face when you talk about him."

"I care about him, is that a problem?"

"No, except you told me that Simon wants to marry you, but the only man you've mentioned in the past ten minutes is Beck. And, you're watching the door like you're expecting someone to walk by. Or walk in. And I don't mean Shay. *That* is a problem," Josie said.

"I know."

I jaywalked across Main Street to the park. The clouds made the sky look as if gray paint had been dragged across it. I crouched and touched the grass. It was dry so I sat, and dug into my camera bag. I lay on my back, crossed my ankles for propriety, and looked up, camera pressed to my face. I saw nothing but those painted clouds floating past my lens, as if late to an appointment. A chill washed over me with the warm, light breeze. *Simon.*

I sat up and pulled out my phone. It was still morning in San Francisco. Was Simon in San Francisco today? I hadn't checked his travel schedule, or asked. I called his cell instead of the office.

"Good morning, stranger."

I heard the smile in his voice, sensed his movement—likely he was making his way to the window where he often perched to talk on the phone. I cringed. Why did he say that? But more importantly, why was that the wrong thing to say? He was being playful. He was teasing me.

"I've only been gone a few days, Simon. We've been apart longer than this for work."

"But this isn't work."

"No, but it's important to me . . ."

"I'm kidding, but it's not the same here without you."

"I talked to Henry," I said. "I think they're going to book next year's benefit gala in New York. I told him the ballroom would be finished by then. Will the ballroom be finished by then?"

"If we get to charge a thousand a person, you bet it will. Did you tell him you'd get it covered on 'Page Six'?"

"That part's not my job, you know that. I said I'd be there myself taking pictures and posting to social media all night, and that I had an in with Lucy Cartwright."

"Lucy Cartwright?"

"The society blogger? The one you want to stay out of *your* business but in everyone else's in New York?"

"Yes!" I heard one big five-hundred-thousand-dollar clap. "Wait till you hear what else is going on here."

"There's a lot going on here too. I'm entering a photography contest." I kicked up my voice an octave, hoping to sound nonchalant, yet excited. It wasn't until that moment that I'd known for sure.

"Why?"

"Because I'm a photographer, Simon."

"The best wedding photographer in San Francisco, maybe in the country."

"It's not that kind of contest. It's a contest for photos of Ohio."

"What's the prize?"

"I don't know." Was there a prize? I wished he could understand that while I cared about every bride, CEO, and event in the moment, that those photos left me a bit hollow. The photos I'd taken in Chance in the past forty-eight hours had started to refill a well I hadn't realized was near empty.

"Annie told me you wanted the clothes from the cleaners you left at my place, so I took them over to her. You could've asked me to send them, you know."

"I didn't want her to bother you. You can forget it, I don't need them." I could go shopping. Or I could wear any of my dresses to Miles and Violet's wedding. The wedding Shay didn't want to happen.

"Annie has everything ready to go."

"Okay, thanks."

"I take it you're having a good time? I mean, if you need more clothes than you already packed."

"Yes, I am." How I wished that I wanted to ramble about Shay and even about Beck. Or tell him about Josie and her kids, or the car. Or the gossip girls, Nettie's on Lark, or the mall. I knew I should let him in, even just a little. I needed to remind myself we had a connection that went beyond work. Beyond work and sex. "It's just hard to be here. I grew up here. I left kind of suddenly and—"

"And you'll be leaving again."

"I guess so." I saw Cameron and Morgan across the street, walking out of the library. Suddenly I wanted to appear nonchalant and unencumbered.

"Si, I've got to go."

"Annie's waving at me, says she needs to talk to you. Hang on."

"I can't. Not now. I have to take care of something." I waved and Morgan lifted her hand in a half wave. She swatted Cameron

189

and he turned. He spoke to Morgan. She continued up Main Street toward Poppy Lane and then he walked across the street to the park.

"She says it's important."

"I'm sure it is, but so is this."

I lay back down, and again, held my camera to my face. I shouldn't have allowed work to intrude on my week, or Simon to muddle my thoughts and my mood.

A shadow fell over me, and then Cameron's face appeared in my viewfinder.

"Earth to Teddi Lerner!"

I smiled but felt shaky and unsettled as I lowered the camera to my side and sat up.

"Feeling more chipper today?" he asked.

"Yes," I said. "No, not really. I want to apologize for yesterday."

"No apology necessary. What's wrong?" Cameron sat and crossed his legs the way we had in elementary school.

"Don't you have to go home with Morgan?"

"No, she can be home for a while on her own. What's going on? Is it Beck?"

"Actually, no. It has nothing to do with him."

"Want to tell me?"

"Not right now."

"Did you get any good shots?" Cameron pointed to the camera.

"No, I wanted to take some pictures here in the square—but don't tell anyone, I'm uninspired this morning. Everything looks kind of, well, blah."

"Oh, that could be the new town motto. I don't know why we didn't think of it before. Welcome to Chance. Land of the free and home of the blah. Should bring in lots of tourists."

I laughed. "That's not what I meant. I just meant that I think I'm trying hard to find just the right thing, at just the right angle, for just the right picture."

"The right picture for what?"

I pulled the contest brochure out of my bag and handed it to Cameron. He studied it.

"I have a diagnosis," he said.

"Oh, you do, do you?"

"Photographer's block. It's like writer's block. I know it well."

"Somehow with all those ideas flying at you at the cemetery, I doubt it."

"I haven't written the book yet, have I? Not the easiest thing to admit, I must tell you. But it's a fact. I have a lot of ideas and a little bit of follow-through." He looked at his hands as if looking for something—a pen, an idea, a muzzle. "I mean I don't have follow-through with writing my book. I have great follow-through with everything else."

"I'm sure you do."

"I do. I swear. I also have a great cure for lack of inspiration."

"Do tell."

"Come with me."

"No way, Mr. Davis. I know where you like to get your ideas."

He stood and reached out his hand toward me. "I promise. This has nothing to do with cemeteries."

"Nice, isn't it?" Cameron shifted his car into park at Jasper Pond. "It's a really great place to think."

"Or make out."

"Ha! Well, if you say so . . ."

"You don't know what this is, do you?"

"Don't tell me. It's an ancient burial ground, and a kiss from someone you knew when you were ten breaks the spell."

I chuckled. "Good try. It's where kids park."

"Yeah, so . . ." Cameron shook his head and then his eyes widened and he blushed. "Oh, you mean *park*. Know it well, do you?"

"I'll never tell."

"I know Deanna runs on the path here; she never mentioned seeing anything."

"It's a late-night-in-the-dark thing."

"It is, is it?"

"Can we change the subject?" I never should have brought it up, but I seemed to say things around Cameron I shouldn't. "Aren't we here to find our creative inspiration?"

"Ah yes, come with me."

We walked across the gravel lot toward Jasper Pond. A new purple playground stood where the picnic area had been, and new picnic tables flanked a dock for remote-control boats. The meadow where Celia and Miles were married had been replanted as a community garden. A sculpted walking path wound around the pond and through some of the trees, with stations for stretching and pull-ups and squats.

"Want to keep walking? Or we could sit? We don't have to talk."

"Whatever you want to do is fine."

"Teddi, I'm trying to help you find your creative center. Work with me here."

"Let's walk."

Cameron slipped his hand into mine and led me to the shore of the pond like an excited child. His hair even flopped like a boy's, and if I were his mother I'd lick my hand and try to glue it into place. His whimsy lightened my mood and I scampered to keep up.

Stones lined the shore and I let go of his hand, then reached down and grabbed two. One perfectly flat and able to skip halfway across the pond, another smooth and round to tuck in my pocket as both a memento and a promise. I did this without looking at Cameron, not wanting to answer any questions he would ask.

"I saw Beck."

"You saw him or you talked to him?"

"I talked to him."

"That's good, right?"

"He told me about Shay." I turned toward Cameron and looked him in the eye. "About what she did. How she behaved."

"You know it wasn't my place to tell you, don't you, Teddi?"

"No, I'm not saying you should have told me. I guess I just wanted to thank you. You let me rant and ramble about Beck and Deanna and all the time you were probably thinking I was a lunatic who knew nothing. And you would have been right."

"I never thought that."

"You're living with your sister and your niece, probably because of the mess Shay started. I don't know why I feel like I should apologize for her, but I do."

"It's not your fault."

"Maybe it is. Maybe if I'd been here, or been more present— oh, I hate that word—this wouldn't have happened. None of it."

"You're being a little hard on yourself, don't you think? Or maybe overestimating the impact you could've had on her?"

"That's not all. But you can't repeat this. Promise?"

"I promise."

"Shay has this crazy idea that I should marry Miles."

"She told you this?"

"No, Beck did. And I have to figure out what to say to her." My thoughts tumbled like socks in a dryer. If I were around more—if I were here—if I hadn't stayed away—that never would have entered her mind. "I have to talk to her about it before Sunday . . . I think not having a mother, and Miles getting re-married, it's too much for her. I'm not making excuses . . ."

"But you are."

"I guess I am. Wouldn't you? If it were Morgan?"

"I don't know. Maybe I would. Anything to what Shay says about you and Miles?"

"Me and Miles? Are you kidding? No, absolutely not! Miles was my best friend's first love. He's like a cousin to me. We're not close anymore but I'll always care about him. So, no. And eww."

Cameron shook his head and smiled. "Very mature, Teddi."

"You said I was the same as when I was ten. Guess you were right."

Cameron and I sat on the stony ground, which made it easy for me to scoop a scant handful of pebbles and let them trickle through my fingers.

"Hey, watch this." Cameron positioned himself into a batter's stance, drew back his arm, and flung a stone into the water, but away from the paddle and paper boat platoons. The stone skipped twice.

"Not bad," I said.

"I can teach you how to do it."

I stood and then removed three stones from my pocket, and

replaced two. I blew on the remaining stone and rolled it in my hands as if I were holding lucky dice. I walked back about three paces and bounded forward with a skip and flicked the stone. Six skips.

"You're a stone-skipping savant!"

"That is the nicest thing anyone has ever said about me. Especially in the past two days. Hell, in the past two months."

I laughed. Then Cameron laughed. Then I laughed again. The laughing was contagious and cathartic. We ended up holding our sides, wheezing, and gasping for breath. I lost my footing for a second and stumbled. He caught me before I made a fool of myself by landing on the ground, but not before he wrapped me in a momentary bear hug, then set me upright.

"I needed that," I said. "The laugh. I really needed that laugh."

"Should we get away from the pond before someone reports us to Park Patrol for reckless endangerment of rocks and photographers?"

We sat on the swings but didn't swing. I held the steel chains and my heart still pounded from the laughter—a release that felt more like a cleanse. I didn't remember the last time I'd laughed so hard my cheeks hurt.

I rose from the swing and lifted my camera to my face, then swung around and snapped a picture of the pond, rimmed by the clouds, touched in the corners by passersby on the trail. Then I took a picture of Cameron's hand wrapped around the chain of the swing. The tips of my Keds surrounded by sand. An empty picnic bench. Stalks of sunshine landing in the parking lot, the gravel shimmering like diamonds. I walked to the path and around the pond alone. I stepped on the heel of my right shoe and pulled out my foot. Then I repeated with the left. The grass and the stones were cool, the water and the sun were warm. I skipped another stone into the pond. I'd visited many beautiful places but none of them rippled to my heart like this one.

I walked back to Cameron. "Thank you," I said. "I love it here. I'd forgotten how much."

"I'm glad. Maybe we could come back."

"Do we have to leave?"

Chapter 16

PERK WAS ALMOST EMPTY when I arrived in the middle of what I assumed was the midday slump.

"Two large peach iced teas."

I carried the cups to a table in the corner. Shay would arrive soon, just in time for a short visit before dinner. That's when I'd mention Simon. I'd never have to tell her I wasn't interested in Miles, because I'd tell her I was already involved. *A couple. Spoken for. Committed.*

Simon and I had never used any of those words.

I picked up the same *Chance Gazette* I'd read once before and feigned nonchalance, as if my leg wasn't bouncing sixty miles an hour under the table. I stomped it as the off switch. I skimmed "Chancelist" on the back page, my small town's version of Craigslist, offering babysitting, lawn mowing, hauling, and tutoring.

Cameron would be a great history tutor, pencil tucked behind his ear, notebook in hand. He had the patience of a saint, if saints were inclined to wear khaki shorts and T-shirts. He'd sat on that swing for nearly an hour. He hadn't questioned me or rushed me.

He left me alone, which left me feeling connected.

I shook my head to scramble the thought and texted Annie.

Me: Did you ship my clothes?
Annie: It's under control.
Me: Thanks.

My phone buzzed with a new text.

Shay: I'm going to hang out with Rebecca and Chloe. ☺ CYA l8r?
Me: Did you ask your dad?

Chloe's mother had been scheduled to drop Shay off at home.

Shay: Vi drove me to Rebecca's house. She has a pool. And a dog.
Me: Ok! Have fun! ☺

I wanted to see Shay. I wanted to show her my pictures from Jasper Pond and tell her I was entering the contest. I didn't want to tell her about Simon, but I would. This, though—a change of plans to be with her friends—this is what should have been happening. A girl on the cusp of adolescence should have wanted to hang out with her friends, not sip iced tea with her "aunt." I was leaving in a few days, but this was what I wanted for Shay— the age-appropriate bond of friendship. Maybe she'd burst into seventh grade with two BFFs and without the need to bully anyone. Maybe realizing she could make friends would help her ease into a new family dynamic.

I tapped my fingers on the table and glanced out the window toward Chance Square and its midday lull void of miniature baseball players.

If I'd been at a Hester property, or back in San Francisco, I'd revel in my newfound time alone. I'd relax on a balcony or walk on a beach. I'd disguise myself as a guest and sit at the pool wearing a large floppy hat and dark sunglasses.

But now I didn't want to be alone. I didn't want to go back to my room, or walk around Chance on my own. I didn't want to call Annie and talk about work, and I couldn't call Josie because she was at work. I wanted to talk with someone, not to someone. About anything. I had always been able to call Celia and just say, "What are you doing?" Her answer might have been anything from formulating a plan for world peace to folding the laundry, but it didn't matter. We always parlayed into a conversation about anything, nothing, and everything at the same time.

I folded the thin newspaper and placed it on the table for the next customer. The door opened and Lorraine walked in, but without Cousin Maggie. She waved and walked to the counter. Steaming mug in hand, she sat at a table on the other side of the coffee shop. Lorraine wasn't reading or talking on her phone or even gazing out the window or at the shelves full of mugs. I envied the peacefulness I presumed.

I approached Lorraine's table, one hand in my pocket, one hand holding Shay's abandoned cup. Lorraine smiled wide.

"Hi, Teddi. I hoped I'd see you again."

"Me too."

"Do you have time to sit?"

I nodded as I sat on the chair across from Lorraine. "How are you?"

"No complaints."

"Glad to hear it." I wished I could say the same thing. "Where's Maggie today?"

"Today's my day off. Maggie usually spends the day with her library friends."

"She's okay to do that?"

"Oh yes. I'm really just a companion for her. No one likes to be alone all the time." I sipped the iced tea through the straw. I was going to float back to Nettie's if I didn't stop drinking tea soon. "Are you waiting for someone?"

"Not anymore. Shay was going to meet me here but she's with her friends."

"As it should be, at her age." Lorraine stirred a honey stick into her tea.

"I guess. I was just looking forward to the company—not that you're not very nice company, that's not what I meant."

We laughed.

"I didn't think that's what you meant, no worries. You're welcome to sit with me as long as you like."

"I don't want to intrude."

"Oh, sometimes I wish people would intrude a little more. When I was growing up on St. Thomas, my family all lived close by and we just popped in on each other. The problem wasn't having company, it was having time alone. And now everyone is too concerned with respecting personal space, so no one takes a chance. I'm glad you did."

"Sometimes my personal space is just too spacious."

Lorraine laughed and covered her mouth with her hand, as if she'd been taught that was ladylike. "That's why I like spending my days with Maggie. She's a tough nut, but she's mine."

"Do you live alone?"

"I do. I'm divorced and my daughters are grown. One lives in Philadelphia and the other lives in New York. I was just here, in Chance, working part time, and I realized I was alone too many hours every day. The Internet is not a sufficient replacement for a person."

"No. And just being around other people isn't the same thing as being *with* other people."

"That's why I agreed to spend time with Maggie. I like talking with her."

"I never realized how much I relied on having someone to talk to all the time until I didn't."

"Celia."

"Yes."

"I didn't know her but I've heard that she was lovely."

"She was." I sipped as much tea as I could before I swallowed. "Losing her derailed me."

"Of course it did."

"And at the same time, it set me on the path I'm on today."

"That's a difficult thing to come to terms with."

"It is."

"You can talk to her, you know, even though she's gone."

I cocked my head, and inched my way back as I waited for Lorraine to convince me she was a psychic/clairvoyant/medium/good witch and that for the tidy sum of a zillion euros she could channel Celia right through the coffee beans.

"I don't believe in *that kind of thing.*"

"In what kind of thing?"

"Spirits."

"That's neither here nor there. You can talk to her no matter what you believe."

"I'm not a fan of cemeteries."

"You're overthinking this, Teddi. Just talk to her inside your head. You can do that anywhere. Right here, if you want. Go ahead. I'll wait."

I stared at Lorraine. "Um . . ."

"I'm kidding!" She laughed as she reached across the table and rubbed my arm. "Relax."

"That's the problem. I can't relax. I feel like I really screwed things up and I'm too late to fix them." I gathered my cup and napkin, and stood. "I'm sorry, I didn't mean to lay all this on you."

"Sit. I don't mind. You don't have to talk if you don't want, but stay. Unless you have somewhere you need to be."

Lorraine and I sat in a companionable and soothing silence. The sounds of Perk simmered around us—the hiss of the espresso machine, the swoosh of the broom, the scrape of chairs as they were pushed into place.

"Since you have two daughters, can I talk to you about something?"

"Of course."

I slid my chair closer to Lorraine's.

"Shay's only twelve, but I have to have a difficult conversation with her and I don't even know how to start."

"Are you sick?"

"No, why would you think I was sick?" Did I look sick? I thought I looked okay.

"She's a little girl whose mother died. If you approach whatever this is by beating around the bush, she is going to think the worst. And it's not the worst, is it?"

"No."

"She's been through the worst."

"Yes, she has. Which is why I don't want to make anything harder for her. And I don't want her to hate me. I couldn't stand it if she hated me."

"Kids fling words around they don't mean sometimes, remember that. They do it for effect. Be direct, but kind. And you can tell her it's hard for you to talk about, that it's not easy for you to disappoint her or upset her. For some reason teenagers think we enjoy making them miserable. Just ask your friend." Lorraine tipped up her chin toward the door so I turned around.

Josie bounded through the door as if pushed by the wind. "I *so* need a latte." She placed her briefcase, handbag, and shopping bags at my feet and hurried to the counter even though no one was trying to outmaneuver her.

"She's a firecracker, that one," Lorraine said.

"How do you know Josie? Oh, that's a silly question." I laughed at my own naïveté. Everybody knew Josie.

Perk's tempo rose to meet the end of the day and the need for caffeine. Josie placed a plate of cookies in the middle of the table.

"What are these for?" I asked.

"Lorraine loves the lemon cookies here. I'm so glad you two met. Didn't I tell you she was great?"

"Who?" I asked.

"Lorraine."

"You didn't tell me anything about Lorraine. We met the other day when I walked past my cousin Maggie's house. And Lorraine was none too pleased at first, I might add."

Lorraine smiled, and covered her mouth again.

"Then it was kismet!" Josie said.

"I have no idea what you're talking about."

"Lorraine is the counselor who helped us with Jonathan. You didn't know? I gave you her card!"

"No, I didn't know. I, uh, sorry. I didn't really look at it yet." I turned to Lorraine. "You're a therapist? I had no idea. Why didn't you tell me?"

"You didn't ask."

"That's how you know Shay."

"I really can't say yes or no."

"Why do you work as my cousin Maggie's caretaker if you're a therapist?" I half expected that to be the answer. That cousin Maggie needed a psychologist, not a companion.

Just then someone poked me in the back between my shoulder blades. "Because she likes me."

I turned around to see Cousin Maggie.

"I didn't mean anything by that, I just didn't think—"

"That I'd want to be around someone well read and educated who didn't treat me like an invalid?"

"No, that makes perfect sense." It actually didn't really make sense to me at all, but I didn't want to be chastised by Cousin Maggie. She harrumphed and walked to the other side of Perk with her librarian friends.

"I'm going to leave you two to chat some more. Call me later?" Josie tapped my shoulder and gathered her bags.

"Sure."

Josie walked out of earshot. "It's none of my business why you're working with Maggie," I said to Lorraine. Had she been trying to hide something from me? "Like my mother used to say, 'Grown-ups get to make their own decisions.' I hated when she said that, but it's true."

"Chance is the place you ran away from."

"Uh-huh." I gulped.

"Chance is the place I ran *to*."

Lorraine replenished her tea. She talked about the private practice she'd built and the daughters she'd raised with her husband in Shaker Heights.

"We had everything but the picket fence. And that was next on the list."

"Sounds too good to be true."

"It was. Vincent had always had a temper but it got out of control when the girls went away to college. I took on more patients and worked longer hours, just to be out of the house. He accused me of having an affair."

"Did you?"

"I could have, but I never did. I filed for divorce without telling him, and maybe I shouldn't have done it that way. There was just no reasoning with that man. I knew I'd need a plan to minimize the fallout, so I had everything ready. He was never physically abusive but he was making me question my sanity. Me! There's no one saner than me." Lorraine wrung her hands. Time was still working to heal her wounds. "His whole family was born and raised in Cleveland, and with them, Vincent would always be the good guy they thought he was."

My phone buzzed. "Answer it, it might be Shay," Lorraine said.

I glanced at my phone. A call from Annie. I tapped Decline. Another call came through almost immediately. Annie again. I tapped Decline and shut off my phone. "I am so sorry. It's work and they don't know when to leave me alone. I shut it off. Continue."

"What if Shay calls?"

"She'll call back. Please continue."

"Thank you," Lorraine said. "My mother-in-law was not loving like you might think a mother-in-law might be if she's never had a daughter. But when the girls were in elementary school, she said something to me while we were cooking Thanksgiving dinner. She'd continued peeling potatoes and then turned on the faucet and said, 'If Vincent gets out of hand, you leave his ass, you hear me? You go far away. He won't follow you. He's not motivated enough for that. But you are.' Then she turned off the water and never mentioned it again until right before she died, about eight years ago. 'You go if you need to go.' I thought she wanted me to leave the hospital room but she grabbed my hand and looked me in the eyes, which she never had, not in the more than twenty years I'd known her. I thought maybe she'd finally decided to thank me for taking care of her, since Vincent did nothing at all, but then like a smack in the head, I remembered the first time she'd said it. My whole body got cold and I started shaking, even though the temperature in the hospital room had been turned up to almost tropical. She'd known it wasn't going to stop, that he wasn't going to stop, that it was only going to get worse."

"So you left."

"The day after she died."

I shivered. "And you chose Chance?"

"Chance chose me. I took a position as a psychologist at Union County Hospital for a year. About six months in, I found a house I loved here in town; it's the small Victorian on the corner of Grand and McGuffy. I moved in right before Celia was diagnosed. I only met her once in passing."

Lorraine and Celia had been neighbors. They would still be neighbors. They would have been friends. I was sure of it.

"I bet your mother-in-law would be happy that you have a nice life here."

"I think she would. And I think Celia would be happy you have a nice life away from here."

The sun warmed the top of my head, the line of my nose, and the apples of my cheeks, but I didn't seek shade. Sometimes I needed to feel the sting of the sun, to close my eyes and still see light, to warm myself from the outside in. Sometimes I was on a beach. Sometimes I was on a mountain. Today I was on the sidewalk outside Nettie's. I wouldn't burn, but I'd slathered ample sunscreen anyway, to be safe.

Like Lorraine, I calculated my risks when I could manage it.

Chapter 17

"AUNT TEE, YOU DON'T really seem like the bowling type."

"What? These red-and-blue-striped shoes aren't my style for a night out on the town?" Shay chuckled while she tied her shoes. "Well, I am! It'll be fun. Did you know your mom and I used to come here all the time when we were your age? They've renovated it and renamed it a few times, but it'll always be Big Top Alley to me."

"Big Top Alley? That's lame."

"There is nothing lame about a circus tent logo and a poor excuse for Bozo as the mascot for all the bowling teams."

"What's a Bozo?"

I was officially old, and all because of a clown.

"Oh, it doesn't matter. What matters is that we didn't have gourmet food or neon lights or electronic scoring. Everything was old-fashioned. But it wasn't fake old-fashioned." I motioned to the retro-chic bar and soda counter. "It was fun because we were here together and with our friends."

"So my mom was like, perfect, *and* she bowled."

I lifted the ball from Shay's hand and placed it on the rack. "Your mom wasn't perfect, but she was the perfect friend for me.

I'll tell you a secret, okay? We didn't really bowl so much as distract the boys who were bowling."

"Aunt Tee!"

"It's true, but don't worry. It was before she started to like your dad."

Shay laughed and bowled a gutter ball. "So my mom thought this was fun when she was my age?"

"You're not having fun?"

"I didn't mean . . ."

"I'm kidding, Shay. It isn't always about the what, it's about the who. This would be fun with Rebecca and Chloe, right?"

"I guess."

"This was also the site of one of the only fights your mom and I had."

"You and Mom had a fight?"

"We both liked Derek Jones." I drew my hands to my heart. "He was fourteen and a freshman, so very *old*. He didn't know either of us existed but we fought about who was going to marry him. I mean, we argued and didn't talk for hours that night. Then I decided your mom could have Derek and I'd marry Jeffrey Scott."

"You can't know who you're going to marry when you're twelve."

"You're smarter than we were."

"Hardly."

I bowled an intentional gutter ball and turned back to Shay. "You're amazing, you know that, right? Your mom would be really proud of you."

"I doubt that."

Shay sat on the molded turquoise plastic line of chairs. I stacked up my own insecurities between us and sat next to them.

A server stepped into our lane and set a tray on the table in the corner. "Small cheese pizza, cheesy fries, and two lemonades."

In between bites of pizza Shay chattered about her collage, her art teacher, the kids in the class and their collages. She rambled off names of the crazy-talented kids and the regularly talented kids, who she admired, and who'd complimented her work. I was just so relieved not to hear her berate or belittle anyone. Maybe Beck had been exaggerating. Maybe "mean girl" had been just a short phase and not a character trait.

"Want to see the pictures I've taken since I've been here?" I lifted my camera out of my bag and handed it to Shay without telling her to be careful. "Push that button and you can scroll the other way through the last pictures I took. It's my secret stash. Just things I've seen since I've come back to Chance."

Shay smiled. "You're entering the contest!"

"I am. It's kind of scary, but I'm taking your advice and being brave."

"This contest is scary? C'mon!"

"I thought it would make me sad. I thought it would remind me of—"

"My mom."

"Yes. But I took pictures for over two hours at Jasper Pond yesterday. And it was amazing." I didn't mention Cameron's encouragement. Or Simon's lack of enthusiasm for photos for art's sake. Those weren't the most important parts. Not for Shay. "I was doing something your mom and I did together. I'd take pictures, she'd paint or sketch. I thought about her, but it didn't make me sad."

Shay nodded slowly, in time to my words and memories.

"When did you know you wanted to be a photographer?"

211

Shay stared at the little screen, smiling, her mouth shaping into oohs and aahs as she scrolled.

"As soon as my dad gave me my first camera; I think I was ten. It was a little black disposable one and you had the pictures developed at Fotomat." Disposable camera. Pictures developed. Fotomat. Did Shay even know what those were? "I took pictures of everything. Lots of pictures of my toys—I set them up in scenes with your mom and she would sketch and I would snap. Then we'd dress up, even when we were too old for that, and I took pictures of her. We laughed like crazy! There were no selfies back then, so if we wanted a picture of the two of us, someone else had to take it, and when Cousin Maggie gave me my first real camera, it had a timer. And I wasn't much for letting go of control of my camera."

"Not like now."

"I don't hand that over to many people, believe me."

"I understand," Shay said. "I don't like when anyone touches my art supplies. Vi tried to organize everything once. She thought she was helping me but then I couldn't find anything and when I went to reach for something, it wasn't there."

"Do not mess with the artist's tools." As soon as I said it, I knew I shouldn't have.

Shay chuckled. "Exactly. She doesn't get it. She doesn't get me."

"She'll learn, but you might have to help her. She's going to be your stepmom."

I slid onto the seat between us, knocking some of my fears out of the way. I took Shay's hands and turned her toward me.

"We're friends, right? Friends that are like family, right?"
Shay nodded.

"We need to be honest with each other, okay?"

She nodded again.

"I'll start. Uncle Beck told me what happened. At school." Shay's eyes opened wide.

"They made such a big deal out of it. I was just joking around."

"Hurting people's feelings isn't a joke."

"No kidding. I got in a shitload of trouble. They suspended me."

I pulled back. "Shitload? Really, Shay?"

"Sorry. I got in *a lot* of trouble. And I am sorry about all of it. I know it was wrong. But I was just joking around but then they all turned on me. It still pisses me off. Oh crap. Makes me mad. I mean, not oh crap. Sorry. I'm not supposed to curse. Damn."

Shay apologized so many times I wondered if she thought it didn't matter what she did as long as she said she was sorry. I didn't have experience with the good-job-you-did-your-best-everyone-gets-a-trophy-for-trying culture of parenting but I'd witnessed it aplenty in Chance and at the Hester hotels.

"This have anything to do with your dad and Violet?" I knew it did. Did Shay realize that?

"That's what they tell me. I'm 'acting out' because of all the 'changes' going on."

Shay's air quotes added teenage sarcasm to the therapy-speak.

"I really am sorry. And I get it. That's why they don't trust me. That's why I like Rebecca and Chloe. They don't know what happened so I don't have to worry that they'll change their minds."

"About what?"

"About being friends with me."

I pulled her into a hug. "Oh, Shay-Shay. They'll want to be friends with you, and so will lots of other people, for your whole life. You just got a little bit lost. Happens to the best of us. Just be your best self." Now I sounded like a therapist. Or maybe just like a grown-up.

"My best self is still a freak in this town."

I stepped back. "What are you talking about? Did someone call you that?"

"No, but not only do I have no mother but I have no brothers or sisters or cousins. I don't play sports, I'm not in band, and I'd rather stare at a tree and paint than hang out at the ballpark gawking at boys."

"Oh, sweetie, if there's one thing you're not, it's a freak. You're an artist, like your mom."

"A lot of good that does me. She's not here, is she?"

"No. But I am."

"You have no clue what it's like."

"You are so wrong. Why do you think I was always at your mom's house? I had no brothers and sisters either. And then when I grew up I didn't get married and have kids like all my friends here—including your mom. I had a career that took me away from here on weekends when they were doing married and baby things. It made it really weird for me sometimes."

"Did it make you mad?"

"Maybe, sometimes. But that wouldn't have been an excuse to be mean or to make anyone feel bad. I think it would have made me feel worse. I also had something a lot of them didn't have, the way you have your art. You're lucky, and so was I." *Thank you, better-late-than-never revelation.* "It's one of the reasons it was a good idea for me to leave Chance." My chest quivered as Celia's wish for *me* transferred to her daughter. "Just like it's good that you made new friends in an art class. You're expanding your horizons. You're finding what's right for you. And who's right for you."

"But you said you didn't really make a lot of new friends."

"I was wrong not to make friends when I left. And I was wrong to leave so many friends behind. I know that now."

"You should make friends who are photographers like you. Or like you somehow. That's what I like about Chloe and Rebecca. They get it. They get me."

"That's really good advice, kiddo."

"You should also get married and have kids. You should definitely have kids. Or at least get married."

Shay's tone had shifted from wise to wistful. I knew where she was headed, but I wasn't going there. Not tonight.

"Maybe someday some of that will happen, but none of it is happening any time soon."

I said it without thinking, which was usually when the truth revealed itself most plainly.

Back at the house, I felt steady; no longer shaken by the past, with a new understanding having settled between me and Shay, even if she did want me to get married.

"I'll meet you in your room. I'm going to say hello to Violet."

Shay ran up the stairs and I walked to the kitchen. "Hey."

"Hey," Violet said. "I heard you two come in. Did you have fun?"

I watched Violet pretend to dry a dish with a paper towel. "We did. I also told Shay I knew about what happened with those girls at school."

"Miles told me you knew. What did she say?"

"She said she was sorry."

Violet turned around. "She's doing better, but it's been a rough year. Once everything at school calmed down we really believed that planning the wedding would be a good way to distract her, but it just seemed to make things worse."

"It didn't seem so bad the other day. Except for the hating-the-shoes part."

"It's getting better. We got along great until—"

"Until you were going to be her stepmom."

"Yeah."

I stood across from Violet, her eyes cast downward. "It'll get better," I said.

"I know."

Violet looked at me. When she spoke, the words rolled out without effort, as if she'd said them a thousand times before. "The counselor says Shay will have to see that I'm not going to erase all parts of Celia from their lives. I would never do that. Part of the reason I fell in love with Miles was because I could see how much he'd loved her. I wasn't trying to take him away from Celia's memory, but he was ready to move forward."

"And you met him in a grief support group?"

"I did."

"Can I ask . . . I mean . . ."

"My older sister, Lily."

I gasped.

"She was my very best friend."

"I'm so sorry."

"I know you are," Violet said. "Because you understand. Miles has told me how you and Celia were like sisters."

We reached across the empty space and held hands. I nodded.

"I'm going to talk to Shay, maybe I can help a little with all this. But not tonight. It's already been a long day. Could I spend tomorrow night with her? Do you have anything planned?"

"Miles is going out with his friends—a pseudo bachelor party at the microbrewery in Jeffersonville. I was just going to have my younger sister, Heather, come here, but I could meet her for dinner if you wanted the house to yourself with Shay. I think she'd rather be with you anyway."

"Thanks," I said.

"I'm glad you're here. And not just because of the pictures."

"Me too."

I sat on Shay's bed and scooted back to the headboard. It was the same bed she'd slept on when she was three. The only thing that had changed was that the ballerina bear comforter now was purple with polka dots.

Shay lifted a sketch book off her desk, opened it, and laid it on the bed next to me.

I leafed through the pages of pencil sketches, watercolors, and even some cartoons that looked like they were drawn with Sharpies. I left my camera on the floor, in the zipped-up bag. I wanted to just be with her. I would remember it with my heart, not by looking at something outside of myself. The silence lingered, likely just a few extra seconds, but it seemed like hours. Maybe we didn't need any more words tonight. Perhaps the images we created in our minds were enough. The soft colors in her floral watercolors that so closely matched the garden in fall, with orange that looked like a match had singed the edges. With green rimmed in deep purple. I captured the scene in my thoughts. I wished there were Hester properties in New England. Or even here in Ohio. I'd never before realized that I missed feeling like I was *not* on vacation. Even working, I sometimes didn't know what month it was because the weather didn't match my internal barometer for seasons. January in

Scottsdale was lovely but messed with my Midwestern sensibilities.

I looked back at Shay. This was not the time for my wishes, or for Shay's.

I turned the page and saw a pastel drawing of Celia's house— Shay's house.

"That's your house. Shay, it's perfect. Better than a photograph."

"Not really."

"Yes, really. Has your dad seen this?"

"No."

"Has he seen any of these?"

"Some."

"You should show him. He'd go crazy. They're amazing."

"You should show him your pictures too."

"Those were private. Just between you and me, okay? I only shared them with you because of how special you are to me. And I knew you'd appreciate them. And you know what?" I pulled out my camera and scrolled through the photos. "I'm going to enter that one into the contest." I pointed. "I'll use this address on the entry form, since I travel so much. Uncle Beck will know it was all my idea, I promise."

"When you win you'll have to come back."

"I'm coming back even if I don't win, but a ribbon is a nice incentive." I smoothed Shay's hair.

"Can I tell my dad about the contest?"

"Let's keep it between us for now. He's got enough on his mind."

"Why? He'd be really happy you were coming back; I know he would be. It feels normal when you're here, Aunt Tee. I think he feels that way too."

I turned and half crossed my legs on the bed. "I have amazing memories of your dad and mom and me. And you. All of us together. But it's different now. That doesn't mean it's bad."

"I know, but you said you didn't really make a lot of new friends, and you said you didn't have a new best friend, so why couldn't my dad be your best friend? It's not healthy to be alone. I think I heard that on the news one day. You need a special friend, Aunt Tee."

"I have you."

"That's not what I meant and you know it."

"I promise I'll work on having more friends if you'll promise the same thing."

"Stay here, Aunt Tee. I don't want you to leave. We're friends. Best friends. You said so. You gave me my mom's necklace."

I moved next to Shay. "I'll see you tomorrow night. Violet said she's going to go out with her sister so you and I can have a girls' night in. Sounds great, right?"

"I mean don't leave and go back to San Francisco!"

"I'm not going to leave forever, Shay. Those days are over. I'll be back a few times a year or more, and I've already mentioned to your dad about you coming out to San Fran to visit. You'll love it there."

"But I don't want you to leave."

"I know you don't. But when school starts you're going to be super busy. You're going to keep taking art classes, you'll be studying for your bat mitzvah, and you'll be figuring out this whole new family with your dad and Violet. She loves you, Shay. And I love that."

Shay rolled her eyes.

"Your mom would want you to give Violet a break."

"How do you know?"

"Because your mom always wanted what was best for you."
And for me.

"If my mom wanted what was best for me she wouldn't have died."

I heard a tap on the door and then it opened. Shay slammed shut her sketchbook and shoved it under her pillow.

"I don't mean to be a party pooper," Violet said, "but it's getting late and Shay has an early class tomorrow. Plus, your dad's on his way home from that campaign event and I'm sure he'll want to tell us about it. You two can continue this tomorrow night. Okay, Shay?"

"Whatever."

Chapter 18

THE DREAM ENDED. I knew it would. That's the downside to being awake inside a dream: you know the end, the curb, the cliff, is coming and that there's nothing you can do to stop the inevitable except wake up, which in this case, wasn't what I wanted at all.

I'd talked to Celia.

Celia's voice had been her voice. Celia's face had her face. She'd talked to me, she'd given advice. We'd laughed. I swore my side hurt.

I'm not even sure she was alive in my dream but I'd talked to her, on the phone—one with a cord. Was there one like that here? Now? I looked around. No. But I was sure of it. I rubbed my arm where I'd wrapped the pink cord around it. There were no marks.

"You sound good," she'd said.

"You too."

"It's okay, I promise . . ."

Her voice faded. Then my memory of the words faded as well. I squeezed my eyes tight as the images grew smaller. Me on the bed, Celia on—on what? A chair. A rocking chair. I was watching her on the phone talking to me. What was okay? What

I'd done? What I hadn't done? Or where she was? I opened my eyes and lay there, my hair across my face, my arms wrapped around me under the comforter.

Don't go yet.

I waited to be sad and instead, I smiled. I couldn't help it. I covered my face with my hands and shook my head, then I placed my hands together as if in prayer and slid them between my cheek and my pillow. I was calm, my limbs heavy and warm.

I felt as if I'd talked to my best friend.

I sighed, mindful of Celia's fresh footprint on my heart.

Or maybe it was a swift kick.

I flung open Perk's door like I was late for an appointment. Just in case I saw someone I knew, which was more than likely, I stopped and adjusted the waist of my dress and smoothed my hair, ran my tongue over my teeth to insure I'd brushed them, as if the minty freshness wasn't enough of a clue. The coffee aroma filled my nose and I heard the ticking of the wall clock I'd never noticed before, as well as the swish of the espresso machines, matched by the shuffle of the few newspapers.

Today's score: sensory overload, *one*; Teddi, *zero*.

I hurried into a line three people deep. I turned around and looked for Josie in the clusters of coffee and tea drinkers. We hadn't planned to meet, but she ended up at Perk almost every morning either post-run or pre-work or just because. It was almost nine; maybe Cameron would be free after his shift and sit with me. I reached into my pockets, touched my stone with one finger, and shimmied my dress a little lower on my waist, adjusting the neckline accidentally on purpose.

I stepped to the counter and in front of a teenaged barista. Not Cameron the man-barista.

"Welcome to Perk! How can I perk you up today?"

"Uh." I glanced to her left and then her right. "Uh. Oh, sorry. I'm just . . . is Cameron Davis working this morning?"

The barista smiled but shook her head. "Nope."

"Oh, okay. I thought he worked mornings."

"Not today!" She said it with what I now believed was the mandatory Perk perkiness.

"Do you know if he's working tomorrow morning? I'm just curious."

"Nope!"

"Okay, then." Thank you for absolutely no information whatsoever. "Espresso macchiato. Two shots. Can I leave a message for him?"

"For who?"

"For Cameron."

"No need. Just turn around."

No. I turned around as a generic please-don't-let-me-look-like-a-fool prayer dashed through my thoughts. Whew.

The door was closing behind Cameron and Deanna as they stepped into the coffee shop. I waved, they waved, and I turned back to Ms. Perky and paid my $3.50 in penance.

I sipped and read the same issue, perhaps the only issue, of the *Chance Gazette.* I'd almost memorized it when Cameron walked over, cup in hand. Deanna followed.

"Hi, Teddi, this is my sister, Deanna." He looked at me as if to say, *You know, the one you darted away from when you saw her with Beck.* "Deanna, this is Teddi Lerner."

"Nice to meet you, Deanna." I stood and shook her hand.

"Nice to meet you, too. How does it feel to be back in Chance?"

I opted for honesty. "It feels good. And a little strange."

"I love it here for me and Morgan but I bet it doesn't compare to San Francisco."

"San Francisco's a great city, that's true."

"The restaurants, the Bay, Chinatown, Fisherman's Wharf, the views . . ."

"It's a wonderful place to work."

"You do a lot of traveling, too." Deanna rolled her eyes. "Chance must feel like a step back in time. Bet you can't wait to get back to real life."

"We should go, Dee. See you soon, Teddi?" Cameron tapped my arm once, and I nodded.

"It was so nice to finally meet Cam's crush," Deanna said.

Cameron shook his head. "My sister has a big mouth. Gotta love her, though. She's keeping a roof over my head this summer."

I chuckled, softened by Deanna's familiarity and Cameron's playfulness. I turned to Deanna. "Cameron told me that I broke his eight-year-old heart. I apologized profusely, I promise."

"His eight-year-old heart too? Is that so?" She winked at me and nudged her brother. "I had no idea."

I sat on an Adirondack chair in the midst of the butterfly bushes in the garden behind Nettie's. I drew my knees to my chest and draped the skirt of my dress down to my ankles. No missed calls today, but two from Annie from yesterday. I exhaled as a monarch flitted by.

"I'm sorry, I couldn't talk yesterday. Things are a bit crazy here. Was it important?"

"Taken care of. Rescheduled Arturo for the tux shoot."

"The what?"

"The tux shoot? The designer who's using La Jolla as their set for the shoot for his spring collection? Arturo. You gave them the tour of the property, Teddi. What's up with you?"

"Oh, right. Nothing."

"Something's up. In the five years I've known you it has never taken you two hours to return my call, let alone twelve. Can I help?"

"Did you send my clothes? It's important that I have my clothes."

"They will be there, pressed and ready to go."

"And if they aren't?"

"They will be."

"Did you—"

"Yes, I packed two of everything in case some tipsy Aunt Eloise bumps into you and spills her cosmo."

"I'm going to ask you something but you can't tell Simon I asked."

"My lips are sealed."

"Has Simon said anything about me while I've been gone? I've only talked to him once."

"You mean like 'It's quiet around here'?"

"Very funny."

"No, really, he misses you. You two spend a lot of time together."

Do we?

"He said you two make a great team."

"Why did he say that?"

"He was buzzing around his office, the door was open, and I walked by. He called me in."

"He never calls anyone into his office."

"He asked me if you were happy here."

"Here where? Here meaning Hester Hotels? Or here meaning him?" Annie and I had never outwardly acknowledged that I was sleeping with Simon, but it was understood after the first time he and I returned from a three-hour lunch and then ordered takeout.

"I wasn't sure. He said he's left-brain bossy and you're right-brain bossy and that makes you two a great fit."

Were we?

I just wanted to drive, but wished I had a convertible, a head scarf, a pair of cat-eye sunglasses, and my best friend.

I headed out of Chance anyway.

The sky was blue with few clouds. The landscape was peaceful, flat, and green in this part of the county. It wasn't filled with landmarks or anything notable, and I found it inviting, but not in the let-me-post-it-on-Instagram way. The farther I got from Chance the more familiar it seemed, as if bits of the past had scattered and I was gathering them.

I turned and headed back to town, for no other reason than I didn't want to run out of gas in the middle of the country where there was spotty cell reception and no gas stations. Then, as if by chance, yet not at all, I ended up on the most western end of West Avenue, heading toward the cemetery. I pulled into the parking lot facing the grounds. I looked across, my line of vision skimming the tops and around the edges of headstones. There was Cameron, walking toward me, scribbling onto a notepad, turning away from the sun to shade his face and guard his words.

I lifted my hand. He turned as if to look behind him, and then turned back toward me. *Yes, I'm waving at you, not the dead people.*

"We really have to stop meeting like this." Cameron pressed his forearms onto the open window.

"Did you find the story you're going to write? The dash you want to fill in?"

"I think I have."

"I'm glad."

"What brings you here, Teddi? This isn't your usual hot spot."

"I was looking for you."

I pulled on the door handle and Cameron stepped back two paces. He walked closer and stood in front of me. I should've shut the door. My heart pounded. The breeze had died down but I pushed back my hair, in case it was thinking of going anywhere. If I stepped forward I'd bump into Cameron; if I stepped back I'd be in the car. I'd confined myself. I had no one else to blame. Or thank.

"Why were you looking for me?"

"You make me laugh."

Wow, it was that simple. And not simple at all. He made me laugh. And that's what I'd missed as much as Celia herself. The laughing.

"That's a lot of pressure."

"Oh, I didn't mean it like that . . ."

"I'm kidding, Teddi. Take a walk with me. I can't promise a stand-up routine but I might be able to take your mind off whatever's bothering you."

"How do you know something's bothering me?"

"You're parked at the cemetery?"

I smiled.

"Well, I can't walk in there," I said.

227

"We can go wherever you like."

That sounded nice. A walk, maybe back at the park or around the square. What was I doing? Nothing. Walking was nothing.

Until it wasn't.

I shook my head. "I'm not sure where I want to go. I'm not sure of anything. Cammy, you've been so nice to me."

"A second ago I made you laugh and now I'm Cammy and I'm nice? Ouch."

"You are nice!" I took Cameron's hands. "I guess . . . I guess I don't want you to get the wrong idea about anything. I think I'm almost engaged. And you live here in Chance. And I, I don't."

"You *think* you're *almost* engaged to who? Beck?"

"No. Simon Hester."

"Well done."

"What is that supposed to mean?"

"I just think it's a little strange that we've had two or three intense conversations in less than a week and you've never mentioned a millionaire fiancé, Teddi."

"I don't have a fiancé."

"Oh, right. An 'almost' fiancé."

"It's a long story."

Cameron walked around the car and opened the passenger door. "I've got all day."

I pretended the last five minutes hadn't happened and I drove around Chance like a tour guide, espousing history I'd learned at Chance Elementary and on every Fourth of July during the reenactment of the town's founding and important scenes from Chance's history.

I turned onto Fern Street at the edge of Chance's downtown.

The street was partly residential and partly commercial, as if it couldn't decide if it wanted to be home to people or things. The grandest Victorian in Chance was on Fern Street, painted now in deep grays, soft whites, and muted pinks. I'd heard the home had been sold to a family from New York. Simon had moved from New York to San Francisco as a child. I wondered how he'd have fared in Chance, if he'd still have grown up to build a hotel mini empire. The people inside those walls, though? I wondered if they knew the house was rumored to have been a speakeasy during Prohibition, while masquerading as a dancing school. It was probably why my mother never let me take ballet, even though in the eighties, lessons were across town in the basement of Chance Hall, and even though liquor was legal and the house had been home to respected Chance families since 1933. No one in Chance talked about the 1920s' speakeasy history, though everyone talked about the World War I history when the house doubled as a rehab hospital for army officers and was staffed by local nurses. I prickled with pride I'd forgotten. My great-great-grandmother had been one of those nurses. Still, when Celia and I were in high school, we turned down the coveted roles in the Fourth of July play. We regretted it by the time we turned twenty.

"I'm surprised a history teacher doesn't know all this history."

"It's not really relevant, but I do agree, it's interesting."

"Not relevant, really? If you've put roots down here it is relevant."

"I don't live here, you know that, right? I'm just here for the summer."

"Where do you live?"

"Oakland."

"Oakland, California?"

"Yes."

Oakland was right across the bridge from San Francisco. I shook my head and smiled. I think it was a stupid, lopsided smile, the kind I couldn't control that came when I daydreamed or planned or when I was surprised. "Maybe we can get together for lunch or something." Really? Ladies lunch. Men—men eat lunch too. And I'd just told Cameron about Simon.

"And what would your almost-fiancé think of that?"

"Who?"

"Simon? Remember him? It has been about ten minutes since you mentioned him and your mysterious nonengagement engagement."

"I was focusing on the house."

Cameron smirked.

"What? Just say it."

"I've only known you for a week, but I'm here to tell you it's a really bad idea to marry someone you don't love."

"How do you know I don't love Simon?"

"Do you?"

"He's wonderful to me."

"I'm glad."

"You are?"

"What do you want me to say, Teddi? I like you. I think you're cute. I like the way you lift your hair off your neck when you think no one's looking and stick your hands in your pockets like they're full of treasures. I'd love to get to know you again. I'd like to take you on a date. But *not* if you have a fiancé. Or an almost-fiancé."

I parked in front of Perk. My cheeks burned.

"Thanks for the tour," he said. "And the history lesson. And good luck with your maybe engagement."

"I like you, Cammy. I do. I wish things were different."

"You get to decide, you know."

"Decide what?" Was he asking me to choose between him and Simon, right here and right now, before we'd even gone on a date?

"Your dash, Teddi. You get to decide."

Cameron walked up Main Street. I wished I could reach into the glove box and pull out the phone that connected me to Celia in my dream. Instead, I closed my eyes and squeezed my memories together to extract the right tempo, pitch, and cadence of her words.

I knew exactly what she'd say.

Chapter 19

"PUT THEM IN THE oven and in thirty minutes I'll show you the next step," I said to Shay.

Shay slid the cookie tray into the oven and I set a timer. When the door was closed I turned on the oven light. I had always liked to watch the mandel bread loaves rise and expand as I waited to slice and then bake them again.

"So, you ready for the big day?" I asked.

"I guess. Unless they cancel it."

"Shay, they're not calling off the wedding! You know that, right? Your dad and Violet love each other. A lot. "

Shay ignored me. "Can I show you my storyboard for my comic book? It's my next project for art class." She left the kitchen and walked toward the stairs. I followed to her bedroom. Sketchbook pages were clipped to twine that crisscrossed her room like a clothesline.

The drawings were rough and in pencil, yet whimsical, the thought bubbles waiting to be filled.

I stared at one sheet without seeing it. "Remember you said you wished I had a special friend, like a boyfriend?"

Shay nodded. "Then you wouldn't always be alone, Aunt Tee."

My heart tugged. She was worried about me. I didn't remember the last time I felt like someone worried about me.

"Remember hearing me talk about Simon? The man I work for? I've talked about him before."

"Daddy says he owns the hotels."

"He does."

"Is he rich?"

"It doesn't matter to me how much money he has."

"So, he's your best friend?"

I'd never thought of Simon that way, but I supposed he could be. If I let him. "I'll tell you something not a lot of people know." Shay opened her eyes wide and nodded. "I've been dating him. We have a lot of fun together. He's really nice."

"He's your boyfriend?"

"I think he's going to ask me to marry him."

"What? No!" Shay rose from the bed, bending at her waist and yelling, "No, no, no, no, no!" She yelled it so many times I lost count, and then she just sat on her desk chair and put her hands over her ears.

I had no idea what to do, what to say, what to think.

Maybe it was too much information, too much sharing. She was only twelve. What was I thinking? I just didn't want her to worry about me—I'd have someone, I wouldn't be alone, it would be a nice life.

I didn't know who I was trying to convince.

Shay looked at me, but stayed folded in half. "Are you engaged?" She lifted my left hand in hers. "You don't have a ring."

"He didn't ask me officially. Not yet anyway."

Shay exhaled. "Oh."

"But if he asks—when he asks—I think I'm going to say yes."

She wrapped her arms around herself and stood. "No. You can't do that. You'll ruin everything." She yanked the papers off the twine and let them fall to the floor.

"I don't understand, Shay. Talk to me. Remember? We're being honest. Tell me what's wrong. You'll like Simon, I know you will. And you will be in the wedding. I was thinking you could be my maid of honor."

She turned to me and shook her head. Tears streamed down her face. She gasped for breath and I released one I didn't know I was holding in.

"What about Daddy?"

"Daddy can come to the wedding too." Sure, why not. We were building the foundation of a new friendship, one that would include Violet. Shay looked away.

Oh God. No. I reached out and turned her toward me. "Honey, your daddy and I aren't going to be anything more than friends. I told you that."

"Why not? It's perfect. You've known each other for so, so long and if you and Daddy were together you would be my stepmother. I love Vi, I do, but you're already family. And you and Daddy both miss Mommy like I do. It would be like we were all still a family, not something new that doesn't have anything to do with her."

"Your dad loves Violet. I care about him, but not like that."

"But you were best friends with Daddy."

"I was best friends with your mom, sweetie. Being a couple with your dad would be like having my brother for a boyfriend. And that's just not right." *Shut up already, Teddi, before you blurt out every bit of irony left in the county.*

"But you can try, right? What if you told my dad you wanted to stay and be a family with him and me? Think about it, Aunt Tee. You already fit with us. I know you said your job is in San Francisco and I was thinking maybe we could just move to San Francisco and be there with you."

"Honey, your dad and Violet love each other. Your dad and I don't."

"But he has fun with you and we can talk about Mommy. We can't do that with Violet."

"Yes, you can. She doesn't want to take your mom away from you."

"I don't believe you."

"You have to trust me. It's going to be okay. It might not seem like it, but it is. It's a lot, I know. You've made new friends and your family is going to be new, but it's all good new. I'll do anything I can to help make it easier. Anything. I promise."

"You're just going to leave. That's what you do. I hear what the grown-ups say."

The timer on my phone went off. The mandel bread was done with its first bake.

"Go," Shay said. "Take the stupid cookies out of the oven. They don't make you like a mother, you know. No matter what you think."

Shay inhaled deeply, her shoulders and chest rising.

I reached over and Shay lurched back. My body quivered with the recollection of the first time she reached for me from Celia's arms. Maybe at this moment she needed a little space. I knew I did.

"I'll be right back. Maybe we can look at the calendar and decide a good time for me to come back to visit."

"Whatever."

I needed to help Shay find a place of peace even if it was just for the weekend. Then I'd be gone. Like Miles had said, I wasn't her parent.

Downstairs, I laid the cookie sheet on the counter, sliced the small loaves, and arranged the cookies on the sheet to bake again. I filled a kettle with water. I'd take up two mugs of tea. I wouldn't attempt anything maternal. Was tea too maternal?

I decided it was not, and carried two mugs up the steps. Shay's door was closed, my invitation to take a breath and then purposefully intrude, but my hands were full.

"Shay? I'm out here with tea. Open the door. Please."

Silence from the other side of the door. I rolled my eyes. Good thing the door was closed, because I was sure that was the incorrect response. "Shay, please, honey. Open the door. We can talk about this. We can talk about anything."

Still no answer, no noise, no movement noises. I set the cups on the floor and turned the doorknob, expecting it to be locked, but it wasn't. I pushed open the door and stepped inside.

"Shay?" She wasn't on the bed. She wasn't next to the bed or under the desk. I checked the closet but it was empty. The bathroom was empty. The guest room and Miles's bedroom were empty. I opened the door to the attic and pulled on the light. I ran up the wooden steps. Nothing.

Back in the hall, I set my hands on my hips. "Shayna Rose! This isn't funny." I sounded like a mother but I didn't care. Fear propelled me down the stairs. I jumped the bottom three. I opened the front door. "Shay!" I left the door open and ran back through the house to the kitchen and slid open the back door. I stepped out onto the deck and looked at the vacant swing set and scanned the bushes. "Shayna!" The sun hadn't set so I ran around the house, looking into the car even though I'd locked the doors. I looked in the garage. Back in the house, Shay wasn't under the tables, in the closets, in my car. Jeez. I opened the dryer, the fridge, the freezer in the basement.

I texted her.

Me: Where are you?

No answer.

Shayna was gone.

My head pounded and my pulse raced. Hereditary catastrophizing kicked in even though not more than three minutes had passed. How far could she have gone? Where could she have gone? She had no friends to run away to or with. What else hadn't Miles told me about her? What didn't I know? Had she done this before? Would she hurt herself? Was she coming back?

Shay could not end up on a milk carton.

I dialed Miles's cell phone. It didn't matter what he thought of me or if Shay was somewhere in the house I hadn't thought to look. All I cared about was finding her.

Miles picked up on the first ring. The background noise was raucous.

"What's wrong?" A confidence-building greeting that was right on point.

"I can't find Shay."

"What do you mean you can't *find* Shay? I thought this was girls' night in. Where are you?"

"I'm at the house, but Shay's gone. I checked everywhere.

We had an argument, more of a misunderstanding—or so I thought—and she was really upset. I didn't realize how much."

"I'll go get her."

"You know where she is?"

"I'm pretty sure."

"You have no reason to trust me at this point, but please tell me."

"I think you've done enough, Teddi."

"Please, Miles. I upset her but it's not about me. Shay needs me to be the one who finds her. Please, Miles. I need to fix this. Please let me help Cee's daughter."

"I don't think it's a good idea, Teddi."

"It's the first good idea I've had in six years, Miles. Please."

Miles didn't answer me.

And then, I knew.

I drove to the West End Cemetery, pulled into the parking lot, stepped out of the car, and looked off into the distance, with its muddy, creeping darkness, its deafening silence.

Be brave.

I heard the words clearly inside my head, but this time it wasn't Celia's voice I heard. Or even Shay's.

It was my own.

I ran onto the path that led up and down every aisle of graves. I jogged up and down each path, looking straight ahead, seeing the monuments only in my peripheral vision. The marble blurs were streaked with sadness I ignored. The streetlamps had just turned on, and shined enough light for me to see where I was going. My chest burned by the time I saw her, standing, with her hands inside the apron she hadn't taken off. I looked down. Neither had I.

I kept quiet, conscious that any word I spoke carried the weight of a thousand stones.

"Can I come closer?"

Shay shrugged. My yellow light to proceed with caution. I stood about two feet behind her. I also faced Celia's headstone.

CELIA STILLMAN COOPER

DAUGHTER, SISTER, WIFE,

MOTHER, TEACHER, FRIEND

ARTIST

הבצנת

Now there was no pretending it didn't exist. No hoping or praying or wishing it away.

Celia's headstone was the biggest one on the row. That would have been Miles's doing. Gray granite with a deeply etched Star of David and the customary Hebrew acronym for "May her soul be bound up in the bond of life."

Celia's certainly was.

"I've never been here before," I said.

I just stood, feet firmly planted in the last place I'd expected to be tonight. Shay said nothing. I was going to wait her out. She was going to understand that I wasn't leaving.

Shay looked up and muttered a few words I couldn't hear. They weren't meant for me, but for the universe. She released them into the sky and onto the wings of birds and butterflies so they could carry her thoughts away. Then they would hurt less.

"I don't remember her." This time, Shay said it louder. "I can't hear her voice in my head. We have videos, but that's what I remember, not the real person. I don't know what she smelled like. Nothing reminds me of her."

I squeaked to hold in my cries. I was the lucky one. I was the selfish one.

"Can I come closer?"

Shay nodded, so I walked up behind her and put my arms around her. We stood at Celia's feet, I imagined. I didn't like the idea of standing on her head. I hoped that Celia knew Shay and I were together, connected by her, and through ourselves. I dipped my hand into my pocket and pulled out my stone.

I stepped to the side and held out my hand. "I've been carrying this around for a long time." I flipped the stone over. *Tulips*. "I wrote that when I saw the tulips at Butchart Gardens on Vancouver Island. I took out my phone to call your mom and tell her about them and—"

"And you couldn't."

"And I started to cry."

"In front of other people?"

"A lot of people. But I didn't care. I had to make it all mean something. The new job, the traveling. I couldn't believe I was doing so much and your mom wasn't part of it. So I took this stone from the ground. I knew one day I'd leave the stone here as proof."

"That you never stopped thinking about her."

"Ever. Even when it doesn't seem like it."

"Go ahead, Aunt Tee."

"Do you want to do it?"

"I think you should."

"Are you sure?"

"You don't want to do it, do you? You don't want to touch it or go closer. It's really not so bad. At least it's something real."

I placed the stone on top of the marker, the word facing down. No one else needed to know what it said. Or that I'd left it. I stepped back to Shay and held her hand.

"I came here to tell her Daddy is getting married on Sunday. Do you think she already knows?"

I nodded.

"I knew you weren't going to marry Daddy, Aunt Tee. But . . ."

"It seemed like a good idea?"

"Sometimes. I just don't want to forget about her, and Violet doesn't know anything about her."

"She can. You can tell her. I can tell her. Violet loves you, Shay. She doesn't want to take your mom from you. I promise."

"That's what she says."

"You should believe her. She's a good one. I can tell."

Shay turned and looked at me. "You like her?"

"Yes, I do."

"Do you think my mom would be okay with all of this?"

"Yes," I said.

"How can you be so sure?"

I gulped and remembered my dream. "She told me."

Shay just nodded.

"Do you think you're going to marry that guy? Simon?" Shay furrowed her brows.

"I don't know."

But I did know. Not once while I was looking for Shay or standing with her in the cemetery had I thought of reaching out to Simon. Not once had I heard his voice inside my head whispering words of encouragement or pictured his face for strength and comfort.

Cameron was right. I didn't love Simon.

Three cars doors slammed. Neither Shay nor I turned around.

"Everybody okay?"

Shay nodded and walked into a hug with Miles. Violet joined them.

Thank you, Violet mouthed to me.

Beck stood off to the side.

Shay looked at me and waved. "I think we burned the cookies."

Miles and Shay walked ahead to the car.

"This has been a long road," Violet said.

"She loves you," Teddi said.

"I know she does, and I'm grateful for that every day."

"I can tell."

"Coming?" Violet said to Beck.

"No. I'll ride back with Teddi."

"Wait!" I ran over to Shay and grabbed her hands. "Strawberry ChapStick."

"You want some? I have it in my pocket."

"No, that's not what I mean. *That's* what she smelled like, Shay. Your mom. She smelled like Strawberry Chapstick. Just like you."

Chapter 20

Beck said nothing. I said nothing. Again.

We walked into Nettie's and Beck settled into the corner of the settee in the foyer.

"Sit down, please." His voice was soft, yet stern.

I gulped away hesitation as I sat in the opposite corner. If only the cushion between us were enough space to muffle my thrashing heart.

"Shay really scared you, didn't she?"

"I never felt anything like that before." And I hadn't. "I had no idea where she was and I imagined the most horrible things."

"You know it's not your fault, right?"

"How can you say that?"

"Because you didn't push her out the door, Teddi Bear."

I bent my neck, stared at my hands in my lap, and clenched my lips to keep the sounds inside. I'd cried in front of, and with, Beck countless times. But that was then. We were different then. I was different then.

"Do you want to tell me what you said to her?"

I shook my head. My hair flung onto my face. Beck reached over and pushed the hair away and left his hand on my cheek.

He stared at me. I looked away but I knew he was still staring. He slid closer. I counted to ten inside my head and then laid my head on Beck's chest, on the space I'd left behind. I indulged myself and rested heavily on him, releasing any resistance. He wrapped his arms around me.

Minutes passed. We stayed silent as the past crept into the present, threatening to tangle up the future. We stayed still as it relinquished its claim.

I looked up and sat against the back of the couch, Beck's arm still around me. "What happened to you while I was gone?"

"I got arrested."

"No you didn't." I waved my hand, dismissing his ruse.

"I did. I went to a bachelor party and was too damn stubborn to let the designated driver take me home. It was too soon after Cee for me to be out partying. I got a DUI."

"Was anyone hurt?"

"No."

"Is that when you stopped calling?"

"I stopped before that, because you didn't answer me. But that was a wake-up call. I lost my driver's license and had to come back from Columbus and move in with my parents, and they drove me where I needed to go. AA meetings, mostly, over in Tuckerton. Otherwise, I walked everywhere. That's easy here. As you know." I just shook my head.

"You being out of the picture really was the least of my problems at that point, Teddi. If it hadn't happened, and I hadn't moved back, I wouldn't have the relationship I do with Miles and Shay, and I wouldn't have bought the inn, and both have been good for me. Even when I moved back to Columbus, I knew where my anchor was."

"You're lucky." I gasped. "I didn't mean that."

"I get it. And you're right."

"So, you're okay?"

"I will be in about five seconds."

Beck kissed me twice, but didn't linger.

I pulled back gently. "Why didn't anyone tell me what was going on with you? Miles could've told me. Your parents could've told me."

"I didn't want them to. It wasn't their story to tell, it was mine."

"I wish I'd known. Maybe . . ."

"You couldn't have stopped anything from happening. Just like you couldn't have stopped Shay. If she didn't do this tonight, it might have been tomorrow night, or when Miles and Violet are on their honeymoon. Shay likes to be near her mother, which is fine, except she can't go there without telling anyone, and she knows that. None of it is your fault. You have to trust me."

"Still, I wish someone would've told me. About you."

"Except for Shay, you made it pretty clear you didn't want to know what was going on back here."

I suppose I had.

I couldn't fall asleep. I lay on the bed on my side and stared at the wall. My head hurt so bad I was either drunk without drinking or getting a migraine from six years of pent-up feelings that had just burst through the dam I'd built around them.

Beck had needed me. Shay had needed me.

And no one knew why I'd gone away.

I slid to the floor and reached under the bed, pulling out the suitcase that didn't fit into the closet. I unzipped it and lifted out a drawstring bag.

When Miles had lifted my suitcase into his car, he'd joked that I had bricks in it. When I told him rocks, I hadn't lied.

I emptied the bag into the well of my lap. Twenty-two stones tumbled out. Twenty-two testaments to friendship. I'd started with the one from Butchart Gardens, which would never settle in my pocket again. I picked up a small white stone and flipped it over. *Gecko.* I'd picked it up off the ground in Sabino Canyon in Tucson, when a gecko ran across my path. I jumped and ran away, knowing that Celia would have wanted it to come closer. I missed having someone who challenged my sensibilities but never asked me to change them.

I could barely see the writing on a flat black stone, but I knew I'd written the word "peppers." I'd lifted that one out of a cactus plant in our Albuquerque hotel, after I'd had some of the spiciest food of my entire life. Food that Celia would have loved, without flinching or without drinking a quart of milk.

I'd gathered stones in Boston, Malibu, Seattle, Miami, St. Louis, Philadelphia, and Savannah, but the stones weren't meant to honor cities or hotels, or to serve as reminders of overarching sadness.

These stones were moments. Twenty-two breathtaking, side-splitting, heart-wrenching moments from my travels I needed to carry with me, carry to Celia, so I'd tucked them into the pockets I'd had sewn into every dress.

I gathered them back into the bag, slipped on my robe, and walked upstairs. Light shone under only one door. I knocked and Beck opened it.

"I need to show you something," I said. "And tell you something."

He stepped aside but touched the small of my back as I walked inside.

Beck's room had caramel-colored walls and majestic draperies and linens, and warm brown leather furniture.

I knew it had once been two rooms—two large bedrooms. Now the bed was separated from a sitting area in an alcove. Ticking-striped drapes framed the walnut headboard.

I sat on a chair and Beck sat on the end of the bed closest to me.

No matter the distance, there was a bond between us that pulled at my heart, that made me not take my eyes off him even when I looked away. I couldn't believe I'd allowed, no, forced myself to stay away so long, so long it would have been forever had Shay not unwittingly come to my rescue. What had I been thinking? I couldn't outrun it no matter how hard I tried.

"I'm sorry." Too little, too late. I knew this.

"It's not your fault what happened to Shay. I wish I could say it was, but it's not."

I shuddered from his misinterpretation. "That's not what I'm sorry about."

He just stared, daring me. He wasn't going to make it easy. He shouldn't, but I wished he would anyway.

"I'm sorry I left without saying good-bye. I'm sorry I didn't answer your calls or respond to your texts. That was wrong."

"Yes, it was."

"I'm sorry for all of it."

"But you're not sorry you left."

"No, I'm not." The truth. "I am sorry about the way I left."

"You made a choice. We all do it, and we pay for it sometimes. I should know."

"I didn't feel like I had a choice back then."

"I'm done being mad, Teddi, but it's time to own what you

did. You packed up your car and drove away and didn't look back. You forgot about all of us. Including Cee."

"I felt like half of me died *with* her—but I didn't have the right to feel that way. I wasn't family. I didn't lose a sister or a daughter or a mother or a wife. Your loss was deeper than mine. But it didn't feel that way to me. I was empty and lost and there was no book or prayer or support group that could help me, because friends are at the bottom of the list. People wanted to know why I was late for work. Why I looked so sad. Why I had no appetite and didn't shower. Losing Celia was the biggest thing in my life, and my grief was invisible." I handed Beck the bag of stones. "And I didn't forget about her. I carried her with me every single day."

He opened the bag and spilled the stones onto the bed, spreading them out with his hand. He lifted each one and examined it before setting it down.

"When I found the first one, it was something to hold on to that was part of my new life but that kept me connected to Celia. I planned to come home and place it on her headstone. But I couldn't bear the thought of any of it. So, I just kept waiting for the next perfect moment and the next perfect stone. Eventually, I stopped feeling like a balloon that was floating away."

"You wouldn't have felt so disconnected if you were here."

"It would have been worse."

"How can you possibly think that?"

"Because Cee wanted me to leave Chance."

"No. She would have wanted you here for Shay. For Miles, too. Even for my parents."

"Well, she didn't. I turned down a job in Chicago and she knew that, so she wanted me to go out and find something else. She was the only person who knew all the things I wanted to do and all the places I wanted to go. And you know what I did when she wanted me to promise I'd leave? *I said no.* To my dying best friend. It was the only thing she asked me to do for her and I couldn't do it. I wouldn't do it. I told her I was going to stay in Chance and shoot local weddings and schools and Little League teams and become a Wagoneer and volunteer at the freaking library sales."

"And that's not what she wanted for you."

I shook my head. "She was so disappointed in me."

"She loved you. And she was really proud of you and of your work."

"You didn't see her face that day when I said no. She thought I was kidding. But how could I say I would leave when Shay was here? When *you* were here? I couldn't fathom it. And then . . ."

"She was gone."

"And I could only think one thought. I had to do what she wanted me to do. Especially since deep down, I knew she was right. But it took her dying to get me there. Do you hear me? My best friend had to *die* for me to start living. That eats away at me every single day." I slowed my thoughts and hoped my breathing would follow. "And I doubt she meant 'go away, don't talk to anyone, and come back six years later.' That part? All me."

"You could've told me why you were leaving."

"I didn't want you to stop me. And I didn't want you to be mad at Cee."

Beck looked down and fiddled with the stones. "I loved you, Teddi. I'd have wanted you to go if that's what you needed. I would have understood why Celia wanted you to go. At least I would have tried."

Beck had loved me?

Beck *had* loved me. Past tense. I stood as *why didn't you tell me* screamed at the back of my throat and exploded in my ears.

It was better that I hadn't known.

Beck rose from the bed and hugged me around my shoulders with a strength that wasn't mine to absorb. I didn't move in too close.

"I couldn't have gotten through those six months without you." I looked up as he kissed the top of my forehead, but didn't linger. "I'm not staying away anymore."

"I'm glad."

"And I don't want to lose you again. I know it's not like before, but . . ."

"Me either," he said.

I walked out of the room and heard Beck push the door shut behind me.

"I loved you, too," I said, loud enough for him to hear.

Chapter 21

I AWOKE AS THE sun was lifting away darkness, and slipped a dress over my head and quiet shoes onto my feet that wouldn't click or flap. I pulled my hair into a ponytail and slipped my camera over my neck. I turned the doorknob slowly and opened the door with gentle ease.

My velvet bag was on the floor, a note attached.

T—YOU SHOULD PUT THESE
WHERE THEY BELONG.
B

I tucked the stones into my camera bag and walked outside.

The porch was damp from morning dew. I held the banister and looked out at Lark Street, then closed my eyes to snap a mental picture. I touched my camera to make sure it hung around my neck even though I'd just placed it there.

I shook out one leg. I needed to move, to walk, to run. I skittered around to the side of the house, through the white gate, under the weathered trellis covered in purple clematis, and into the garden, shrouded from Lark Street by high bushes and draping trees. I looked at the stepping-stones but walked on the grass, examining the flowers and bushes. I clamped my lips in defiance of my mother, who used to ramble off every species and insist I repeat them. It took me six months not to read the signs with the plants at Hester hotels, to just look at the plants and flowers and stones and grasses and photograph them. I did not want to get caught in the academic details of beauty. I snapped a few photos through the morning mist, with the light offering just a peek at what was to come. I slipped a stone into my pocket that had been hidden beneath a cluster of black-eyed Susans. There were weeds to be pulled there as well, but I wasn't in the mood and it wasn't my job.

Celia would have done it anyway.

I stood in the garden longer than I ever had before.

My stomach grumbled. Perk would have just opened a half hour ago. I could take my tablet, set myself up at a corner table, and review the wedding schedule and shot lists. Today I would be on my own. Josie was helping set up for an open house. Miles and Violet and Shay were tending to post-trauma and pre-wedding details with family. I was happy and sad. I was hopeful and fearful.

I was also eager to see Cameron, and tell him that I'd decided about my dash. And to ask him to be part of it.

I opened the garden gate and walked to the front of Nettie's. Someone was standing on the porch facing the house.

"Miles?"

He turned around. "Look who I saw walking on Main Street."

A man rose and came into my line of vision, blocked momentarily by a pillar and by a tightening in my stomach. My hand touched my side as my brain arranged the visual puzzle pieces. Taller than Miles, slim, but broadened by a sport coat, meticulous hair, a familiar gait. The man turned and held up a garment bag. "Special delivery!"

I stopped at the bottom of the steps. The knot in my stomach cinched and stomach acid lurched into my throat. Simon! In Chance. On the porch. With Miles. The puzzle pieces fit together in my head. I wasn't ready. "What are you doing here?"

"I wanted to surprise you."

"It's eight o'clock in the morning?"

"I took the red-eye."

What had Annie done?

"I just wanted Annie to send the clothes. You didn't have to fly all the way out here."

"I wanted to talk to you, Teddi."

"I found him in line at Perk. What luck, right?" Miles said, missing all the cues that I wasn't happy about his discovery.

I walked up onto the porch but stood near no one. Miles linked my arm and coaxed me closer to Simon.

"How's Shay?" I whispered. "I was going to text her a little later."

"Still asleep, of course. We were up late talking. She'll be okay, Teddi."

I leaned over to Simon and more nudged him than hugged him. He hugged me with his one available arm, still holding up my clothes with the other. I took the garment bag and laid it over the railing. "You should have waited, Si. I'll be back on Monday. You should've waited."

"But then I wouldn't have met him, and your boss here has already given me some great insights on luring a hotel chain to Union County. I'm disappointed he doesn't think it's right for a Hester, but I understand. Business is business. He's been very generous," Miles said.

"You could've told me about the land, Teddi. You know I'm always interested in possible opportunities," Simon said.

"It wasn't the right time for business."

"It's always the right time for business," Miles and Simon said in unison.

"I like him, Teddi," Miles said.

I told you so. I couldn't believe Miles was pitching a hotel for Union County the day before his wedding. Yes, I could.

"I'll leave you two to your unfinished business." Miles shook Simon's hand. "Maybe I can pick your brain later?"

"Call me anytime, Miles. Happy to help."

"Thank you," Miles said.

"When Shay wakes up, tell her I love her," I said.

"Who's Shay?" Simon asked.

"He doesn't know about *Shay?"*

Right then I knew Shay had told Miles about Simon, the impending marriage proposal, my possible yes, and maybe even about Shay being my maid of honor. Miles shook Simon's hand again. "If you're here tomorrow, you're welcome to come to the wedding, considering."

"Miles, stop. Simon isn't staying." I turned to Simon. "You're not staying, are you?"

"I guess not."

"I'm sorry, I didn't mean it that way."

"Should I know who this Shay is? And why didn't you tell me you were shooting your best friend's husband's second wedding? It wouldn't have mattered to me."

Exactly.

I shook my head as if that were a way to align right and wrong and good and bad and sense and nonsense.

"Teddi, are you okay?" Miles said. "You look pale. You never look pale."

Miles motioned to the swing, and I sat, hoping neither he nor Simon would join me. Miles held on to the pillar nearest to the step and swung himself back toward me. "Call me if you need something before tomorrow. I have to go check flowers and napkins." He rolled his eyes but smiled wide, bounced down the steps, and almost skipped to his car. Simon and I said nothing. Heart-shaped exhaust may have spewed from the tailpipe as Miles drove down Lark and headed for home.

"Tell me what's wrong, Teddi," Simon said.

"Just about everything." That was the most honest I'd been with him or myself in the past six years.

"I didn't realize you'd grown up in such a small town." How could he? "When did you leave?" he asked.

I watched Simon sway as he waited for my answer. His frame was broadened by his sport coat. I knew beneath the tightly woven linen were shoulders that fit neatly into a men's medium.

"I lived here until six years ago. Until I moved to Chicago and started working—for you. I haven't been back here since."

"Wow. Why not?"

"It's complicated." I fidgeted to pass seconds that felt like hours.

"You don't want to tell me," Simon said. I shook my head and pushed off the ground with my toes, swinging back and forth. "I'd never pressure you to tell me something you don't want me to know, Teddi."

"I know that, Si. But don't you think that's a problem?"

"That *what's* a problem? That I won't pressure you?"

"No, that we're *involved* and I don't want to tell you everything about me and my life, and that it doesn't bother you?"

"I wanted to talk to you about us being involved, Teddi. That's why I'm here. I didn't want to wait until you were back at work. We never really attached a label to it, so maybe it's time—"

"Don't say it."

"Don't say what?" Simon sat next to me on the swing. Why was he making this even harder?

"Don't propose. I can't marry you, Simon. I thought maybe I could. I like you a lot. We have a good time together. You're so smart and kind and fun to be around. I love working for you. But I don't love *you*."

"Teddi?" Simon squeezed my hand and tugged on it. I summoned my bravery and looked at him. He deserved that.

"Yes, Simon?"

"I don't love you either."

The words floated around me. "You don't?" I lifted my hand from his.

"I was never going to ask you to marry me."

"You weren't?" I shuddered. *Now I wasn't good enough to be the first lady of Hester Hotels? All our time together has meant nothing to Simon?*

"My proposal is completely professional," he said.

"Are you kidding?"

"I carried your dry cleaning across the country. Does that sound like I'm kidding?"

"No."

"You thought I wanted to marry you? Really? I don't mean you're not great, but we never talked about anything like that."

"I know, I just assumed when you said you wanted to propose something . . ."

"Oh, I'm sorry. I have a business proposal for you. A new job.

A promotion, really. If you want it." I didn't know what I wanted. "Have you been worrying about that the whole time you've been gone? Is that why you didn't want to talk to me? I thought you were going to come back and quit. Or that you weren't going to come back at all."

"And that's why you came all the way here." I looked away, my cheeks burning from humiliation. Simon tapped my shoulder and I turned back. "I'm so embarrassed."

"Don't be. I'm flattered that you would even consider it. You were considering it, weren't you?"

I shrugged. "Maybe a little." I couldn't lie. "Not really. We had a lot of fun, though, didn't we?"

Simon nodded and held my hand again. "We certainly did. But I think our best times were when we were talking about work, brainstorming, collaborating. And I saw what you had to offer the company." He opened his eyes wide. "You're not going to quit now, are you? Can we talk about the new job? Whenever you're ready, of course. Not here, not now."

"Am I interrupting?"

I stood as Josie sashayed onto the porch. I hadn't even seen her coming. My throat was dry and tightness edged over my shoulders. "Josie, this—is Simon Hester. My boss. Simon, this is Josie Fields. My friend. My dear, lifelong friend."

Josie curtsied and Simon bowed with Hester flair.

"I wondered what was going on when I saw Miles and Mr. Hester at Perk. I had a feeling. I usually do when it comes to handsome men, you know." Josie winked at me. "But speaking of handsome men . . ." Josie tipped her head toward the sidewalk, toward Cameron walking up Lark Street.

Cameron walked up one step, holding a paper cup with the Perk logo on it. I'd implied I'd stop by to see him. Now his shift had ended and he'd come to find me. I knew the cup in his hand was a latte. For me.

I sat on the top step as he approached. "I'm sorry I didn't stop by," I whispered to Cameron. I felt Josie walk across the porch behind me, and sensed that she and Simon were listening. "A lot has been going on."

"Just thought I'd see if you were okay," Cameron said. "But I see you are."

"It's not what it looks like . . ."

"Simon Hester," Simon said as he reached down the steps and shook Cameron's hand. I tilted my head from side to side to stretch my constricting neck muscles. My temples pounded. Josie looked at me with a trademark Josie smirk.

"Cameron Davis."

"Nice to meet you, Cameron. Nice town you have here."

"Not my town, but thanks."

"No? Where're you from?"

"I live in Oakland. Right across the bridge from you."

"That's great! You'll come out and have dinner with me and Teddi."

"He doesn't mean *us* us, like a couple us," I said.

"He doesn't?" Josie asked.

"No," I said.

Beck walked out onto the porch. "Having a party without me, Teddi?"

Josie smiled, then covered her mouth.

"I really just wanted to tell you that I was going to visit my parents in Akron, but I can see you're busy." Cameron set down the latte and waved in the general direction of the porch. As he walked away I followed him with quick, short steps. He quickened his pace.

"I'm not marrying Simon. You were right. I don't love him. And it's really funny but—he didn't even want to marry me. I want to see what can happen between us. You and me, us."

"So I'm second choice?" He looked at the porch. "Or third?"

"Neither. Oh, that's not what I meant. Can we talk? Please?"

"Teddi!" Simon yelled from the porch. "Your friend here is a graphic designer? Why aren't we using his firm for some of our work?"

"I've got to go," Cameron said.

I stopped. He kept walking, then turned toward me.

"Can we talk when you get back? I think you'll understand."

"I thought maybe you weren't over Beck, and then I believed you were. I was convinced you didn't love Hester, but no matter what you say, he flew across the country to see you."

"It's not how it seems."

"Look, it's no big deal if I got the wrong vibe."

"You didn't get the wrong idea. Wait—no big deal?"

"We only just met, Teddi. I'm not sure me chasing you around thirty years ago really counts."

"It totally counts. Will you come say good-bye before I leave?"

"Maybe."

Cameron walked down Lark Street and didn't turn back again. I didn't chase him or call after him, hanging on to my one shred of pride left intact.

I stomped back onto the porch. "I like him and now he thinks he's my *third choice*."

"Seems like a decent guy," Simon said. "And not like he'd be that far away. Assuming you're coming back to San Francisco."

"Not now, Simon," I said.

"You *like* Cameron?" Beck asked.

My stomach flipped, and not because it was empty. Yes! I liked

Cameron. I hadn't been *just flirting* and it wasn't *just fun* to hang around him. I really liked him. And now I didn't know if I'd see him again.

"I do like him," I said aloud. "Is it okay that I like him?"

Beck and Simon stared at me, but neither man said anything.

Josie to the rescue. "There is only one person on this porch who should answer that question."

"Are you sure you don't want me to come with you?" Josie asked.

"I'm sure. But will you wait right here in case I change my mind?"

I knew she would. I stepped out of Josie's car and walked through the open gates of West End Cemetery. I watched the ground as I walked up the main path. As sunset neared, I walked faster. My heart pounded—not from fear, but from resolve. The headstone loomed large and I stared. I closed my eyes to saturate my memory with the image, to remember the swirl in my stomach, the lump in my throat, and the unexpected grateful tug on my heart. Eyes open, I reached into a canvas bag I'd slung across my body. I removed my bag full of stones and one by one I placed them on the ground close to the front of the headstone, lined up like the tulip bulbs Celia and I had planted in our hand-dug trench in my mother's garden. I'd placed the words facedown, as if tempting them to seep into the soil, as if urging them to grow. Pictures bubbled to the surface of my thoughts and faded away. I didn't philosophize, or pray, or apologize. Words failed to come, except for three.

I was here.

Chapter 22

A STRING QUARTET PLAYED as wedding guests filled the roped-off lawn around the gazebo in Chance Square. The temperature and humidity had dropped throughout the day, and the sky was a bright Carolina blue even though we were in the middle of Ohio.

I kept myself off to the side of the crowd, half out of sight behind meticulously placed flowers atop decorative columns. I snapped candid photos of unknowing guests with my long-range lens. When it was time, I took my stance next to the beginning of the aisle where I'd take all the ceremony photos. And I waited, sweeping not only the ground with my foot but the memory of Celia and Miles's wedding off to the side. Celia would be happy for Miles. I was happy for Miles. Miles was happy. Shay was adjusting. That was what mattered.

Soon, the seats were filled and a flutist replaced the string musicians. First, the rabbi walked toward me, turned, and walked up the aisle toward the chuppah, the hand-embroidered wedding canopy that had been in Violet's family for generations. Miles approached the aisle with a parent on each side, traditionally linking arms with him. He smiled and looked my way long enough to allow for a proper photograph, but that was all. Then, the groomsmen walked toward me—Violet's brother and one of Miles's cousins, dressed in taupe linen pants and a matching vest pinned with a double white-rose boutonniere, each wearing a Tiffany-blue tie to match Violet's color scheme. When they were halfway up the aisle, Beck stepped into view. He winked at me and my breath caught, but my pulse remained steady. I held my camera to my face and he stepped closer, leaned into the lens and then toward my ear. I shivered.

"Go for it," he said, and then he kissed my cheek.

As Shayna stepped toward me, I inched back to take it all in, to take in all of her. Celia's daughter, with her Tiffany-blue floating tulle skirt that skimmed the top of her knees and swayed as if starring in its own secret ballet. Shay's hair hung loosely curled down her back, the sides lifted and accented with sprigs of baby's breath. I glanced at her dyed shoes and smiled. They were perfect. Shay swung her ribbon-wrapped roses by her side and walked up to me. It was then I noticed a shiny heart around her neck, perhaps a gift from her father and her new stepmom.

"I'm so glad you're here, Aunt Tee. Thank you for this." She touched the necklace. It wasn't new. It was the half heart I'd given her at the mall, the half that had belonged to Celia and had marked our friendship, and now marked my relationship with Shay. The charm glistened as it dangled from a delicate chain that sparkled in the sunlight. "Vi had this cleaned and bought me the chain," Shay said. "She said she'd be honored if I wore it today so that a little bit of Mom is here with me."

I swallowed. "Your mom is with you even without the necklace. You know that, right?"

Shay nodded, lifted her bouquet into place at her waist, turned, and disappeared into a haze of my watery eyes.

I blinked hard as Violet and her parents came into view. She wore a delicate wreath of baby's breath and tiny white roses. Her face sparkled. The ivory lace sheath wedding gown looked both antique and brand new. When her parents kissed her on her cheeks I snapped a picture. The light was perfect. Here, in Chance, without glimmering seas or majestic mountains or crystal chandeliers. No one here needed that. Or wanted it.

Violet stepped toward me and whispered. "I saw it."

"What?" I whispered back.

"Gretchen Halliday tweeted best wishes for *my* wedding day. Can you believe it? That had to be you, Teddi. That was so thoughtful. Thank you."

"You're welcome." *Thank you, Simon.*

As the ceremony ended, I captured a wide shot of Miles breaking the glass, and then a few of Miles and Violet running back down the aisle holding hands as the crowd roared with "Mazel tov." When they ran past me, I walked backward on the grass and then onto a small patch of gravel, jarred by the uncertain footing.

I picked up a handful of the ragged white stones. The past, the present, the future, the people, the places, the joy, the sorrow, the possibilities. It all slipped through my fingers into the pocket of the periwinkle dress I'd chosen instead of my waiter uniform. With one hand I swept the surface of the fabric. The bumps and edges tickled and pricked. Then, as I turned to face the crowd gathering for cocktails, I smiled. The stones were safe and sound, and there was room for more.

I settled into my bed for my last night in Chance. Beck was upstairs in his room and Simon was in the room down the hall. It was just about ten o'clock Pacific time on a Sunday night. I called Annie anyway.

"I'm so sorry!" Annie said, instead of hello.

"Don't be. It all worked out for the best."

"If you say so. But that's not why you're calling."

"No. I just wanted to tell you that I changed my flight, so I need you to reschedule the Horton/Brady meeting until next Monday. They're in the city; it should be fine if you do it first thing in the morning."

"But—"

"No buts. My new motto is family and friends before work, whenever possible. Without losing clients, or sanity, that is."

"Don't worry about the Hortons, it was just a formality. You've shot every event for that family in the past five years and that's not going to change."

"Is that so?" I laughed.

"I'm glad you're staying in Chance a bit longer, Teddi."

"I'm not staying in Chance," I said. "I'm visiting my parents in Portland."

My phone clattered with Josie's new ringtone.

"I'm up," I said.

"Be ready in about half an hour," Josie said. "You know, I'm really going to miss you."

"I'm coming back Columbus Day weekend to stay with Shay, while Miles and Violet go to New York for a mini-moon, courtesy of Simon."

"Wow. I should get married again if it means a free vacation."

"And if I win that contest . . ."

"I can be your plus-one to the award dinner! I'm a really great date."

"I'm sure you are."

"It won't be the same here without you."

"You can visit me whenever you want, but I'll never get out of here if I don't get off the phone and finish packing. See you soon."

"Be waiting outside, okay? I don't want to have to drag you out of there."

"Oh my God, Jos, yes, I'll be waiting outside."

A half hour later I stepped out onto the porch for the last time. Next time I'd be staying with Shay. The time after that, I'd promised Josie I'd stay with her. I made her promise that her book club would read a book and that the gossip girls wouldn't be invited. I felt hollow as I watched the quiet street, drumming my fingers along the railing with impatience. I was going to miss this place and these people. I always had.

I left my bags near the steps and walked back inside, ran my hand along the mantel, the back of the settee. I could walk around the garden one more time.

A blue compact car drove down Lark Street and parked. It wasn't one of Josie's cars. Maybe Beck had booked another guest. Maybe one of the Wagoneers had thought to bring me a goodie bag for my flight. Then, Cameron stepped out of the car, turned, and smiled. He walked around the car toward the sidewalk. His pace quickened and I sprung down the steps and onto the path, where I scampered until we met, somewhere, but not exactly, in the middle.

"You're back from Akron."

"I came back last night."

"I know." I laughed.

"In Chance, someone always knows." We both said it and snickered. I forced myself to stop.

"Josie?" Cameron asked.

"Deanna," I said.

He shook his head and chuckled. "Beck texted me. He explained that things were cool between the two of you. I also got a call from Simon and one from your assistant, Annie. Josie has texted me about two dozen times and has launched an all-out campaign to make me understand the confusion on that porch." He pointed as if accusing the porch itself for the mayhem. "I also know you're going to Portland for a week."

"People in Chance aren't known for being subtle."

"Or discreet." Cameron held his arms behind his back. "A lot of people love you, Teddi Lerner."

I blushed. "Josie's on her way."

"No, she's not."

"She better be or I'll miss my flight."

"I'm going to drive you to the airport if that's okay."

"It is." God bless Josie.

"I'll be back in Oakland in about a month. Maybe we can have lunch? Or go for a walk?"

I nodded again. "I'd like that."

Cameron brought his arms around front, and when he opened his hand, I saw a small stone. "Bet you never thought you'd have a stone all the way from Akron."

"How did you know about my stones?"

"Because you put me to shame at Jasper Pond. How quickly you forget crushing my stone-skipping soul."

"I will *treasure* it." I said it without an ounce of sarcasm, but then I inhaled and told Cameron about Shay and the cemetery, and about writing on twenty-two stones for Celia.

He lifted my right hand, laid the stone in it, and closed my fingers around it. "I wish I'd known her for longer," he said.

"I wish I'd known her longer too."

I reached into the pocket of my dress, released his stone, and pulled out another. This one I'd picked up in the garden right before The Porch Invasion. I opened my hand and showed the smooth stone to Cameron. It was not flat enough to skip in the pond, but sat perfectly still in the middle of my palm, as if floating.

"Maybe you'll leave that one for Celia one day," he said.

"I will when I come back. It won't be the same if I don't carry it around for a while first."

"Maybe by then, you'll have written my name on it."

I already had.

I'd been back at work for a month, but today was different. Today I walked into the lobby of the San Francisco Hester Hotel carrying a briefcase. I reasoned (or was easily swayed) that as creative director of Hester Properties, I needed this accessory. Josie had helped me choose the perfect indulgence—Burberry in mineral blue. We'd shopped online in tandem, Josie sending photos and links across the country as if she were whisking me around the mall.

"Good morning, Fiona." I stopped at the round glass table in the center of the lobby and waved to the hotel's morning manager. Yellow, lavender, pink, and peach tulips dipped in unison over and around the sides of a glass vase large enough to hold a watermelon. "There must be two hundred tulips in here."

"At least." Fiona smiled. "I wonder who could have said she liked tulips."

"I wonder who!"

"Someone starting in her new position today, perhaps?"

"Perhaps." I walked to Fiona and laid my hands on the counter. "Thank you. It was a nice surprise."

"Don't thank me," she said. "Simon wanted to make sure that your first official day was perfect."

When I stepped out of the elevator on the twelfth floor, home of my new office, a vase of red tulips stood on the dark wooden hall table beneath a large round mirror. My hair was down and loose. I set my briefcase on the floor between my legs and adjusted the crew neck of my simple peach knit A-line dress. I smoothed the pockets, flat and empty.

I walked into Annie's new space, a converted alcove, decorated with sleek wood furniture and a soft green settee—a definite upgrade from a cubicle. A vase full of peach and yellow parrot tulips sat at the edge of Annie's desk.

"The tulips are amazing. I'll have to thank Simon later."

"He's in Miami until Wednesday. He said to tell you to enjoy the view."

"It really feels like the first day of something brand new and exciting," I said. "Like everything up until today has been leading right to now."

"Because it has."

Annie walked over and hugged me and I hugged her back. She was my assistant, now an executive assistant, but that didn't mean we couldn't be real friends to some degree. She was fifteen years younger and always made me laugh, as well as question my pocket-dress style, with her lavender pixie-short hair meant to show off her unalome tattoo on the back of her neck, a spiral that opened to the left and meant female spiritual enlightenment. In contrast, as always, Annie's dress was a conservation navy-blue knit wrap, her shoes nude vegan pumps. Only I knew she had a pair of one-dollar flip-flops tucked under her desk.

Annie nodded and tipped her head toward my office door. I opened it and stepped inside. The unadorned wall-width window faced downtown and a summer sky had settled on top of the skyscrapers. In the middle of my teak desk sat an oversized glass vase packed with pink roses and tulips, accented by deep green leaves. I stepped back into the alcove.

"Those flowers are gorgeous, Annie. Thank you. I didn't expect more!"

"They *are* gorgeous," she said. "But don't thank me."

I walked back into my office and shut the door. As if possessed, my desk chair swiveled around. And there was Cameron. He smiled a crooked smile and pushed his hair away from his eyes.

"You're here." My voice cracked and my hand touched my chest as if I were saying the Pledge of Allegiance. I blushed, but in that moment I also knew I needn't be embarrassed at all. "I thought we were having lunch next Tuesday."

"We are. I hope."

"Oh, yes, absolutely."

"I don't have to be at school till this afternoon, so I thought . . ."

"I'm glad you did."

Cameron gently tugged a tulip from the arrangement, walked around to the front of the desk, and handed the flower to me. I buried my nose in the bloom, knowing tulips had only the faint scent of freshness. I felt Cameron's stare and looked up.

I inhaled a deep breath of emotional courage and talked fast. "I'm glad you're here now. I would have been carrying around

271

my phone for the next week in case you called—waiting for you to call—hoping you weren't going to cancel—and driving Annie, and Josie, crazy."

"Then I'm really glad I didn't wait. The world does not need a crazier Josie."

I laughed. "Agreed."

"But that's not the only reason I'm here. I have something to show you."

Cameron pulled an envelope from his pocket and handed it to me. It had already been opened. "It's from the Union County Art Council. It was mailed to Shay, and Miles sent it to me. She wanted you to see the official letter, but not to read it alone."

I didn't win.

And it didn't matter.

What mattered was I was part of Shay's life, and not just once a year. Josie and I texted every day and had chosen a book for our new Web chat book club. I'd started apartment hunting and only looked at units with two bedrooms. Cousin Maggie and Lorraine planned to visit in November and my parents were coming in December. I even thought about Beck, just for a second, and exhaled a peaceful sigh. I noticed a photo of me and Celia, one that Annie had apparently taken out of storage and placed on my bookshelf in a simple frame. Best friends' arms draped over each other's shoulders, heads thrown back in unsuspecting laughter. I smiled and shifted my gaze to the tulips and roses on my new desk, then to the man standing in front of me with hair in his eyes and a pencil behind his ear.

Picture perfect.